SEP 23 1997

6/18
T-46
2015-1
2016-1
2017-1
L 8/17
3-20(48)

DATE DUE

Death in
Lovers' Lane

Carolyn Hart

Death in Lovers' Lane

WHEELER
PUBLISHING, INC.
ROCKLAND, MA

★ AN AMERICAN COMPANY ★

Published in Large Print by arrangement with Avon Books,
a division of The Hearst Corporation in the United States and Canada.

Wheeler Large Print Book Series.

Set in 16 pt Plantin.

Library of Congress Cataloging-in-Publication Data

Hart, Carolyn G.
    Death in lovers' lane: A Henrie O mystery / by Carolyn G. Hart.
        p. (large print) cm.(Wheeler large print book series)
    ISBN 1-56895-467-0 (hardcover)
    1. Large type books. 2. Women journalists—United States—Fiction. 3.
Missouri—Fiction.
I. Title.
[PS3558.A676D446   1997b]
813'.54—dc21   97-25061
                                                                CIP

My thanks to my old friends and J-School buddies, Eve K. Sandstrom and Mack R. Palmer, for sharing their expertise. And with fond memories of a long-vanished newsroom, a tip of a pica pole to the class of '58 and to the memory of LBM.

Death in
Lovers' Lane

one

"Waking up alone has all the excitement of interviewing a hamster breeder. And none of the action." Jimmy's tone was cheerful, but I didn't miss the message.

"We've brought each other some comfort there, these last few years." I chose my words carefully and kept my voice light.

The silence on the line built.

I could picture Jimmy in his hotel room in Los Angeles. Tall and lanky. In Levi's and a sports shirt. He would be draped casually over an easy chair, a book open on the coffee table. His face is long and lanky, too, with that deadpan quality that often fools those he interviews into thinking him placid, perhaps a tad obtuse. It wasn't a mistake they'd make twice.

Jimmy likes gourmet meals, art museums, small towns, and parties where people know each other.

No wonder he felt lonely.

Los Angeles is a sprawl of broken dreams and lost opportunities, disconnected souls and entertainment junkies. The sunny skies and graceful palms don't redeem jammed roadways to nowhere.

1

But it wasn't simply that he was in L.A. on a book tour.

"Henrie O." Jimmy's voice is a pleasant tenor. A nice voice. A nice man. An old friend. A sometime lover. "Henrie O, I've been looking at a house in Cuernavaca. You'd like it." Eagerness ran the words together. "I've been wanting to tell you about it. I'm going down there next week. I want you to come with me."

He paused.

Suddenly, I knew what was coming. And I was totally unprepared.

Since we'd both been widowed and become reacquainted, we'd taken a number of holidays together. And enjoyed them and each other. But—

"Henrie O, I want to build a life there. With you. As my wife."

"Jimmy..." I didn't know what to say. I'd not thought about where we were going. I'd not actually thought we were going anywhere. I'd seen our occasional meetings—Acapulco, New York, Paris, Charlotte Amalie—as interludes: sensual, satisfying, self-contained; a lovely enhancement but not a basic component of my life.

Yet I've never seen myself as an opportunist. Certainly not in connection with people for whom I have great respect and liking. I'd just never figured Jimmy Lennox into the equation of my life. At least not on a permanent basis.

"Think about it, Henrie O." The words were still casual, but his voice grew huskier. "We'd have fun. You know that."

2

"I know that." But there is a world of difference between occasional liaisons and a permanent commitment.

"I'll be here until a week from Friday."

And that was all. I was left holding a buzzing line.

As I walked briskly across the campus, I saw it with a more thoughtful gaze. This had been a healing place for me, after Richard's death. We are none of us ever prepared for the loss of a beloved partner. When the loss comes without warning, the devastation is complete.

Richard's last call had ended, "I'll be home Monday. Love you, sweetheart."

But when Monday came, Richard, my sure-footed, athletic, graceful Richard, was dead from a fall down a rugged cliff. He came home from the island paradise of Kauai in a coffin.

One day I'd been Mrs. Richard Collins. The next I was a widow, a widow remembering how bitterly she'd grudged his island visit.

Nothing softens that kind of loss.

The common wisdom urges no changes for a year. I'd stayed in our Washington apartment, but the joy was gone.

Millay's verse was a refrain in my heart:

Oh, there will pass with your great passing
Little of beauty not your own,—
Only the light from common water,
Only the grace from simple stone!

Richard and I had freelanced for a number of years. We'd taken assignments where and when we wanted, as long as we could work together. Without Richard, none of it mattered. It was months later when a good friend who taught journalism called on me to take over her classes while she recuperated from a broken hip.

So I'd come to the little town of Derry Hills, Missouri, to Thorndyke University, and joined an unusual faculty made up primarily of retired professionals.

That was four years ago.

Now Derry Hills was home, or as close to home as a wanderer would ever know. Thorndyke was a thriving, prosperous school. I liked the weathered limestone and ivy-laden brick buildings, the curving paths among towering oaks and sycamores, the old redbrick bell tower.

Most of all, I enjoyed seeing students, young, old, scruffy, well-dressed, smiling, scowling, but all of them purposeful, going somewhere fast. It might be to a class or the mailroom or for a beer, but they were racing ahead. And whether they knew it or not—and many of them did— they were starting the lives they would one day lead, building the habits of success or failure, happiness or despair.

I relished being a part of that. I enjoyed this hilly, wooded Missouri terrain, the misty curtains of fog in autumn, the crunch of snow underfoot in winter, the gentle greening in spring. I found each season invigorating, especially winter. But I always move swiftly, no matter the season, a woman in a hurry though the days of hurry are past.

It wasn't simply the beauty of the campus that pleased me, though it was spectacular now as the November leaves blazed. In some ways, I was like an old dog luxuriating in a sunny spot, drawing strength from the vitality that surrounded me. An almost seismic sense of expectation emanates from a college campus. That is the true elixir of youth: the grand, the glorious, the magnificent hopes and dreams because all things—*all* things—are yet possible.

I quickly passed the granite statue of Joseph Pulitzer, a scrawny figure with a beaked nose and thick stone glasses. Coattails flying, he forever lunged forward, a pad of paper in one hand, a pencil in the other.

Thorndyke's Journalism School—more formally, the School of Journalism and Mass Communications—was housed in Brandt Hall, one of the University's earliest buildings, three squat stories with crenellated towers on each corner and leaded windows. Steep stone steps led up to a ponderous oak door that had once graced a medieval monastery.

There was a swift clatter behind me. Maggie Winslow darted through the doorway before the heavy panel wheezed shut.

"Mrs. Collins, do you have a minute?" Maggie's brisk voice was pleasant, but imbued with just the faintest undertone of arrogance. And there was arrogance in every line of her slim young body and smooth, confident face.

"Sure," I told her. Maggie was one of my independent-study students this fall in a one-on-one course on investigative reporting. Only top seniors were eligible to enroll. It was a struggle every Tuesday to tamp her down, keep her leashed. Maggie Winslow's instinct was to dominate every situation.

I was equally brisk. "Let's go in my office."

My office is one of a series that rim the newsroom of *The Clarion*, the newspaper which serves as both the official Thorndyke University organ and the town paper for Derry Hills.

We were at the open doors to the newsroom. Maggie gave me a brilliant smile. "Thanks, but I've got to get to the copy desk. I'm due on in just a minute. I just wanted to let you know I've come up with a topic for my series. Here's what I'm going to do"—she handed me several sheets of paper. She swung away, then paused. "Oh, and I'm going to tell Mr. Duffy. I think he'll be excited."

I watched Maggie stride into the newsroom. Shoulders back, head high, she moved like a queen, unassailable in her confidence.

Every man in the room noticed her, of course.

The other women glanced up, and I saw my wariness replayed in their faces.

Maggie knew she was noticed. She liked that. She reached up to straighten the patterned chiffon scarf knotted at her throat. The silk accessory—splashed with golden peonies and swirls of mauve—set her apart, as did her navy

6

gabardine suit, the slim skirt circus-spangle short. Most Thorndyke students slouched around in faded jeans, T-shirts, and down-at-heel Reeboks. Not Maggie. She could have walked onto the five-o'clock news as a co-anchor any night, midnight-black hair cupping a Nefertiti face.

I gave a little shrug and folded the papers she'd thrust at me. I had been, in effect, dismissed by Maggie Winslow. I'd decided early on in the semester that her every move was calculated. So, I wondered, why? But I didn't focus on it. I had other things on my mind.

I crossed the newsroom, nodding to reporters and editors. As I unlocked my office door and flicked on the light, I had a sudden vision of a hotel room in Paris with aged stone walls just like these. But in the hotel, almond-colored light from bronze sconces cast a soft golden glow and Jimmy was turning toward me, arms outstretched.

I slipped out of my cardigan, hung it on the walnut coat tree. I suddenly saw my reflection, wavering and a little ghostly, in the glass fronts of my bookcases. My black hair is streaked with silver, my face strong-boned and stubborn. My eyes are dark. They have seen much and remembered much in almost fifty years of newspapering.

Sunlight streamed through the window behind my desk. I keep the blinds up all the time. Yes, I like plenty of light. I settled in my chair, welcoming the sun's warmth on my back.

I still held Maggie's sheets in my hand. I stared down at them, my glance cool. I don't like being manipulated. Then I shrugged and began to read.

When I finished, I aligned the pages. Hmm. Obviously, Maggie had absorbed enough of my philosophy of reporting to be well aware I wasn't going to like her plans. But if she thought I'd come storming into the newsroom for a public confrontation with her, she still had a few things to learn.

I was grading a stack of editorials—"Should Spanish Be a Second Language?"—when Maggie arrived for our two-o'clock appointment.

I greeted her pleasantly and saw the sudden look of surprise in her eyes. And satisfaction.

Oh, Maggie, don't underestimate your opponent.

That quick thought surprised me. I hadn't realized just how irritated I was.

So perhaps we both stopped for an instant to reconsider.

Maggie sat a little sideways in the oak armchair, her beautiful legs crossed. "Duffy's crazy about my idea."

I could have told her a classy bridge player never smirks when trumping an ace. I could also have pointed out the reason why: it takes more than one trump to win most hands.

Instead, I picked up her proposal and held it out to her. "Good. You can do these stories for him."

8

She didn't take the papers from me. "And for my series. For you."

"No." My voice was still pleasant, but quite definite.

She swung around, both slim feet on the floor. She leaned forward, "Duffy thinks—"

"Duffy runs the newsroom. I run my courses."

"But he—but they've got everything!" In her intensity, Maggie jabbed a scarlet-tipped finger toward me. "Sex, money, human interest."

"Right," I said agreeably. "All they lack is a reason."

"Mrs. Collins, this is the kind of story AP might pick up." Her eyes met mine boldly. Her unspoken judgment hung in the room. *Oh, lady, you're Ice Age. Don't you know anything? Gonzo journalism, that's what makes it in today's world.*

Maggie's derisive look challenged me. "If I do it—and I will do it, Mrs. Collins—I can have my pick of jobs."

Shark pools are recreational havens in comparison to the job-hunt arena for new college grads, especially journalism graduates. Or communications majors, as they are called today. Colleges across the country spew out thousands of these graduates annually, and there are newspaper and television openings for hundreds. You do the math.

Give Maggie ten years and she'd look hard. The sharp appraisal flashed in my mind like pinball lights.

I suppose my face spoke for me.

Her jaw tightened, accentuating the dramatic

9

planes of her face, the hollowed cheeks and deep-set eyes. "I thought—" She broke off.

"You thought I'd roll over and play dead if Duffy liked the stories. Even though you're smart enough, good enough to know this isn't the kind of series I want. This is lazy, Maggie. All you've got here is a plan to rehash some sensational crimes. That's not investigative reporting. And if you think this is a ticket to a big job, you're wrong. This is fluff."

The silence wasn't pleasant.

"Look, Mrs. Collins, I know I've got something here." Once again her voice was intense, abrasive. "Three crimes that shocked Derry Hills, crimes that were never solved. I can do interviews with the people who were involved and describe the scene and the background. People will eat it up. I've—"

"Wrong on all counts." My voice was level and crisp. "All you'll have is a roundup from old stories. And that's not good enough. Not for me. I want real investigative reporting. I want a series of articles that bring out information nobody has, information that will benefit the public, information—"

"Mrs. Collins, wait a minute." Her malachite eyes glistened with excitement. "Will you agree that if I come up with information about these crimes, information nobody else ever found, that it would be investigative reporting?"

"Sure, but that's not what you're talking about." I rattled the papers. "All you've got here is a *Where-are-they-now* mishmash."

Maggie's eyes narrowed in concentration. A crimson-tipped finger pressed against one cheek. "I'll gouge to the bone. There *has* to be stuff the police didn't find. And I can find it. I can do it." She spoke with utter confidence.

And yes, her face was hard, but I felt a sudden spurt of—well, if not liking, certainly admiration.

And God, how I envied her certitude. I know some things without qualification.

Love transfigures.

Yesterday never ends.

No one with friends will ever be poor.

I'd bet my stake on any of these any day. But not on much else.

And now, was a clever, bright, hard youngster playing me like a drum?

In part, Maggie Winslow's instincts were right on. Everybody loves an unsolved mystery. Think Judge Crater. Think D. B. Cooper. Think Jimmy Hoffa.

Maggie surged to her feet, her cat-bright eyes alive. "I can do it." Her tone was exultant.

"Be sure that you do, Maggie. I won't accept anything less than careful, thorough, meaningful discoveries. Do you understand me?" *In other words, young lady, I'll flunk your beautiful ass if these articles are long on stale news and short on investigation.*

"Oh, yes." Maggie's metallic gaze was just this side of insolent. "I've already got some ideas. The thing is, Mrs. Collins, somebody always knows something. All you have to do is shake them up a little."

two

One theory holds that right-brained creative people are very much attuned to physical delights. I firmly believe that. Excellent morning coffee is definitely a major physical delight, I thought as I poured my first cup of the day. But there are others.

It was 4 A.M. in Los Angeles. Jimmy sleeps in boxer shorts and a T-shirt. He flings his arms and legs wide. He would be sprawled across the hotel bed, face nudged against a crumpled pillow.

I wished him, across the miles, a good day, a happy day, then briskly shook open the Wednesday morning *Clarion*. Images jostled just below my conscious focus on the head-lines.

BOMBS EXPLODE NEAR SPHINX

Bougainvillea cascading in splashes of crimson over golden hacienda walls in Cuernavaca.

VOLUNTEERS AID LOST WHALE

Richard and Emily and I decorating Bobby's grave on the Day of the Dead.

Richard hunching over his Olivetti, typing so furiously the undercarriage rattles against the desk.

And then I reached page 4 and the boxed quarter-page ad.

**If You Know *Anything* About
Howard Rosen and Gail Voss
Candace and Curt Murdoch
Darryl Nugent
WHAT HAPPENED? WHEN? WHY?
Call 330-9800 immediately.
All replies confidential.**

I reached for my cordless phone, punched the numbers, listened to the recorded message:

"Hello, I'm Maggie Winslow, a student at the University. I'm writing an article about three famous unsolved crimes in Derry Hills. If you know anything about those who were involved, please leave a message after the tone. I will return your call promptly. Thank you."

I hung up.

By God, what a clever, intriguing, *effective* ploy!

And further proof, if I needed it, of Maggie's flamboyant forcefulness. She definitely had the chutzpah and inventiveness of an investigative reporter.

Maggie might have the last laugh, after all.

I often jog during my lunch hour. And yes, at

my age, it more resembles a summer stroll by an armadillo, but I cover the ground, and *Runner's World* promises it is distance, not time, that matters. I end by walking a mile. I was in the second cool-down lap when Angela Chavez joined me. Everybody relies on Angel to keep the Journalism School humming. Her official title is chief office administrator. Unofficially, because of her good humor and her willingness to go the extra mile to help both faculty and students, she's the J-School Angel, reliable, pleasant, unfailingly good-humored.

Yes, that was Angel. But the news business had taught me early on that every living creature experiences passion and fear, love and hatred, that there is a story, often dark, always compelling, in every human heart. With Angel, I suddenly realized I'd succumbed to surface appearances.

Bleak lines webbed her Raggedy Ann face. There was no trace of her usual placidity. She didn't even say hello. The words burst from her. "You have Maggie Winslow in independent study." It was a statement, not a question.

I looked at her in surprise. "Yes." I tugged at the sleeves of my sweatshirt. The wind had veered to the north and there was a winter feel to the gusts. Dust devils swirled from the track's reddish clay gravel.

Angel's sandy hair streamed in the wind. "Did you see that ad?" It was hard to define the tone in her voice. Anxious? Disgusted? Angry?

I stopped and faced her. "You called the number?"

14

"No." Her reply was clipped. She pressed her lips tightly together, then added jerkily, "No. But people will. I know they will." She glared at me, anger breaking through the thin veneer of control.

"Why shouldn't they, Angel?"

"It's awful, to bring things up when they're over with and people have forgotten." She wrapped her arms tight around her torso.

"Those involved won't have forgotten, Angel. And if any answers can be found, they should be found." Windblown specks of gravel stung my face.

"But it's all over with. Finished." Her voice was shrill.

I looked at her curiously. Angel wanted to believe the unsolved crimes were over with. Why should Angel care?

"Which crime do you know about, Angel?"

"I don't know anything about any crime." She stared at me defiantly. "Everyone's so obsessed with crime. It's so *sick*."

"So you think Maggie will receive a lot of calls?"

"Oh, yes. Of course. People are pigs." Her tone was contemptuous. "They listen to those radio shows, they watch those dreadful TV programs. Anything goes, the nastier the better. And this is a small town. Everybody knows everybody."

Like all exaggerations, this one had a kernel of truth.

Communities have circles of acquaintanceship. Sometimes circles intersect or overlap. Definitely the University was a circle with its own internal groups.

I came back to the central point. "Which crime do you know about?" I moved back and forth on my feet, trying to keep loose.

The wind tugged at Angel's thick blond curls. Her pleasant face was drawn and unhappy. She shook her head stubbornly. "Henrie O—" She paused, then asked sharply, "Can you stop Maggie?"

I suppose my surprise was clear in my face. My surprise—and my immediate displeasure.

A dull flush crept into Angel's cheeks. "I know that sounds odd. But this is going to cause trouble, Henrie O. I know it is. And for no good reason, no good reason at all." She ducked her head and plunged away from me.

A smooth-weave navy sports coat. Khakis with a crease sharp enough to slice cheese. A rep tie.

The sartorially splendid young man beamed at me as I walked up to my office door, key in hand. I'm sure his mother would consider it a lovely smile.

"Mrs. Collins?" His pleasant tenor voice was just a shade pleased with itself.

"Yes." I unlocked my door.

"I'm Jeff Berry. From the president's office." Another engaging smile. "President Tucker would like to see you this afternoon. At two o'clock." A considered pause. "If that would be convenient."

I smiled in return. "And if it isn't?" So I have a rebellious nature.

16

It didn't faze him. "Is there another time that would be better for you? Today."

My, my. I'd met David Tucker only once—at a reception for new faculty several years ago. He'd greeted each newcomer with a graceful comment that indicated he'd prepped for the occasion. He'd asked about my series that had traced the connections between pharmaceutical companies and doctors in a small Texas town. The series made the Pulitzer short list. And earned me the undying enmity of both the industry and the doctors.

I'd taken away from that faculty reception a memory of a big man with a booming laugh, a hearty handshake, and ice-blue eyes that glittered with keen intelligence.

"Actually, two will be fine," I told Jeff Berry. "And," I added, smiling, "please tell President Tucker I'm looking forward to visiting with him."

I had only forty minutes before my appointment with President Tucker. I went straight to *The Clarion* morgue. It didn't take long to find what I wanted: three extensive files that would take a great deal of effort to explore thoroughly. I didn't have time to read all of the materials, of course, but even in a brief overview, names began to take on a reality and pathos that Maggie's ad had not conveyed.

I began with the most recent crime, the 1988 murders of Thorndyke students Howard Rosen and Gail Voss in Lovers' Lane, a secluded road in a wooded area of the campus.

They were found shot to death in Rosen's car. Rosen was twenty-two. Voss was three months shy of twenty-one. Their yearbook pictures were inset in a three-column photograph of the car, doors open, the front end nosed against a flowering dogwood. They both had smiled for the class pictures.

The second crime had no apparent campus connection. Candace Murdoch was charged with the fatal shooting of her wealthy businessman husband, Curt, on July 23, 1982. Her 1983 trial ended with a directed verdict of acquittal.

But the third crime—if crime it was—occurred in the heart of the campus. One early evening in 1976, Dean of Students Darryl Nugent disappeared from his office in Old Central. A photograph taken the previous fall at a faculty softball game showed a handsome, smiling man in his mid-thirties. A big blond with a broad grin, Nugent was rounding the bases in a victory jog, vital, vigorous, virile.

I jotted down some facts on my legal pad. As a young reporter, I'd started off with small steno notebooks, but in later years I switched to the short-size legal pads, lots of paper and a firm back.

Three cases, three sheets.

I made swift, neat notes.

Then I set out to respond to the imperial summons.

Caleb Thorndyke, a Methodist minister, founded Thorndyke University twenty years before the Civil War. For many years, the school was housed in one small Tudor-style redbrick building. That building was twice destroyed by fire, but the 1870 building, Old Central, still stands. It has three Gothic stories crowned by a square bell tower. The campus grew in spurts, sprouting two-to-three-story limestone buildings. More redbrick structures blossomed in the fifties and sixties. The President's Office is in Old Central in the middle of the original campus.

Broad, shallow stone stairs, marked by a century of eager footsteps, lead to enormous double wooden doors. Inside, there is a hushed air, the mixture of dignity and reverence you find in capitols and cathedrals.

It's interesting to speculate how architecture affects lives. The grandeur of this building, with its marbled floors and magnificent paneling, is in unmistakable contrast to today's glass-sheathed towers with their low ceilings and flammable polyurethane moldings.

The anteroom to the president's office is at the end of the west corridor. The brass doorknob felt like iced silk, it was worn so smooth by generations of hands.

I stepped inside a narrow room. Tucker's secretary looked up in polite inquiry. She was an indeterminate age, somewhere between thirty and fifty, a slender, graying woman with precise features and huge gold-rimmed glasses. "May I help you?" Her voice was as muted as her beige sweater and high-necked white cotton blouse.

"Yes. I'm Henrietta Collins. President

Tucker is expecting me." I glanced at the nameplate on her desk: Bernice Baker.

"If you'll take a seat, please." She offered a brief smile and pushed back her chair.

I sat in one of a line of curved-back, black wooden chairs embossed with the University seal as the secretary walked the length of the narrow anteroom to a golden oak door, knocked once, then entered.

Above the chair rail, running the length of the room, hung portraits of all eleven Thorndyke presidents, beginning with the bearded Reverend Caleb Thorndyke and ending with round-cheeked David Tucker.

The portrait was of Tucker as a much younger man.

I rose and walked closer to the painting. Hair as pale and fine as corn silk fringed a domed forehead. The pale blue eyes glittered with vigor, intelligence, acuity, their bold stare as sharp-edged and dangerous as a Prussian saber. The thin lips were slightly curved, an ice-man's version of a smile.

The shiny metal plaque at the bottom of the ornate frame read:

DAVID LOOMIS TUCKER
PRESIDENT FROM 1974–

The door clicked open.
I turned.
"President Tucker will see you now." Bernice's voice was as tepid and colorless as aquarium water.

I stepped into his office. The door clicked shut behind me.

Soft-hued Oriental rugs were islands of delicate color against the glossy parquet floor. The walls were paneled in walnut, with floor-to-ceiling bookshelves on two sides. Deep rose damask hangings framed the enormous windows behind David Tucker. Sun blazed through the southern exposure.

He stood to greet me. Instead of a desk, Thorndyke's president worked at a massive Georgian marble-topped table. The marble sparkled in the sun. An issue of *The Clarion* lay next to an antique silver pen set. It was the only material on the table.

I glanced at the newspaper. As can all newshounds from the hot type days, I easily read upside down and backward. I saw the lead headline. It was today's issue.

My steps made no sound upon the antique rug.

"Mrs. Collins." Tucker's mouth formed a smile. I've seen mortuary slabs with more charm. "I appreciate your willingness to come on such short notice."

"I'm glad I was able to do so." I met his challenging gaze and held it. He was as accustomed to deference as any general or titan of industry, but I'm too old to let my glance slip away subserviently.

A huge hand reached over the marble expanse to enfold mine. His grip was firm and unpleasantly warm.

"Please be seated." Tucker nodded cour-

21

teously, so it was his glance which fell first.

I settled in yet another crest-emblazoned, curved and decidedly hard armchair. Folding my hands in my lap, I looked at him pleasantly.

David Tucker filled his oversized maroon leather chair. He was balding now, with only a few tufts of graying hair. His eyes were deep-set in fleshy folds above plump, smooth, rosy cheeks. But there was nothing avuncular about David Tucker. He had the aura of an old lion, king of his domain, quiescent until challenged, still capable of ferocious attack.

One massive hand picked up a cherrywood pipe. He held it in his palm, his thumb caressing the stem. The pipe was empty of tobacco.

"Mrs. Collins, as Thorndyke University's leader, I believe it is vital for me to know my faculty members. I like to explore their sense of the University's mission."

His eyes bored into mine.

I looked at him steadily.

"I understand you are especially gifted at teaching investigative reporting." The empty pipe bowl glistened richly in the sunlight.

It didn't take a blaring Klaxon to alert me. But it came as no surprise. Why else would I have received this summons?

"That is a specialty of mine."

"What is your definition of investigative reporting, Mrs. Collins?" His tone was pleasant, deceptively bland. He placed the pipe neatly in a pristine, amber-colored glass ashtray.

I like to dance, but not the minuet. I prefer a Charleston.

And yes, I'm impulsive.

"To discover facts that are important to the public. Often, these are facts which have been deliberately hidden." I pointed to *The Clarion* on his table. "Perhaps I can best illustrate my point by describing work one of my independent-study students is currently doing." I rose and reached for the newspaper.

"If I may—" I opened the paper to the boxed quarter-page ad and pointed to it. "Perhaps you noticed this announcement in today's paper?"

He was a quiet, brooding presence, arms folded now across his bulging chest. His flesh-ringed eyes watched me somnolently. But there was a flicker deep in their paleness.

I thought it might have been a flash of admiration, the kind a German ace would accord his prey just before annihilation.

"I did happen to see it." His deep voice was thoughtful. "It looked to me like a dabbling in sensationalism, Mrs. Collins. Surely raking up these sad old stories for no discernible reason— to the distress of so many in our community— doesn't accord with your definition?"

Tucker had honed in on exactly the element that concerned me.

But I didn't like the blandness in his moon face.

And I definitely didn't like where this conversation was leading.

Real men do what men have to do.

Real women love beyond reason.

Real reporters never turn tail.

"Of course it would not," I said firmly. "But that definitely isn't the case in this instance, Dr. Tucker. My student, Maggie Winslow, is pursuing leads which may reveal what actually happened in these three crimes. She is bringing a fresh eye to the facts. Maggie is an extraordinarily resourceful reporter."

Oh, by God, Maggie, you'd better not let me down.

"Indeed. I can see that she has persuaded you of that. But, Mrs. Collins, I urge you to rethink this assignment for your student. I know Ms. Winslow has confidence in her abilities, confidence you apparently share. But, frankly, I see no reason to believe Ms. Winslow can discover anything that the authorities, who are also extremely capable, failed to bring to light."

I felt I couldn't do better than quote Maggie's parting shot to me. "President Tucker, somebody always knows something."

"Nonetheless, you could assign her to another topic." His tone was casual. He might have been discussing the weather.

"I could, Dr. Tucker. But I won't." My tone was as pleasant as his. "There's a small matter of academic freedom to consider."

His ice-blue eyes widened in mock surprise. "Mrs. Collins, I would never infringe upon any Thorndyke faculty member's freedom to teach as he or she sees fit. Certainly not." He pushed back his chair, heaved to his feet. His thin mouth stretched into a cold smile. "I'm delighted we had this opportunity to visit." He came around the table and took

24

my elbow to walk me toward the door. I could smell pine-scented aftershave. "You have certainly brought a distinguished presence to our University."

"Thank you." We were almost at the door.

Tucker looked down at me. "It's wonderful for the University to have faculty with so much professional expertise." His huge hand was hot on my elbow. "But, of course, you are not a *tenured* professor."

This time I didn't say anything.

He held open the door for me. His expression was quizzical. "Do you enjoy teaching at Thorndyke, Mrs. Collins?"

Dennis Duffy is big, blond, brash, a first-rate city editor, and a sexist asshole.

"Henrie O, sweetheart, how's God's gift to the Fourth Estate?" He grinned, but his putty-colored eyes glistened with malice.

"I'm fine, Dennis." I was almost past his desk when I paused and asked, as if it were a casual afterthought, "Oh, Dennis, did you enjoy your talk with President Tucker?"

For an instant, Duffy's pudgy face froze; then he shrugged. "What the hell, lady, gotta take the heat if you want to play in the kitchen."

"When did Tucker call you?"

Duffy glanced at his computer, typed a command. "The big dude got on the horn early. Woke me up. But it shows he starts the morning with our newspaper. Can't beat that."

"And you couldn't wait to tell him I assigned the series to Maggie."

"True. Or false. Not an essay question." His tone mocked.

"And you'll be running the series, of course."

"Sure."

"Dennis?" I waited until he looked away from his computer and up at me. "You're tenured, aren't you?"

His eyes twitched away from mine. "What's that got to do with it?"

But he knew as well as I did.

At my desk, my eyes slid past a recent photo of Jimmy and me climbing the steps of the Pyramid of the Moon at Teotihuacán. Instead, I reached for the silver-framed photo of Richard. Holding it, I could feel some of my anger and frustration seeping away. I could hear his voice, as I heard it so many times for so many years, "Easy does it, Henrie O, easy does it."

Richard always counseled patience and restraint. At the same time, he enjoyed my volatility. It was Richard who gave me my nickname, saying I packed more surprises into a single day than O. Henry ever put in a short story.

What would Richard do? I sought my answer in the face which had meant the world to me.

I grinned. Richard loved that old newspaper saying, "Your mother says she loves you. Check it out."

Check it out.

three

The hallway outside *The Clarion* morgue hosts a row of vending machines. True to the spirit of the nineties, I didn't break for dinner. Instead, I retrieved an apple, a box of raisins, a bag of peanuts, and a can of orange juice. The juice tasted disagreeably metallic. I ate as I continued to work. It was a far cry from long-ago newsrooms, where shiny glazed doughnuts and asphalt-black coffee reigned supreme. Or shared honors with fifths of bourbon stashed in bottom desk drawers.

The Clarion morgue isn't staffed after five. The silence was broken only once. A sports reporter thudded in, seeking the obituary file of an alumnus who had led the football team to a bowl championship in 1954. Otherwise, I had the place to myself. With the doors to the hall closed, it was as quiet—as a morgue.

The 1988 Rosen-Voss murders and the 1983 Murdoch acquittal were on computer. I had to dig among dusty bound ledgers for the 1976 coverage on the disappearance of Darryl Nugent, dean of students.

I started with the Rosen-Voss case, scrolling up the coverage of Sunday, April 17, 1988:

STUDENTS SHOT TO DEATH IN LOVERS' LANE

Generations of Thorndyke students have found romance in Lovers' Lane. Friday night, graduate student Howard Rosen and senior Gail Voss met death there.

According to Derry Hills police, a jogger discovered their bodies about 6 A.M. Saturday in Rosen's car on the secluded road. Police Lt. Larry Urschel said Rosen, 22, and Voss, 20, apparently had been shot to death.

Police theorize that the couple was slain on Friday night. Rosen and Voss were last seen at the Green Owl, a café near the campus, at approximately 11 P.M., according to police.

Lt. Urschel refused to speculate on who fired the shots that killed the couple. No weapon was found at the scene, Lt. Urschel said.

Rosen was a 1987 summa cum laude graduate of the School of Journalism and Mass Communications. City Editor Dennis Duffy said Rosen had served as deputy city editor of *The Clarion* for the spring semester of 1987. Duffy said Voss was currently deputy LifeStyle editor. *Clarion* student editors work in tandem with professional journalists. *The Clarion* serves both the University community and the township of Derry Hills.

Alma Kinkaid, University registrar, said Rosen was from Kansas City and Voss from Derry Hills.

Police described the crime scene as an unfrequented area. The asphalt road leads from the quadrangle behind Frost Memorial Library to a

Grecian amphitheater and Lake Boone. The road's official name is Frost Lane, but it is commonly referred to as Lovers' Lane. The road winds through a thickly wooded forest to the sylvan open theater above Lake Boone. There are no other structures in the area and no streetlights.

Rosen's roommate, Stuart Singletary, from Dallas, Texas, a senior, expressed shock. "I can't believe it. Why would anybody kill Howard and Gail? It's crazy!"

Singletary was awakened by police this morning and asked to identify Rosen. "I didn't realize until then that Howard hadn't come in last night."

Singletary insisted neither Rosen nor Voss had enemies. "That's ridiculous. It must have been a vagrant, something like that."

Police revealed that Rosen's billfold and Voss's purse were found in Rosen's 1987 Range Rover. Both the billfold and purse contained money and credit cards.

Lt. Urschel said police would be interviewing friends of the murdered students. He asks anyone with information concerning the deaths to contact the Derry Hills Police Department at 303-9900.

That was the lead story. But I read all the coverage, the sidebar features about Rosen and Voss, and the speculative comments of a University criminology professor. ("If I were the cops, I'd look for a rejected suitor or a jealous woman. Derry Hills isn't the Bronx. The odds of a random killing are next to none.")

In later issues, I found the coverage of the two funerals, with stark photos of the bereaved

29

and bewildered families, the reassurances by President Tucker that the Thorndyke campus was indeed safe for students, the daily progress reports by Lieutenant Urschel of the Derry Hills Police Department.

The stories hung on to page one for a week; inside, for several more weeks. But as the days of spring and the academic year dwindled, so did the coverage, until, finally, it was old news, the unsolved campus murders in the spring of '88.

I gleaned a few more facts from the follow-ups.

According to Gail Voss's roommate, Linda Lou Kelly, Rosen and Voss were unofficially engaged, but a wedding date hadn't been set.

Police announced Rosen and Voss had spent most of the evening at the Green Owl. The couple had been deep in conversation. "Laughing a lot," a waitress recalled. "He kept raising a glass and saying, 'Here's to Joe Smith,' and she'd smile and say something like 'Joe's my guy.'"

I knew the Green Owl. It was just a block from Brandt Hall and was still one of the most popular hangouts for students and faculty, a combination restaurant, bar, and coffeehouse. Members of the English and philosophy faculties were especially likely to be found in the game-room area, around old oak tables with inlaid squares for checkers and chess.

On the final night of their lives, Rosen and Voss ate in one of the wooden booths at the far back. "They were regulars," the waitress said.

But when I'd read all the stories, the bottom line was that the murder weapon was never found and no suspect in the murders was ever named.

The in-depth profiles pictured Howard Rosen as boisterous and outgoing, with a booming laugh and a penchant for practical jokes. Gail Voss was described as serious, intense, responsible. Both were superb students. Rosen had been named a Fulbright scholar and planned to spend the following year in Berlin, studying the subversion of the German press in the decade preceding World War II.

I studied their pictures.

Howard Rosen exuded the vitality of a buccaneer. In another age, he would have been at home in an elegant doublet and brandishing a sword. His wickedly merry eyes gleamed with deviltry, and his full, sensuous mouth stretched in an appealing grin. Any woman would love to smooth his thick dark curls. No sweet maiden would have been safe from his blandishments.

Gail Voss stared shyly into the camera. Smooth hair framed a heart-shaped face. Her lips curved in a sweet smile. She was the girl next door, your kid sister, Miss America.

Anger flickered within me.

Howard Rosen should be jumping to his feet at a press conference, his voice raised in demand, or straddling a chair at a coffeehouse, regaling fellow reporters with ambitious plans to climb a mountain or run a marathon.

Gail Voss should be hurrying to meet a

deadline and, perhaps playing the dual role of many of today's young women, thinking about dinner and picking up the baby at day care.

They should not be moldering bones and desiccated flesh in corroding coffins.

I fished the last peanut from the bag and swiftly scrawled several questions beneath the heading "Rosen-Voss." Then I turned back to the computer, punched in "Candace Murdoch," and pressed the search key.

The first story in what became the Murdoch case ran on Thursday, July 22, 1982:

CIVIC LEADER SLAIN AT HOME

Curt Murdoch, president of Murdoch Brothers Concrete, was shot to death Wednesday night in the garden of his Derry Hills home. Police have not named any suspects in the murder of the well-known Derry Hills civic leader.

Police said Murdoch's body was found slumped on a stone bench near a reflecting pool. Lt. Ralph Forbes said a .38 pistol was found on the terrace behind the house, approximately twenty feet from the bench. Lt. Forbes said shots were heard by a next-door neighbor, Gerald Trent, at 10:05 P.M.

Trent told police he had just opened his back door to let out the cat when he heard the shots. Police said Trent was certain of the time because he was watching the ten o'clock news.

Police said Trent, a retired colonel in the military police, immediately ran outside and crossed a low stone fence that separates the properties.

Trent reported that he saw a flash of white moving toward the Murdoch house. Trent told police that when he reached the pool behind the house, he found the fatally wounded Murdoch sprawled on a marble bench. Trent immediately returned to his home and called police.

Police said their investigation is ongoing.

Calls to the Murdoch residence have not been answered. Other residents of the home include Murdoch's widow, Candace; his son, Michael; and daughter, Jennifer.

In subsequent stories, suggestive facts emerged: Candace Murdoch was twenty-three years younger than her husband. It was his second marriage. She'd been a masseuse at his health club.

The family cook, Cordelia Winters, told police Mr. and Mrs. Murdoch had quarreled that evening over the death of Mrs. Murdoch's parakeet.

Candace Murdoch was arrested and charged with first-degree murder three weeks after her husband's death. She pleaded not guilty, claiming that at the time the shots were fired she was on the telephone. Murdoch claimed that a representative of a local charity had called, requesting that she place donated items on the front porch for pickup the next week. Murdoch said she couldn't remember the woman's name or the name of the charity because of all the excitement and turmoil attendant upon the murder of her husband. Murdoch issued an emotional plea for the caller to come forward and confirm the conversation.

The trial began in February of 1983. The

prosecution contended that Murdoch had broken the neck of his wife's pet and placed it on her dinner plate that evening, and that they had quarreled bitterly. The prosecution claimed that Candace Murdoch took her husband's pistol from a drawer of his desk in the study and followed him to the garden, where she shot him. Her fingerprints were found on the gun, and the white dress she wore that evening was snagged and grass-stained.

The lead story on February 10, 1983, had a three-column headline:

MYSTERY WITNESS COMES FORWARD, ALIBIS WIFE ACCUSED OF MURDER

Testimony from an unexpected witness shocked the prosecution in the Candace Murdoch murder trial today, confirming the accused woman's statement that she was on the telephone at the time her wealthy husband, Curt, was shot to death last summer.

Angela Chavez took the stand at two-thirty and swore that she was talking with Murdoch at five minutes after 10 P.M. on the night of Curt Murdoch's murder. Chavez further testified that Murdoch suddenly interrupted and said, "I hear shots! Someone's shooting outside. I'll have to get my husband," and then hung up.

When the prosecution asked why Chavez waited until now to come forward, she testified she had left Derry Hills shortly after the murder of Curt Murdoch and had only returned a few weeks ago. Chavez said she had been unaware that her conversation with Murdoch was of such importance until she read the stories in this week's paper.

Prosecutor Wayne Hemblee attacked Chavez's credibility, but, through a blistering cross-examination, the soft-spoken witness maintained her composure. She denied friendship with Murdoch, and, in fact, said, "I've never met Mrs. Murdoch."

The prosecution faced further troubles when Candace Murdoch took the stand, said she recognized Chavez's voice, and, with tears streaming down her face, thanked Chavez for telling the truth. "I will always be grateful to you for coming forward."

Murdoch dried her tears and spoke up strongly as her attorney led her through the events of the evening. She testified that when she heard the shots from the terrace, she broke off the conversation and ran out from the study and darted through the shrubs to see what had happened. "That's why my dress was mussed. And when I saw Curt—oh, God, I couldn't believe it!"

Murdoch admitted she and her husband had quarreled that night, but said her husband had not killed her pet bird, but that he hadn't liked the bird and had put it in the dining room when he found it dead in its cage. "Curt thought he was being funny." The witness's voice shook. "It's so awful now to think I was mad the last time I saw him."

The headline in next day's *Clarion* said it all:

CANDACE MURDOCH ACQUITTED

I only wrote one query on my pad: Angel Chavez?

It was half past six and I was tired. I don't work twelve-hour days anymore. I stood, stretched, glanced at the bound volume of *The Clarion* for March 1976.

No, I had to finish tonight.

And that's when I heard shouts.

My response was instinctive, automatic. Over the years, covering wars, trials, and riots, I've heard every level of human expression, from deep anguish to desperate fear to demonic anger. I know emotion when I hear it.

As I hurried up the hall, a woman's voice rose to a screech. "Where's Dennis? Where the hell is he? Are they in his office?"

I reached the newsroom doorway.

Rita Duffy, the city editor's wife, stood in the center of the newsroom. Her appearance shocked me. Rita glories in the latest fashions, whatever they may be. But tonight she looked slovenly in a wrinkled red silk blouse and tight green slacks. And she wore no makeup, leaving her puffy face naked and splotchy. She shoved Duffy's empty chair hard against his desk. The sound caromed across the room.

Startled faces turned toward her. Only a handful of students remained in the newsroom. It was close to the final deadline and most of the stories were in. Only late-breaking news would be used now.

Eric March, the student deputy city editor,

stopped chewing a mouthful of Cheetos. "Wait a minute, Mrs. Duffy," he mumbled, then swallowed. "Take it easy. Okay? Duffy took the evening off. I'm putting the paper to bed." Eric had a broken nose from intramural touch football, a smear of Cheetos orange on his chin, and a look of exquisite embarrassment. The young editor's job description didn't include handling hysterical wives. He shoved back his chair and stood, still holding the bag of cheese puffs.

Rita darted across the newsroom, flung open the door to Duffy's dark office. "Dennis, you bastard—" She turned on the light, stared into the office, then swung around. "Okay, where the hell are they?"

Eric looked bewildered. "Where's who?"

"Dennis and that Winslow bitch."

The quality of the strained silence in the newsroom abruptly changed.

The sports editor shot a swift look at Eric.

A reporter swung to face her monitor, carefully not looking toward Eric.

Another student—I scrambled for his name, Buddy, yes, Buddy Neville—began to smile. His thin lips curved in a malicious grin.

Eric looked as if somebody'd kicked him in the gut. "No way, lady. You're crazy. Maggie's—Maggie and I— You got it all wrong. I don't know where Duffy is, but he's not with Maggie. He's not." Eric shouted it.

I wished his voice sounded more confident. And I wished there hadn't been a sudden flicker of uncertainty in his eyes.

37

Rita Duffy laughed, and the sound was harsh and ugly. "Oh, you've got a lot to learn, kid. I can tell you about women like Maggie Winslow. They'll do anything—anything—to get ahead. And bastards like Dennis will screw them every time. But this time"—her voice broke—"this time he's not going to get away with it. When I find them, he's going to wish he'd never been born." Rita whirled around. She brushed past me. I don't think she even saw me. Her face was mottled, her eyes glazed.

Eric March watched her leave, then, scowling, he yelled at the sports editor. "You got that story done? Let's get this show on the road." Eric stared down at the desk. An ugly flush surged up his neck, turned his face and ears red. He flung down his pencil. "Buddy—hey, Buddy, put it to bed for me, man." And he plunged toward the hall.

I heard the downstairs door wheeze shut. A moment later, the sound of Eric's clattering steps ended, and the door wheezed a second time.

If I hurried I could catch Rita, perhaps calm her down, encourage her to go home.

I didn't think there was a thing I could say to Eric March.

But protecting Dennis Duffy from the mess he'd made of his personal life wasn't in *my* job description either.

Besides, I was irritated.

I wanted Maggie Winslow to produce first-rate copy, a new, fresh, important investigation of three unsolved crimes. I wanted her series to be exactly what I'd promised Dr. Tucker it would be: painstaking, in-depth investigative reporting.

I wished the stories were mine to do. But they weren't. I was a bystander, a coach, a cheerleader. I had to depend upon a young reporter to do the work. So I wanted Maggie functioning at her best.

What effect would Rita's suspicions have on Maggie?

Very little, if I could help it. Maggie was smart and quick, and now was the time to prove she was tough, even if she might also be in the process of learning the painful lesson that those who play with fire often get burned. Of course, Rita could be wrong. In fact, it would surprise me if Maggie was having an affair with Dennis. But I've been surprised before.

I walked over to my office, unlocked it, and hurried to the phone. I punched Maggie's number.

The answering machine picked up.

My message was short and to the point: "Maggie, this is Henrietta Collins. I must talk to you tomorrow as soon as possible. I will expect you here in my office at eight-thirty in the morning. Thank you."

I locked my office, said good night to Buddy and the others. Buddy arched his eyebrows sardonically, but said nothing.

It was a relief to get back to the morgue. I

had the beginnings of a headache, but I was determined to finish my task.

It didn't take long. The facts were quite simple: At approximately 5 P.M. on Monday, March 15, 1976, secretary Maude Galloway knocked on the door of her boss, Dean of Students Darryl Nugent, to tell him she was leaving for the day. "The dean was writing on a legal pad. He barely looked up when I knocked. He said, 'Good night, Maude.' I closed the door to his office and left."

Darryl Nugent was never seen again.

I replaced the bound volume of *Clarion*s and gathered up my notes.

I had some ideas about how Maggie should begin. Tomorrow I would share them with her.

four

Steam curled from the mouth of the thermos. Coffee gurgled into my mug. I always enjoy using this mug, a gift from my daughter, Emily. The mug is fire-engine red. An arched black cat forms its handle. Inside the mug, a small gray mouse perches on a tiny ceramic ledge. The legend reads "Morning Delight."

I lifted the mug, savored the scent and welcomed the pungent flavor of its contents. Whether it was the stimulus of the caffeine or the excitement of the chase, this morning I felt

I could take on the world—including President Tucker—and win hands down. Gone was last night's fatigue. And I'd dismissed my worry that Maggie Winslow might be too distracted by her personal life to do a good job. Maggie—whether romantically involved with Dennis Duffy, placating her boyfriend, or avoiding Rita Duffy—had an assignment from me that better take precedence.

I wasn't going to do Maggie's work for her, but I could, one way or another, point her in the right direction.

I pulled my legal pad closer and checked the questions I wanted Maggie to explore:

Rosen-Voss case

Did anyone profit?
Enemies?
Quarrels?
Ex-lovers?
Competition?
Why that particular night?
What happened to Howard Rosen and Gail
 Voss on the day they died?
Why Lovers' Lane????

Candace Murdoch

Who else might have wanted
 Curt Murdoch dead?
Previous connection between
 Angela Chavez and Candace Murdoch?
Check Angel's story.

Darryl Nugent
Get his appointments the day he
    disappeared.
Love affair?
Money missing?
Family problems?
Health problems?
Talk to his secretary.

I finished my coffee and glanced at the clock. Forty past eight.

Maggie was late.

I reached for the phone, impatiently jabbed the numbers.

"Winslow residence."

A male voice.

Not Eric March was my first quick thought. And not another student. This was a man's voice, deeper, harder, heavier.

"May I speak to Maggie Winslow, please."

"Who's calling?"

There was a brusqueness to the request that I didn't like. But I wanted to talk to Maggie. "Henrietta Collins."

"Hold on."

I heard the receiver being muffled.

In a moment, a different man spoke.

"Lieutenant Urschel." His voice was hoarse, raspy. "Derry Hills Police Department."

I didn't need the identifying tag.

Lieutenant Larry Urschel. His name was in my notes, the officer in charge of the investigation into the murders of Howard Rosen and Gail Voss.

"Lieutenant Urschel—" It was hard to talk, the words felt like pebbles in my throat. "Where's Maggie?"

I drive fast. It's always hard to keep my MG below the speed limit. This morning I didn't try. I shot beneath a canopy of trees into the dimness of Lovers' Lane and a half mile later slewed to a stop at the barricade. As I got out of the car, a young uniformed patrolman walked up.

"Mrs. Collins?"

I nodded.

This boy didn't look old enough to be a movie usher, but his eyes already had the wary, careful look of a cop, checking out my hands, checking out my vehicle.

I fastened my jacket. It was still cold, the winter-coming chill of a mid-November morning, even though it would soon warm into the sixties. Fog wreathed the trees, eddied in torn swaths over the road.

"Lieutenant Urschel is on his way, Mrs. Collins. He asked that you wait here for him."

"All right." I looked past the patrolman. I could hear movement and voices, but I couldn't see around the bend where the barricade had been set up.

I was familiar with the terrain. I'd attended an outdoor performance of *Blithe Spirit* at the University amphitheater last summer. It was heavily wooded here. Oaks, hickories, and feathery-branched pines fought for space. Oak limbs thick as my body locked above the road. The blacktop wound around several more hills before it reached the amphitheater on a rise overlooking Boone Lake. I doubted that Daniel Boone had ever set up camp by these waters, but it was a local legend highly prized by Derry Hills residents.

"It's been a hell of a morning—"

A dusty green Ford Bronco jolted to a stop beside my MG.

The young patrolman broke off and stood tall and straight. He didn't salute, but the effect was the same.

The driver's door slammed. The man who moved toward us had the broad shoulders and athletic certitude of an old football player. His stride was just this side of a swagger. His waist was still trim, though I pegged him to be in his mid-forties. His close-cropped brown hair was flecked with gray, and his bulldog-square face was heavily lined. He wore an inexpensive brown suit. The jacket was a size too small. Did he stubbornly refuse to acknowledge weight gain? Or was his salary stretched as tight as his suit coat?

When we faced each other, combative eyes scanned me with the rapidity of a carnival barker sizing up the crowd. I read the evaluation in them: *Late sixties, big city, money, sure of herself, handle with care.*

"Lieutenant Urschel?" I held out my hand. "Henrietta Collins."

There was a barely perceptible pause before the homicide detective thrust out a tanned, muscular hand. "Ma'am." His grip was cold,

44

firm, fleeting. Shaking hands with a woman wasn't his style. "Appreciate your coming." His voice reminded me of President Clinton's. Did Urschel, too, have allergies? Or had he smoked too many cigarettes for too many years? "I met you last year. At Don's wedding."

Don Brown is also a lieutenant in the Derry Hills P.D. He is a friend of mine. We'd first become acquainted shortly after I came to Thorndyke and a young woman was murdered in the apartment house where I was staying.

I'd enjoyed Don's wedding very much. But Urschel's memory of the event was better than mine. I didn't remember him. Perhaps I don't scan crowds with the same intensity.

"Yes. Of course. How is Don?"

Urschel's sandy eyebrows rose a fraction. "Okay. I guess. He's on paternity leave." He tried to say it matter-of-factly. He didn't quite bring it off. Between forty-something and thirty-something, there is more than a gap in time. "Okay." His eyes flicked toward my right hand and the wedding band I still wore. "Mrs. Collins. You know Maggie Winslow. Right?"

"Yes, Lieutenant."

"Then if you'll come this way—"

Just around the curve, an ambulance waited, lights blinking. Police tape on stakes fluttered around a twenty-foot square of the blacktopped road.

A woman's body lay in a crumpled heap in the center of this marked-off area. Her magenta suit was sodden from the heavy mist of the night, and the short skirt was hiked up almost to her hips. Her face was pressed against the asphalt. A jade silk scarf poked out from beneath hair that had once been sleek and glossy, and now lay dank and damp on skin no longer living. The scarf cut deeply into her neck. A black leather shoulder bag rested about a foot from the corpse.

A technician within the cordoned-off area looked toward us. She brushed back a strand of strawberry-blond hair with the back of a latex-gloved hand and said quietly, "I'm finished, Lieutenant. They can take her now."

"Not yet."

The tech shot him a cool glance, but said nothing. She got up a little stiffly, moved to unlimber her muscles, then reached down for a blue vinyl bag.

A lanky photographer crouched a couple of feet away. "Just a few more shots, Lieutenant," he called, not looking our way.

When the photographer rose, Urschel jerked his head at me. "Mrs. Collins, she checks out with the photo on her driver's license. But for the record—"

I didn't want to see her face.

But Urschel hadn't invited me here for my benefit. At his nod, the technician eased the rigid body over, gently swiped the dank hair away from the face.

It was as ugly as I had known it would be.

And it was Maggie.

My hands clenched. "Yes." I had trouble breathing. "It is Maggie Winslow."

Maggie Winslow, arrogant, confident, and good. Very, very good at reporting. Maybe not so good in judging the impact of her questions.

But I was the one who'd demanded that she do more than rehash old crimes for the entertainment of readers. I'd insisted I'd accept the work *only* if she turned up new information. I'd even been pleased when I saw her brazen, bold ad in *The Clarion* Wednesday morning. Way to go, Maggie, I'd thought.

Pleased.

Dammit. Oh, dammit, what had I done?

"Sorry, ma'am." But Urschel's tone was perfunctory, and there was no pause before the next question. "You were her professor?"

I stared at Maggie's body, bunched awkwardly on the asphalt. "Yes." Oh, yes, indeed, the professor who wanted fresh facts about crime, very fresh facts. But also the professor who'd worried that Maggie's personal problems might intrude on her work. Had her personal problems led to this ugly finale? For my own peace of mind, I desperately hoped so.

"What was so damn important you left her a message to be in your office at eight-thirty this morning?" The words peppered me like pellets.

My head jerked toward him.

Of course Urschel had listened to Maggie's messages. And the crisp demand I'd left

Wednesday evening—*I must talk to you tomorrow as soon as possible*—wasn't the ordinary exchange between a professor and a student.

His avid eyes watched me like a feral cat tracking a field rat.

"I wanted to speak with Maggie about some articles she was working on under my supervision." Briefly, I described the investigative series Maggie had proposed. When I mentioned the old Lovers' Lane murders, Urschel's square face tightened.

That's when I popped my own question. "Is this where they found Howard Rosen and Gail Voss?" My voice had a tight, thin edge.

Oh, Maggie, was it those murders that brought you to this dank, solitary place?

Lieutenant Urschel looked down the lane. His face creased. "No. Rosen's car was closer to the lake."

In 1988, the dead students were found in a car. But Maggie's body lay in the middle of the road. "Where's Maggie's car?"

"We're looking for it." Urschel blinked as if obliterating a vision of the past, and his stare settled on me. "Now, Mrs. Collins, what was so urgent—"

I'd expected to deal with the problem of Maggie Winslow and Dennis Duffy today. But not this way.

"—that you had to see Maggie Winslow first thing this morning?"

I had no right to keep quiet about last night's ugly scene in the newsroom. As matter-of-factly as possible, I told Urschel about

48

Rita Duffy's furious arrival, hunting for her husband—and Maggie.

Urschel pulled a small notebook from his pocket, flipped it open. "So who are these people?"

I gave him the names.

"Mrs. Duffy thought she"—and he jerked his head toward the body—"was screwing her husband?"

"Yes." I turned my head away from Maggie. I concentrated on the tendrils of fog in the pines.

"This Duffy woman was real mad?" His husky voice was uninflected, but the pen was poised above the pad.

"Yes." In my mind I heard again the clatter of Rita Duffy's footsteps and the asthmatic wheeze of the J-School door.

Urschel made a note. His heavy face looked satisfied. I could read his thoughts. This was going to be a quick one, he had decided, an easy one. But he wasn't quite finished with me. "Where were you last night, between six and eight?"

"Is that when Maggie was killed?" Rita Duffy had burst into the newsroom about six-thirty.

Cops like to ask questions, not answer them.

There was a noticeable pause, then Urschel replied curtly, "Early last evening. Where were you?"

It was like dealing with a boomerang. Every question brought it back to me.

I sketched out my evening.

"These files you checked. They all had to do with the series she"—the lieutenant again jerked his head toward that still figure—"was writing?"

"Yes."

He waited.

Old reporters know better than anyone that one-word answers can keep you out of trouble.

I waited, too.

He had less time than I. "Who saw you?" His tone betrayed his irritation. Urschel still stood a couple of feet away, well out of my space, but I felt pressed.

"Most of the time I was alone in *The Clarion* morgue. That's where the back editions are kept."

"You were working pretty late. Right?" There was nothing ominous in his words, but I felt a prickle of unease.

"Fairly late."

"You go to this kind of trouble for all your students?" He didn't try to hide his disbelief.

I didn't like the question, and I didn't like the implication. "No," I replied pleasantly, "I do not go to this kind of effort for all my students."

Urschel snapped, "What got you so involved, Mrs. Collins?"

"There were special circumstances, Lieutenant." I told Urschel about Maggie's ad. "*The Clarion* is well read. That ad attracted the attention of Dr. Tucker."

Lieutenant Urschel's eyes narrowed. I didn't need to identify the University president for him. Tucker was a Derry Hills mover and shaker.

"Dr. Tucker didn't want Maggie to do the series." I intended to make it very clear that the possibility of bringing those investigations back to life definitely displeased Thorndyke's president. "He wanted me to request that Maggie drop her investigations of the crimes."

I hoped this conversation would lead Urschel directly to the president's office.

But as I talked, I realized Urschel wasn't interested in the series. He was merely puzzled by what he saw as an odd relationship between a student and a professor. When the student was murdered, anything odd blinked like neon.

"In fact, Dr. Tucker was—"

"Yeah, I see," he said abruptly, cutting me off. He snapped shut the notebook.

"Lieutenant." He was dismissing me, but I wasn't ready to go yet. I felt at a huge disadvantage. As a reporter, you have some standing. And a reporter who covers the police beat builds up long-term relationships. This cop will open up. That one can be charmed. Another will kindly respond to respectful inquiries. Yet another is scared of the press. But I didn't know Urschel. I had no inkling how to approach him. But I had to give it a try. "Lieutenant, what counts here is that I insisted that Maggie hunt for new facts for those articles. And now she's dead. In Lovers'

Lane. What if she found out who killed Howard Rosen and Gail Voss?"

"No way, Professor." Urschel's eyes locked with mine. "A kid reporter can't find an answer in a few hours that I couldn't find in months of looking. So you can relax. The Rosen-Voss case had nothing to do with this murder." He turned away.

"Lieutenant Urschel, why was Maggie killed here—in Lovers' Lane—if there's no connection?"

I thought he was going to ignore me. Cops protect facts in an investigation as Woodward and Bernstein protected Deep Throat. But, grudgingly, Urschel looked back at me. "The ME said she wasn't killed here. The lividity's wrong. She was knocked unconscious, strangled, and left lying on her side. Somebody dumped her here an hour or so after death." Once again his gaze flicked down the road. I knew he was remembering another crime scene. He cleared his throat. "Mrs. Collins, this girl was strangled. The students in '88 were shot. You can rest easy, Professor. This murder has nothing to do with the Lovers' Lane murders. Nothing."

Maybe.

Maybe not.

I have no classes on Thursdays. Throughout the day, I graded papers, but it was easy to track the investigation into Maggie's murder by looking through my office window into *The Clarion* newsroom. I kept my office door open so I could hear snatches of conversation.

Buddy Neville had taken over as deputy city editor, subbing for Eric March. Dennis Duffy, his face ashen, stared dully at his computer, apparently leaving most of the work to Buddy. Buddy tried to submerge his pleasure in handling a big breaking story with an occasional muttered "Too bad about Maggie" or "Poor old Eric." But mostly the boy's eyes gleamed with excitement, and he barked orders over the phone to Kitty Brewster, who was covering the police beat.

If only I had the police beat...

The newsroom drew other faculty like a magnet. Everybody wanted to know what was happening. Helen Tracy, the LifeStyle editor, darted from desk to desk like a honey bee after nectar. Even the J-School's normally aloof director, Susan Dillon, dropped by twice. Fortunately, no one knew I'd been to Lovers' Lane that morning.

Helen, who has a story instinct on a Louella Parsons level, poked her lean body into my office about lunchtime. "Wasn't Maggie one of your students, Henrie O?" Her bright, clever brown eyes scoured my face.

"Yes."

Our eyes locked for a moment.

Helen knew—I don't know how, perhaps it was that uncanny journalistic instinct of hers—that I knew more than I would tell, but we didn't have to put this communication in words. She nodded. "Talk to you later," she rasped, and buzzed away.

Every so often, I looked out into the newsroom at Dennis Duffy. He no longer exhibited the self-satisfied air of a plundering roué. Instead, his dissipated face had the stark bleakness of a man trying to find his way through earthquake ruins, all the familiar landmarks obliterated, the smell of death cloying the air. Had Rita Duffy been right? Had Dennis known Maggie a lot better than he should have?

Angel Chavez slipped in during the lunch hour. She stood by the city desk, her back to me.

Of course, the news of the murder was of interest to everyone in the J-School, including the staff.

But somehow I doubted that Angel usually kept abreast of breaking stories. She looked so stolid, wearing a white cotton blouse with a scalloped collar, a navy skirt, and sensible blue leather flats.

That demure demeanor didn't fool me now.

I remembered the sharp feel of the wind at the track and Angel's hair streaming away from a face raddled with anger.

And fear?

Yes, she looked like such an unlikely person to have starred as a defense witness in a notorious murder trial. But appearances do deceive—or mislead. Who would ever forget the scholarly young professor who'd been fed the quiz-show answers?

Reporters have to remember that the surface doesn't reflect the depths.

And I was sure I had no grasp of what Angel thought or feared at this moment.

Buddy was flapping his hands. "...jogger found her body about seven this morning. Out on Lovers' Lane. But Kitty says the cops just picked up Maggie's car from the J-School lot."

Angel said sharply, "A jogger found the bodies that spring."

For an instant, Buddy looked blank. The year 1988 was long before his time at Thorndyke. But he was quick. "You mean those students? Huh."

It was hardly a world-class coincidence. Ever since the Kennedy days, joggers are everywhere, especially on college campuses. I was more interested in the fact that Maggie's car had been spotted in the J-School lot. I wondered if her car keys were in her purse.

"Her car was in the lot. So somebody drove her to Lovers' Lane," Angel said.

"Looks like it." The phone rang. Buddy turned away, snagged the receiver. "City desk." He scrawled notes on a pad.

Angel waited patiently.

Buddy muttered, "Yeah, yeah. Cover it. Okay."

When he hung up, he swiveled to his computer.

Angel moved closer, spoke over his shoulder. "Those articles Maggie was writing..."

Buddy looked up impatiently. "Yeah?"

"Do you know if she'd turned anything in yet?" Angel's face was somber, intent.

The phone rang. "I don't know, Angel. Check with Duffy." Buddy grabbed the receiver. "City desk."

Angel crossed to Duffy's station. "Dennis, do you have Maggie's stories on the old crimes?"

Dennis didn't even look up. He grunted, "No."

Angel waited for a moment, but he continued to stare at his computer. Slowly she turned away.

I glimpsed Angel's round, usually pretty face. Her eyes were dark with worry, her lips set in a grim line.

I turned to my computer and checked to see if Maggie had filed any stories in the series.

I didn't find anything. That would no doubt please Angel.

But that didn't matter. What mattered was the fact that Angel Chavez was worried.

I made a note—"Watch Angel"—then turned back to the papers I was trying to grade. I kept a close eye on the newsroom through my window.

It was almost three when Buddy jolted up from his chair, clutching the telephone receiver.

When I reached the city desk, he'd just slammed down the phone. He stared at Dennis, then blurted, his voice an octave higher, "The cops have brought in Mrs. Duffy."

Rita Duffy's arraignment was at four-thirty that afternoon. That meant the police investigator—Lieutenant Urschel—had convinced the prosecutor's office that there was sufficient evidence to prove the case against Rita. I had a gut feeling there had to be more evidence than we—the press—knew about.

I elbowed my way into the jammed county courtroom.

Rita huddled at the defense table, her face slack with shock. I'd seen survivors of train wrecks and bombing raids with that same look of incredulity. And horror.

Was Rita terrified of this proceeding? Or was she trying desperately not to remember the tautness of her own muscles pulling, pulling, pulling a silk scarf until it would tighten no more?

Rita's pudgy fingers gripped the edge of the wooden table. Her faded blue eyes were blank, her plump face pasty. Her broad shoulders hunched defensively. She was powerfully built for a woman.

Lieutenant Urschel had indicated that Maggie's body had been moved after death. Rita Duffy appeared to be a strong woman, quite capable of that feat.

But why? Where was Maggie killed, and why was her body moved an hour or so later? What possible reason could there be?

I edged to my left for a better view of Rita.

Someone should have told her to comb her hair, put on makeup, sit up straight.

Dennis Duffy sat stiffly in the first row. It was the only time I'd ever seen him without his perpetual sneer. His big hands were clenched tight and his usually cocky face looked scared and perplexed.

The machinery of the law—in the persons

of Circuit Court Judge Edward Merritt and Prosecutor Paul Avery—moved with juggernaut precision. The arraignment took a quarter hour from start to finish.

Rita's lawyer, B. B. Ellison, pleaded her not guilty to the charge of murder in the first degree.

Paul Avery stood. "If it may please the court." The prosecutor approached the bench.

I was familiar with Avery's name from trial stories in *The Clarion*. This was the first time I'd seen him. Gary Cooper, I thought suddenly, the same lean, powerful frame, and bony, quizzical face. Avery's features were memorable—high-bridged nose, cleft chin, piercing light-green eyes. He was about my age, and he moved with an easy, confident slouch. He had the air of a man who never hurried, a man who imposed his tempo on the world.

"If it please the court, the prosecution requests a million-dollar bond. This is an especially brutal crime, Your Honor." Avery had a magnetic voice, not the super-proud slickness of a radio announcer, but the full, rich timbre of a lawyer at ease with an audience of one or a thousand. "The young victim was knocked unconscious"—he paused for a definite beat—"then strangled." Once again Avery let silence fill the courtroom, and the ugly image took shape in every mind. "Your Honor, this demonstrates a cold and deliberate premeditation."

"Motion granted." Judge Merritt's waspish face, beneath a high curl of stiff gray hair, remained remote, untouched. He banged his gavel and rose.

Everyone stood.

As the door to the judge's chambers closed, a deputy gestured for Rita to come.

Rita Duffy would remain in jail. There was no way she and Dennis could come up with enough money to make that bond.

Murder in the first degree.

At the preliminary hearing, set for December 4, Ellison could argue for a charge of second-degree murder.

I doubted he'd get it.

If Maggie Winslow's killer strangled her as she lay helpless, this could not be considered a crime of passion.

Murder in the first degree. If convicted, Rita Duffy could be sentenced to death.

Deputies walked on either side of Rita as she left the courtroom.

Cameras flashed and reporters trotted alongside as she was led down the hallway.

She looked back over her shoulder, her eyes brimming with tears. Her mouth formed a plaintive cry, "Dennis, Dennis!"

And then she was in the elevator. The doors slid heavily shut.

The reporters turned toward Dennis.

A local television reporter pressed forward. "Mr. Duffy"—he stumbled over the name because this was Dennis and they played poker together—"Mr. Duffy, is your wife guilty?"

Dennis's chest heaved. Perspiration beaded

his face. He flung up his head. "Rita's innocent. I'll prove it. I swear to God I'll prove it!"

For the first time in our acquaintance, I admired Dennis Duffy.

Dennis whirled away from the elevator. For a moment, our glances met and held. He still had that punchy look, a man who'd lost his place and had no idea which way to go. He grabbed the arm of B. B. Ellison.

Dennis bent his big head close to the lawyer's and talked fast.

I realized as I turned away that Dennis was looking toward me.

five

My desk was in disarray. In the center were papers I'd tried to grade as I kept tabs on the coverage of the police investigation into Maggie's murder. But to one side was the material I'd spread out early that morning in anticipation of my expected meeting with Maggie. I wouldn't be instructing my student in how to find out more about the most famous unsolved crimes in Derry Hills.

I perched on the edge of my desk, unable to forget the terror in Rita Duffy's eyes. I checked my thermos. There wasn't even a vestige of warmth in the coffee.

I stared at the papers I'd put together for the pep talk that never took place.

Three piles.

The Rosen-Voss case.

The Curt Murdoch case.

The Darryl Nugent case.

Maggie Winslow was murdered as she sought fresh answers to old questions. And Maggie's body was found in Lovers' Lane.

But I knew quite well that *The Clarion* was read by almost every household in Derry Hills. The placement of Maggie's body in Lovers' Lane could have been prompted by her ad in the Wednesday issue.

I'd met Rita Duffy a few times. She was smart, quick, clever, a hearty woman with a booming laugh. She worked for the Chamber of Commerce, knew everybody in town, was interested in every person she met. She wasn't the kind of person to miss an ad as provocative as Maggie's. So, Wednesday night, when she was desperately seeking a place to leave Maggie's lifeless body, Lovers' Lane could easily have seemed a brilliant location.

But why would Rita—if she killed Maggie—take the body anywhere?

That brought up the most puzzling question: Where did Maggie die? In her apartment? Somewhere on campus? Or in someone else's car? Rita's, for example?

I slipped into my chair and stared at the three piles. I should be feeling relieved. If Rita Duffy murdered Maggie, no fault could lie with me.

But—

Why Lovers' Lane?

I pulled my pad close, scrawled "Lovers' Lane," then listed some possibilities:

1. Lovers' Lane chosen because it was the most secluded, remote, private area on campus.

2. Lovers' Lane chosen because Maggie's murderer wanted to link her death specifically to the Rosen-Voss murders.

3. Lovers' Lane chosen because murderers repeat themselves.

The first possibility was the simplest and likeliest. For some reason, it was important to the murderer of Maggie Winslow that her body not be discovered where the actual death occurred, and there was no better place on campus to get rid of a body than Lovers' Lane.

Was the murderer unsophisticated enough not to know the police would determine that Maggie had not died in Lovers' Lane?

Possibly.

Was Rita Duffy that unsophisticated?

I doubted it.

Perhaps it didn't matter. Perhaps what mattered was leaving the body far from the site of death.

The second possibility required a murderer knowledgeable about the earlier crime and quick to take advantage of Maggie's efforts to discover fresh facts about the Rosen-Voss case. It could mean the murderer was involved in the Curt Murdoch case or the Darryl

Nugent disappearance and was trying to focus attention on the Rosen-Voss case.

The third instance meant Maggie had indeed discovered something that could reveal what happened in Lovers' Lane in 1988. If that was true, the murderer was either going back to a pattern that had worked before or was confident only Maggie had an inkling of the truth. In either event, leaving her body in Lovers' Lane was an arrogant, taunting display of power.

None of this led me any closer to knowing whether Maggie died because she screwed the wrong husband or because she'd pressed too close to a previous crime for comfort.

But was it reasonable to think that Maggie in a matter of hours could solve puzzles that had baffled hardworking investigators for years?

Larry Urschel seemed to be a careful and capable detective. He was apparently convinced yesterday's murder and the 1988 slayings had nothing in common.

I remembered Maggie's confident observation: Somebody always knows something.

And her body was found on Lovers' Lane—

My office door opened.

Dennis Duffy was a man in emotional turmoil, his eyes glazed, his skin gray. Patches of sweat stained the armpits of his cotton dress shirt.

"Henrie O, I need help. Please. Jesus, you've got to help me." His outstretched hands trembled.

Gone was the bullying and sarcasm and

snickering suggestiveness that laced his usual verbal assaults.

"Sit down, Dennis." My voice was gentle, but also remote.

He lunged toward my desk, glared down at me, big and mad. "Goddammit, you're the one who told Maggie she had to come up with new stuff. I asked her about that damn ad and that's what she told me. You're the one." It was an accusation.

We stared at each other.

His eyes were wild, beseeching, desperate.

"Sit down, Dennis."

"That cop won't listen to me. I tried to tell him about Maggie's series. He won't listen! You've got to talk to him—"

"I already have."

It was as if Dennis had run as fast as he could, using every breath, every muscle, and slammed full force into a wall.

Slowly, like a pricked balloon, Dennis sagged into the chair. "Henrie O, Rita didn't do it. She couldn't. Never. She's—oh yeah, she explodes. She's got a rotten temper, but to hurt someone—to kill someone—she couldn't do it. I swear to God, she couldn't."

I didn't know Rita Duffy that well, but last night her corrosive anger had shocked the newsroom into immobility.

"Why was Rita so upset?" Implicit in my question was the judgment, So what else is new this time, you sorry, unfaithful bastard?

He clenched his hands, stared down at them. "Yesterday—it was November 15."

I waited.

"The day"—each word was as hard and distinct and unyielding as a granite gravestone—"our daughter Carla died. Of leukemia. Six years ago."

I understood the agony in his statement.

My son Bobby died twenty-seven years ago.

I looked at the photograph in a leather folder on my desk. Bobby is running toward me in Chapultepec Park, his face alight with an exuberant grin. I remembered the laughter in his voice—"Mom, hey, Mom!"—and the way he skidded into my arms, alive and eager and happy. It was his tenth birthday.

The emptiness is as great today as it was then, a void that nothing will ever fill, a grief that will never ease.

I had to believe that somewhere, on a far distant, sunnier shore, Bobby and now Richard awaited me. I had to believe that or sink into numb despair in an empty, meaningless world.

Dennis groaned.

I reached out, gently touched my son's picture.

Dennis's voice shook. "And she thought, Rita thought—" He broke off; his face crumpled.

Rita thought he was being unfaithful yet again on a day that was forever seared into her soul.

"Were you?" My words dropped like ice pellets.

"No." He almost shouted it. "No way. God, no."

I straightened the stack of papers on the

Rosen-Voss case. "Where were you last night?"

He groaned again, pressed his palms against his temples. "No place. I'd told Eric to handle it. There was probably a late story coming in on that hotel explosion in Cairo, but nothing else. The front page was ready to put to bed. I just wanted—I couldn't sit there any longer. I got in my car. I drove around."

"You didn't stop anywhere, talk to anybody?"

"No." He rubbed his face wearily.

"You didn't see Maggie anytime during the evening?"

His head jerked up. "No. Absolutely not." He stared straight at me.

Like the barely heard rattle of a snake on a hot, still day, a warning flickered in my mind. Such a straight-from-the-shoulder, honest, sincere gaze...

Dennis's yellow-gray eyes were opaque.

"Where did you drive around?"

He flipped over his hands. "Everywhere. Nowhere."

"Did you go over to Maggie's apartment?"

"I might have gone that way. It's a small town, Henrie O."

I let it drop, but the buzz continued in my mind. Maybe he didn't see Maggie. But I'd bet he looked for her. So what price to put on his soulful protestations of innocence? "What time did you get home?"

"Midnight, I guess. About that."

"Was Rita there?"

"Yeah." His voice was empty.

"What did she say? What happened?"

"The bedroom door was locked. She wouldn't let me in. She screamed about Maggie. She wouldn't listen."

"What did you try to tell her?"

"That it was bullshit. Bullshit." His voice rose. "I ended up standing there by that goddamned locked door, yelling that I hadn't fucked Maggie, but I sure as hell was going to give it a try."

"Are you telling me you weren't having an affair with Maggie?"

"You got it the first time." His tone had an echo of its old flippancy.

"So what gave Rita the idea? Why should she think so?"

Dennis's putty-colored eyes slid away.

My sympathy curled a little around the edges.

He lifted his hands in elaborate bewilderment. "Hell, I don't know. I had drinks with Maggie a couple of times. I don't know, maybe somebody told Rita about it."

"Why?"

He looked blank.

I spelled it out. "Why did you have drinks with Maggie? That's not part of the curriculum, Dennis."

"Yeah, well." He grew sad. "Maggie was a gorgeous girl. You know? And sexy as hell. So, I gave it a try. Goddamn."

Dennis was too jowly to be called handsome, but it wasn't hard to trace the good-looking young man he had been. His ebullience and hard-driving aggressiveness would make him sexually appealing to most women—unless they prized fidelity.

"Did it ever occur to you to keep your hands off women reporters?"

"I don't rape anybody." His glare was defiant.

But this was not the time for a discussion of sexual harassment, in all its infinite varieties.

"So what did Rita say this morning?"

Dennis blinked, shook his head. "I never saw her. I slept in the den. I got up early and got the hell out and had breakfast at the Green Owl. Then Kitty Brewster called in about Maggie. I couldn't believe it. I thought it was crazy. The next thing I knew, the cops had brought Rita in."

"And you still haven't talked to Rita about what happened last night?"

"No. But, Henrie O, she didn't do it." He looked at me earnestly, hopefully. "That cop won't listen to me. But you can find out what happened."

He heaved himself to his feet, leaned toward me. I smelled sweat and fear and the sweet muskiness of bourbon.

"Henrie O, it has to be one of those old crimes. It has to be. Nothing else makes sense. Listen, you can figure it out." His voice was eager, clear. If he'd been drinking, he was still able to speak distinctly. "You can see Rita in the morning. I talked to her lawyer. He's going to set it up. I'll let you know what time. When you talk to Rita, you'll believe me. She didn't do it."

"Dennis..." I started to shake my head.

"Henrie O, I've never begged in my life. Except when Carla died. And that didn't do any good. But I'm begging you. Because you've covered the news big time. If it's out there to be found, you'll find it. Please. Not for me. For Rita. For Maggie. Please."

I straightened my desk, but it didn't corral my thoughts. I wasn't looking forward to tomorrow. I'd not promised Dennis that I would talk with Rita.

But I knew I would.

I couldn't ignore the kind of plea Dennis had made.

Even though one cold, analytical portion of my mind wondered about Dennis, wondered a lot. Was he a panicked husband determined to save his wife? Or was he a killer posturing as a devoted (in his own fashion) husband?

And I couldn't forget the look of panic and fear in Rita's eyes as she was led away.

But I'm not a reporter anymore. What the hell did I think I could do? Cops don't make an arrest in a capital murder case on a whim. There had to be evidence, and plenty of it.

Irritably, I pushed back my chair. But maybe the truth was that I needed to talk to Rita Duffy on my own account. For my own peace of mind, I had to know what had caused Maggie's murder.

So, if I was going to play in this game, I'd better get some chips.

I looked out into the newsroom.

Helen Tracy's fingers flew over the keyboard of her computer. She thought fast and typed fast. If you want to know what's going on in any small town, who the movers and shakers are, where the skeletons are buried, who's sleeping with whom, take your favorite LifeStyle editor out to dinner. As a guest. Her restaurant of choice.

The doughy smell of pizza and the sour scent of beer washed over us as we stepped inside the Green Owl. We were enveloped in sound, a roar of conversation punctuated by peals of laughter, the bang and crash of dishes, the Beach Boys immortalizing California girls. The Green Owl has an eclectic jukebox—the owner claims it has been in nonstop use since 1938—with every kind of music from Benny Goodman to Hootie and the Blowfish.

Helen was scanning the huge room, waving hello in every direction. The horseshoe bar, reputed to have come from a Colorado mining town, was to our left. Straight ahead was the coffee area. No matter the hour of day—or night—these tables were always nearly all taken, students studying, checker and chess players sunk in concentration, newspaper and magazine readers engrossed. The coffee area was set off from the bar and the main dining area by potted tea palms, which added an incongruous but charming 1920s aura. To our right was a sea of rustic wooden tables with red-and-white-checked cloths. Booths lined the walls.

We settled at a table with a good view in all directions and ordered salads, southwestern chicken pizza, and iced tea.

Helen has a long face and puffy crescents under coal-black eyes. She not only looks like a bloodhound, she'll stick with a story through swamp, field, and forest, baying her findings in a piercing voice. Moreover, Helen knows all the whispered scandals that are never printed, and one of her primary pleasures in life is sharing the unprintable with anyone who will listen.

All I had to do was murmur, "The Rosen-Voss case..."

And Helen was loping down the long ago trail. "...*never* made any sense, Henrie O! For starters, Lovers' Lane!" She peered at me from beneath frizzy, silver-streaked bangs, her mobile face miming incredulity. "I mean, this was 1988, *not* 1958!"

Helen vigorously swirled her teaspoon in her mint-sprigged glass. "*He* had an apartment. *She* had an apartment."

I knew Helen meant Howard Rosen and Gail Voss.

"Oh, they had roommates. But these were upscale kids. Everybody had his or her own room. So, we're supposed to believe Howard and Gail were having backseat romance in his car! I told everybody, *No way, José.* But do the cops ask me?" She shrugged and grabbed a breadstick.

"Were they dressed?" I took one, too. Hot, garlicky, good.

71

"Fully." Once again her tone was scathing. "You'd think *anybody* would see how weird this was. What were they *doing* there? *Why* were they there? Lovers' Lane, give me a break." She took a big bite of breadstick. "But Dennis went right ahead and played the story with the Lovers' Lane angle. I told him, *Sweetheart, this is baloney!* Of course"—and she rolled those mournful eyes, "Dennis is still into back-seats with willing coeds. The Flamingo costs a buck."

Helen thought Dennis was too tight to spring for a motel room. Did that mean he knew Lovers' Lane very well indeed?

The waiter brought our salads. Mine was a Caesar with strips of anchovies.

"So you think it's strange Howard and Gail were in Lovers' Lane?"

Helen speared a radish slice. "Real strange. Weird," she said again. "Phony. I don't know"—she squeezed her face like a quiz show contestant—"like it was staged."

But I scarcely heard. I'd had a thought, and it was ugly. "Helen, was Dennis after Gail Voss?"

"Oh, Dennis, stud man of the newsroom." Her eyes widened, then glinted with interest. She reached out and grabbed my arm. "Speak of the devil!"

I craned to see.

Dennis Duffy, head down, walked heavily toward the bar. He slid onto a stool. His back was to us. He slumped against the counter, despair in every sagging line of his body.

72

"If you sit here long enough," Helen murmured cheerfully, "you'll see everyone you've ever known."

I gave her a swift glance. As far as Helen was concerned, it obviously wasn't Feel-Sorry-for-Dennis Week. ⌐

She chattered on, her voice light. "Even Dennis probably wasn't clod enough to go after a girl like Gail. I mean, who's to say he didn't lust. But Gail was a lovely girl, really sweet. *Not* a backseat type for anybody. And she was crazy about Howard. Nuts about him. I'll tell you"—Helen swallowed—"Howard and Gail were two nice kids. And according to my students, it was just silly to even ask if they had enemies. What normal, nice college students have *enemies?* They didn't have enemies. Oh, one of the girls told me Gail's brother didn't want her to marry Howard. Said he 'wasn't our kind.' So, her brother was a prejudiced drip. But everybody says he loved his little sister. As for the usual motives for murder, money's always at the top of the list. But they didn't have any. They were college students. His folks were rich. I think Howard had an older brother, so I guess he'll inherit twice as many millions. But nobody ever suggested Howard's brother was in Derry Hills that night, and of course the cops would have checked that out. Gail? Her folks were upper middle class. So, what difference does that make? And you can check off all the other reasons—revenge, jealousy, fear, hatred—none of them fit."

73

I didn't have an answer.

Helen waggled her fork. "I knew Gail's roommates. Lovely girls. They were double-dating at an all-night fraternity party that night. I heard the cops really looked at Howard's roommate. That was Stuart Singletary. He's on the English faculty now. Stuart had a heavy date, but he wasn't alibied for the whole night. But why would Stuart kill Howard? Nobody'd ever heard them quarrel. They had no reason to quarrel." Helen retrieved another breadstick. "There was nothing odd in either Howard's or Gail's life. Everyday. Ordinary." Helen munched on her salad, then added thoughtfully, "But you know, Henrie O, ever after all these years I get a funny feeling in my gut when anybody mentions the Rosen-Voss murders. There's something strange there, stranger than hell."

The anchovies were saltier than the crust on a tequila shot glass. I forked over the lettuce, looking for another strip.

Helen took a gulp of iced tea. "So, why are you nosing around?" Her eyes clung to me avidly, the better to retrieve every morsel of intelligence.

Quid pro quo.

"Dennis says Rita didn't kill Maggie." The waitress brought our pizzas. I gave up on the salad. No more anchovies. I pulled free a green-chili-laden wedge of pizza. "What do you think?"

Helen shook Parmesan over her pizza. Her dark eyes were thoughtful. "Rita Duffy's

74

famous for her scenes. Did you know that? Last year she came in here"—Helen pointed toward a back booth—"yelling her head off. Dennis was tête-à-têteing with a nifty little redhead from Topeka. In August, he and Rita had a screaming match at the Faculty Club. That time, it was about a blonde from Omaha."

"So Rita raises hell." It was easy to sound amused, but there's nothing funny about that kind of jealousy. Still..."So how many bodies has she left behind her?"

"None." Helen took a bite of pizza and chewed. "But Dennis picked a bad day to set her off, Henrie O." Of course she knew about the Duffys' daughter.

Helen looked toward the bar. "The jerk." Her face was disdainful. "Oh, hey"—now her eyes were avid—"it looks like stud man's in trouble."

I twisted to see.

Dennis stood, one hand on the barstool for balance. He wavered on his feet.

The bartender was shaking his head. He scooped up Dennis's empty glass, shook his head again.

Bars don't serve drunks anymore, at least not if the owner has studied the liability law.

The back of Dennis's neck flushed an ugly red. He shoved over the barstool and almost fell down after it.

"Oh, hell." Helen was on her feet, tossing down a twenty on the table. "We'd better get him out—" She broke off as a redheaded man hurried from the coffee-bar area to

Dennis's side. In his early fifties, he had a broad, open face spattered with freckles. He slipped an arm around Dennis's shoulder, bent close to him.

Helen plopped back into her chair, but she didn't take her eyes off the bar. "Tom Abbott to the rescue. He used to live next door to the Duffys." She smoothed her hair, surged back to her feet. "Think I'll go lend a hand."

I must have looked astonished.

She gave me a faintly embarrassed smile. "I can carry it off. One J-School faculty member to the aid of another—and maybe Tom will bring me back for a drink after we get Dennis home. I've been trying to figure out a way to hustle Tom for a couple of years."

Abbott's name was familiar to me. He was the chair of the English department. Helen was loping across the room.

I had finished my third slice of pizza when she trooped disconsolately back to her chair. "Tom said he could take care of it. So, I strike out again. Damn, I've put a lot of effort into tracking that man. But I never pick up any vibes. I guess I won't be the second Mrs. Abbott."

"What's so attractive about being the second Mrs. Abbott?"

She flashed me an insouciant grin. "It would be kind of like cozying up to the mint, but sexier."

"A rich English professor?"

"Sweetheart, Tom is Derry Hills's claim to literary fame. His book hit the best-seller list a few years ago, and it's clung like bubble gum on a sneaker. He plays chess here almost every night. I drop in so often, they have me on automatic order. But so far I haven't gotten him to offer more than a grin." She sighed.

I wasn't interested in Helen's pursuit of Tom Abbott and his money. I was interested that Abbott had once lived next door to the Duffys. He might well be a man to see. Then I realized Helen had kept right on talking and I had to wonder about ESP or corollary thought.

"...be good to talk to Tom. His daughter, Cheryl, is the girl Stuart Singletary was out with that night, and they're married now. Tom might know something, or have some ideas. And I'd talk to Stuart and Cheryl, too."

I paid the check and we stepped out into the chilly November night. The silence was almost shocking after the maelstrom of sound in the Green Owl. It was just a block up the street to the campus and the J-School parking lot where our cars were parked.

Our shoes scuffed through leaves on the sidewalk.

Names eddied in my mind. Maggie. Rita. Dennis. Tom. Cheryl. Stuart. Howard. Gail.

Which ones mattered?

Or was it as simple as Lieutenant Larry Urschel believed? An angry wife, an unfaithful husband.

It was up to me to figure it out.

Six

Friday morning's forecast called for a chance of sleet. I chose a turtleneck sweater and navy corduroy slacks. Informal, perhaps, but upscale in a jail, and that's where I would likely be at some point during my day.

It wasn't just the weather that chilled me. As always, I unfolded *The Clarion* as I poured my first cup of coffee.

I had expected the lead story to be Maggie's murder and Rita's arrest. There were an inset photo of Maggie and a two-column shot of Rita, looking unkempt and bewildered, in the corridor at the courthouse.

Dennis Duffy had played the story the way any city editor would have. It must have been the grimmest task he'd ever performed.

Yesterday, I'd agonized for Dennis when the reporters and cameramen surrounded him in the courthouse hallway. Even though they had approached him almost diffidently, it must have been a shock for Dennis to be on the other end of media attention.

But I wasn't agonizing now. Not for Dennis. He was using every weapon at his command, and nobody knows the power of the press better than a city editor.

Blazoned in the bottom five columns on the front page was an interview by Kitty Brewster:

CITY EDITOR CLAIMS OLD CRIMES LED TO REPORTER'S MURDER

Clarion City Editor Dennis Duffy insisted Thursday that his wife Rita is innocent of the murder of *Clarion* reporter Maggie Winslow.

In an exclusive interview, Duffy revealed that Winslow planned to write a series of articles about three famous unsolved local mysteries: the 1988 murders of Thorndyke students Howard Rosen and Gail Voss; the 1982 shooting death of Derry Hills businessman Curt Murdoch; and the 1976 disappearance of Thorndyke University Dean of Students Darryl Nugent.

Duffy explained that Winslow was working on the series under the supervision of Henrietta Collins, assistant professor of journalism.

"I've talked to Mrs. Collins," Duffy said, "and she assured me she'd do everything in her power to find out the truth about Maggie's death. Collins said she will not be intimidated, and she will complete the series, using Maggie's notes."

Collins spent a long career as a reporter for several major newspapers and received acclaim for several investigative series concerning...

A photograph of me from my wire-service days filled two columns.

I crumpled the page. "Dennis, you *are* a sorry bastard."

79

I'd made no such promise. I'd certainly not agreed to write the series. I'd only said I would see what I could find out.

If I'd had any hope of working quietly, Dennis had destroyed it.

I doubted that he cared.

Dennis had only one goal: to save Rita.

I'd do well to remember that.

I seethed all the way to my office. I considered requesting a retraction. But frankly, I didn't know for certain what had happened to Maggie, and yes, I was going to ask questions, to nose about, to poke and prod. That would look odd if *The Clarion* carried a story saying I wasn't doing the series.

So, for now, I'd ride with it.

But Dennis needn't think I'd be coerced into doing the articles. I'd make that absolutely clear. The series had once been important to me, but what mattered now was finding out the truth about Maggie's murder.

I unlocked my door and kicked an envelope that had been shoved beneath it.

I picked up the envelope. My name was scrawled on the outside. I opened it, pulled out a memo sheet.

Henrie O—
You can see Rita at eleven o'clock.
                                        Dennis

Yes, Your Majesty.

But I couldn't afford to worry about high-handedness. I needed information, and I'd do what it took to get it. Eleven o'clock wasn't much time. I had a lot to do before I spoke to Rita.

I went upstairs and posted notes on the doors of two classrooms, canceling my nine- and ten-o'clock classes.

Back in my office, I poured a mug of coffee and turned on my computer. I pulled up class schedules for Margaret Winslow and Eric March. I noted Maggie's Wednesday classes. It gave me some starting points. On a map I could now place her at various times that final day of her life. I rechecked her schedule: 7–9 P.M. W, American Literature, A Popular Cultural Analysis, 1850 to the Present, S. Singletary, Evans Hall, LL1.

S. Singletary.

I grabbed a University directory, flipped to the faculty section: Stuart Singletary, assistant professor of English. According to Helen Tracy, Singletary had shared an apartment with Howard Rosen.

That was certainly a link to the old crime, wasn't it?

So Maggie's final class had been with someone involved—okay, maybe *involved* was too strong—with a man who had been interviewed by the police in the double murder in Lovers' Lane.

On the other hand, Stuart Singletary had had a big date the night of the Rosen-Voss murders. And he had been teaching the night Maggie died.

I wished I had a better sense of when Maggie

died. Lieutenant Urschel had grudgingly said early evening. What did that encompass? I needed to trace Maggie's movements Wednesday night.

Ivy clung to the soft-gray limestone walls of Evans Hall. The turreted battlement looked like something out of Disney by way of an Irish Spring soap ad.

As befitted a junior member of the faculty, Stuart Singletary's office was on the third floor, next to a storeroom at the far end of an ill-lit hall. Old bookcases were stacked haphazardly by one wall.

I tapped on his partially open door.

"Come in, come in." The tenor voice was high and reedy.

I pushed the door, stepped into a narrow office and was startled by the luxuriousness of this enclave. Velvet curtains framed the tall windows. An antique silver filigree clock glistened in a shaft of sunlight on the ornately carved rosewood desk. There was even a small Persian rug tucked into the narrow space between the desk and the door.

A junior office, to be sure, but one with furnishings a good deal more expensive than most assistant professors could provide. Or most full professors, for that matter. Family money? It isn't unknown in academic circles.

Thick chestnut-brown hair, overlong for my taste, cupped a long face with sharply defined features, a thin nose, a pointed chin with a distinct cleft. A bristly black mustache curved above narrow lips.

He looked up.

For an instant, his face was absolutely without expression.

Which interested me enormously. Was he ordinarily so gauche—or did he know who I was and did that worry him?

"Professor Singletary?"

"Yes." That was all he said. The word hung uninflected between us.

"I'd like to visit with you, if you have a moment, Professor. About a student. I'm Henrietta Collins. I teach in the Journalism School."

Stuart Singletary pushed back his chair and stood. He wasn't very tall, about my height. His chocolate cashmere pullover emphasized the velvety brown of his eyes and the vivid black of his mustache. The sweater's smooth thickness gave his narrow shoulders some bulk. "Yes, Mrs. Collins." He sounded politely puzzled, but his eyes were intent.

I pointed to *The Clarion* on his desk. "Perhaps you saw the story on the front page...about the articles I'm writing."

He reached for the paper, lifted it, looked at the page. Stared at the page.

It was a charade. I felt sure that he'd already read the paper and had known who I was from the moment I stepped into his office.

Which was also enormously interesting. And surprising to me. Helen Tracy had indicated the police had looked hard at Stuart

Singletary as a possible suspect in the 1988 murders. But, obviously, they had found nothing incriminating.

So what was making Singletary nervous?

He scanned the article. Taking his time. Making time.

I waited.

Finally, he looked up at me, his narrow face furrowed with distress. "This is all very shocking. Why, I know the Duffys. It doesn't seem possible. But"—he rattled the page—"I can't see how Maggie Winslow's murder could have anything to do with those other crimes. That seems extremely sensational to me."

"Does it?" I moved toward the wooden chair that faced his desk. "May I?"

"Oh, of course. Please." I've seen IRS agents greeted with more enthusiasm.

I sat down.

Reluctantly, or so it seemed to me, Singletary sat, too. He placed his copy of *The Clarion* on the desk in front of him, but his eyes never left my face.

"You know the Duffys. And you knew Maggie Winslow, too."

"Maggie was one of my students." There was a flicker of enthusiasm in his reply. "An excellent student."

"Yes, she was a superb student. That's why I'm here, Mr. Singletary. She was writing the series about these unsolved crimes, including the Rosen-Voss murders, under my supervision. So I'd like to talk to you about the

Rosen-Voss murders—as I'm sure Maggie must have done."

He pursed his thin lips, then said carefully, "We spoke briefly. She caught me after my nine-o'clock on Wednesday morning. But there wasn't much to tell. Nobody's ever figured out what happened. I don't think anyone ever will."

I opened my purse, pulled out a pen and pad. "Was Maggie in class Wednesday night?"

"No." His headshake was firm. "I was surprised when I called roll and she wasn't there. She'd never missed. I don't have many who never cut. You know, they think three cuts are some kind of mandate from heaven." It was a little joke and his teeth gleamed briefly beneath his mustache, then once again his face was somber. "But it means she was with someone, doesn't it? The person who killed her. I told the detective that's what I thought."

It's very easy to have portentous thoughts after an event, but any deviation from Maggie's usual routine could be very important. Why did she miss class? Was she indeed with someone? Seven o'clock. Did that qualify as early evening in Lieutenant Urschel's mind? I made a big "7" on my pad and underlined it.

"I kept expecting her to come in. But she never did. It seems so strange to think I was having fun with the class." Singletary leaned forward, his expression suddenly lively. "I'd asked the class to pretend they were Japanese students studying English, then to tell me how they would picture the United States if the only American novels they'd ever read were *An American Tragedy, The Fountainhead,* and *The Catcher in the Rye.*" He grinned. "Makes you think, doesn't it?" The smile died away. "But, God, that lovely girl..." For an instant, his dark eyes looked sickened.

The young professor sank back in his chair, pressed the tips of his fingers together. He hesitated, then blurted out, "What was she doing in Lovers' Lane? The paper said they found her in Lovers' Lane." He laced his fingers tightly together. "That's where they found Howard and Gail. But what was Maggie doing there? That's weird. Like a cult or something."

I didn't respond to that gambit. I thought a suggestion of a cult was reaching, reaching a long way.

I was finding Stuart Singletary more and more intriguing.

"You talked to Maggie Wednesday morning?"

"Yes. She wanted to know all about Howard and Gail and if I had any ideas about the murders."

"What did you tell her?"

"Same thing I've told everybody ever since it happened." He was impatient, irritable. "I roomed with Howard for about six months. We were both grad students in English. He was going to finish a master's before he went to Germany on a Fulbright. But he wasn't really an academic kind of guy. I think he was just hanging around to be with Gail. They'd met when he was a senior, and he was crazy about her. I never thought he was serious about grad school. But he had all kinds of money, so why not another year in school?" There was an undercurrent of jealousy in his tone.

On my pad, I scrawled "$$$"—and underlined that, too. "How did you and Howard meet?"

He took too long to answer. "Meet?" he echoed.

"Yes." I smiled blandly.

He cleared his throat. "Let's see...I guess Cheryl introduced us."

"Cheryl?"

"My wife." His glance flicked toward a studio portrait of a smiling redhead. "We were dating then."

"How did Cheryl know Howard?" It was like prizing open an oyster shell. So I was on the lookout for a pearl.

"Oh, English department stuff. Her dad's Dr. Abbott. Chair of the English department. They had parties for the grad students. So Cheryl knew all the grad students. She introduced me to Howard. We hit it off. I needed a place to live and his roommate had just moved out."

He spoke more easily the more he said, but I had to wonder whether there was something discreditable about that meeting. Or had Howard been interested in Cheryl? Or Cheryl in Howard? Something here was making Singletary uncomfortable.

"Had Howard ever dated Cheryl?"

He shot me a quick, startled look. "No. Never. She just knew him casually."

"Were you and Howard close friends?"

Singletary smoothed his mustache. "Not really. He was a nice guy. And funny. God, he was so funny." Singletary relaxed back in his chair. "Howard was never serious. He always had some kind of gag going. Once he put a fake mouse in my cereal box. The tail was poking up out of the cornflakes. God, I about fainted." His grin was vivid, though fleeting. He suddenly seemed quite young and likable. "And he told me about one girl he'd dated— this was before Gail—Howard convinced her that he was twins, and he'd act completely different on dates and she'd think she was out with Harold, not Howard." A quick snort of laughter. "See, Harold was a real shy guy, had to be encouraged to even try and kiss a girl. God, how he loved to play jokes. And he was so damn funny. At parties, he'd get everybody started doing emotions: anger, fear, despair, lust. You can't believe how many different ways he could screw his face up. It was hilarious." Singletary spoke now with animation. "Nobody could ever be bored around Howard. And he was always on the move. I think maybe he slept four hours a night."

Howard the clown. Howard the kidder. Who kills somebody like that?

But I asked the question anyway. "Did Howard have any enemies? Anyone who disliked him or was angry with him?"

"Enemies—that's a heavy word, Mrs. Collins. I mean, Gail's brother didn't like him. Howard told me about that." Singletary shrugged.

"A lot of people thought Howard came on too strong. But I can't say anybody would have been his enemy."

"What about the girls he dated before Gail? Anyone who might have been jealous?"

Singletary's gaze was thoughtful. "I don't think so. Howard had dated a bunch of different girls. But as far as I know, he wasn't serious about anybody until he met Gail."

"How about Gail? Was there another man who might have been angry that she was going to marry Howard?"

"I don't think so." But his voice wasn't so confident. "At least, not that I know of."

"Did you see Howard and Gail that night?"

"Howard. Not Gail. He left about seven to pick her up." These words came quickly, as if they'd been said many times. There was no hesitation, no tension. "I think he said they were going out to dinner. Anyway, I invited Cheryl over for pizza." He looked again at the framed photo.

Even at a quick glance, I could see Cheryl Singletary's resemblance to the man who'd hurried to help Dennis at the Green Owl last night. Tom Abbott's daughter had the same open, freckled face. Her lips curved in a warm smile.

Singletary's gaze was proud. He nodded toward another photo. "That's our daughter, Cindy." The little girl had smooth chestnut hair and a narrow face.

Stuart's pleased expression fled. "Anyway, that night Cheryl and I hung out, watched TV.

I took her home around eleven. Then, bam, bam, bam, a knock on the door about six-thirty woke me up. I didn't even know until then that Howard hadn't come in."

"A two-bedroom apartment?" I asked.

"Yes."

"So if Howard had wanted to have Gail over for the night, it would have been okay."

"Sure." He hesitated briefly, then continued. "Sometimes she spent the night. Sometimes, he stayed at her place."

"So why Lovers' Lane?"

He stared at me. Something flickered deep in those velvety brown eyes, flickered and was gone.

I asked, "Do you think they went there to make love?"

"I don't know why they went there."

"Did it surprise you when the police told you where they'd been shot?"

His frown was quick and irritated. "Surprise me? Listen, you can't imagine what it's like. Your roommate shot and killed! I was knocked over. Sick. I don't think I even thought about *where* it happened. It was a nightmare."

Now I was thoroughly at sea. I pride myself on detecting genuine emotion. As a reporter, I had observed people in every kind of stressful situation. My instinct told me that Singletary's unhesitating answer to my question was truthful.

But that was definitely at odds with the sense of strain at various points in our interview.

What caused the swift swings in Singletary's mood?

"Is this basically what you told Maggie on Wednesday?"

"Yes." The irritation bubbled close to anger. "It's what I've always told everybody, ever since it happened." Now his glare was defiant.

"Is there anything else?"

"No. Believe me, if I knew anything that would have helped, I would have told the cops. I never could figure any reason why it happened. And that's exactly what I told Maggie. I told her it had to be a drifter. Somebody on Lovers' Lane that night, somebody who just wanted to kill people. Anybody. For no reason. Things like that happen sometimes. You read about it all the time. People who are so alone, it's like they're sheathed in ice." The words were smooth and quick, almost a patter. "They see other people as stick figures. Not real. Somebody like that. Maybe he killed them just to see life end."

"He?"

His fingers smoothed his mustache. "That's sexist, isn't it? But I can't see a woman doing something like that, walking up to a car with two people sitting there, talking, hell, I don't know, maybe making love, and shooting them dead."

"So you think the murders of Howard and Gail happened for no reason? Simply because they were in Lovers' Lane the wrong time, the wrong night?"

"Yes. Definitely." His reedy voice was truculent.

"Did you tell this to Maggie?"

"Yeah. But she said she wanted to keep on looking into it." His shoulders rose and fell. "So I gave her some names. Gail's family still lives here. Her brother Frank's a lawyer in town."

"And that's all you told Maggie?"

"That's all I know." He spoke with finality.

"When did you last see Maggie?"

"After my nine-o'clock Wednesday morning." His mouth closed into a tight thin line.

I closed my notebook, dropped it in my purse. "Do you know Rita Duffy?"

"Casually. I've seen Rita and Dennis around. The Faculty Club, basketball games. That sort of thing."

"Do you think she could have killed Maggie?"

He stroked his mustache. "Well, she's pretty volatile, and everybody knows he's a womanizer. So"—he frowned—"maybe it happened like the police think." A quick frown. "But why would she and Maggie be in Lovers' Lane?"

I opened my mouth, then realized the morning paper had simply reported that Maggie's body had been found in Lovers' Lane and that she had been strangled.

There was no mention that the police believed the murder had occurred elsewhere.

So I simply shrugged as I stood. "I wish I knew, Professor Singletary."

As I walked out, I glanced at some framed

daguerreotypes of the Battle of Gettysburg. I wasn't a collector, but they looked pricey to me. But my last glimpse as the door closed on the beautifully furnished office was dominated by the uneasy expression on the face of the young professor.

I pre-empted a monitor in the J-School morgue from one of my students. "Ten minutes, John. I promise."

"No problem, Mrs. Collins." John flashed me a grin and moved over to the filing cabinets.

I hadn't intended to come back to the J-School yet. I had other stops I planned to make. But Professor Stuart Singletary had attracted my attention.

He'd been alternately nervous, convincing, uptight, and relaxed.

Of course, it's unnerving to have a close connection to murder. Maybe that's all it was.

And I wondered a hell of a lot about Singletary's expensive clothes and fancy office furnishings. Although I saw no connection between the deaths of Howard Rosen and Gail Voss and Singletary's somewhat surprising affluence, still, it was an odd note, it bugged me, and I wouldn't let it go until I understood.

I punched in Singletary's name.

Good grief, twenty-six stories.

I'd said ten minutes. It took thirty. There were little stories and big ones—scholarship awards, Phi Beta Kappa, awarding of degrees—and then I found the coverage of Singletary's wedding in 1990 to Cheryl Marie Abbott, daughter of Thomas Wheeler Abbott, chairman of the Thorndyke University English department, and Mr. and Mrs. Wendell Blaise Harrison, La Jolla and Chicago.

As I scanned the story and the photos of the wedding reception—flowers and ferns sprouting like the Hollywood version of a rain forest—I was impatient with myself. Of course! I knew where the money came from now. Tom Abbott was not only Stuart Singletary's father-in-law, he was the author of *Listen to Me*, which hit the top of the best-seller charts. So there wasn't any mystery about Singletary's expensive polish. But as long as I was taking the time, I looked over all the entries.

I was almost finished, whipping through the headlines like a gambler shuffling cards when I found a feature by Maggie Winslow that ran in *The Clarion* a month ago. I felt that old flicker of excitement that every reporter gets when there's a nugget in all the grit.

Maggie had interviewed Stuart Singletary after he was awarded a grant from the Thorndyke Foundation to edit a literary magazine showcasing faculty writings. Maggie had done an excellent job, capturing Singletary's no doubt genuine enthusiasm for teaching and describing his well-regarded volume of poetry that had been published by the University Press, but, like a good reporter should, she'd also come up with the unusual and odd fact that provided a different perspective on her subject: Stuart Singletary had a black belt in karate and was an accomplished rock climber.

So the nervous young professor who'd known Howard Rosen and Gail Voss was strong, athletic, and gutsy despite the reedy tenor voice and gaudy office.

And he'd not bothered to mention to me his previous in-depth interview with Maggie.

I would remember that.

The apartment looked like a garage sale: clothes piled in chairs; rumpled blankets helter-skelter on the single bed; a car's jumper cable jumbled in one corner with a pair of skis and a baseball bat; books stacked on the coffee table, the mantel, the window seat. Newspapers littered the floor. Unwashed dishes loaded the kitchen table, poked out of the sink. The air was close, stale, and tainted by a garbage pail that should have been emptied days ago.

Eric March hadn't shaved. That stubble of beard, dark against his pallor, made him look even younger. The muscles of his face were slack, his eyes red-rimmed and dull. He hunched in the corner of a worn sofa like a collapsed marionette, his long, thin arms wrapped around bent knees.

It was cold in the apartment, but he wore only a wrinkled T-shirt and age-whitened jeans. He was barefoot.

"...keep thinking the door's going to open and she'll be there, telling me to get with it, hurry, come on. Maggie was always in a hurry.

And yet, it's funny, every time I looked at her, it was like the world stood still." A shudder rippled the length of his body. "Do you understand that?"

Grief was devouring him. "Oh, yes, Eric. I understand," I said softly.

Most lives are spent like Plato's shadows on the cave wall, ephemeral, unconnected, unconnecting, as vagrant and insubstantial as reflections in water.

But when two minds and souls and bodies truly fuse, a reality like no other is created.

Most people spend their lives seeking that kind of connection. Most never find it.

I was glad for Eric and for Maggie. Even though his life was now bitterly barren, they had broken through the shadows to sunlight.

His sorrow made him look even younger and more vulnerable than he was. But it surprised me a little that the so-cool, so-confident, so-sophisticated Maggie had fallen in love with a young man who still had the awkwardness of early manhood.

"She was—so alive. So alive. And now..." His mouth twisted. "You think that woman killed Maggie?" He began to tremble. "If she did, I'll kill her. I will. I'll get her and I'll take her neck in my hands"—he thrust out his hands, big hands, hands of a basketball player—"and I'll squeeze and squeeze and—"

"Eric!"

Slowly his hands, those big, strong, grasping hands, fell into his lap.

I said quietly, "It may not have been Rita Duffy."

His head jerked up. "Who else?"

"Maggie was working on a series about those unsolved crimes. Did she say anything to you about that?" I shifted in my chair. I'd forgotten how students make do with furniture. A spring poked against my hip.

Eric kneaded his fist against his prickly cheek. "She was excited."

I tensed. Maybe this was going to be the moment I learned something about Maggie's thought processes, where she'd been with her research, where she was going.

"Maggie told me she was having a blast working on the series. She said"—Eric's eyes squinted in thought—"she said it made all the difference when you put everything in context, when you got the big picture."

Everything in context. The big picture.

"That's all she said?"

"She said something about what a difference time made."

"Do you have any idea what she meant? Which crime she was talking about?"

"No." His voice was dull.

"But she was excited?"

"Yeah. And God, she was so beautiful when she talked about what she was writing. That's how she always was about writing. Her eyes would light up—" He broke off, stared down at his hands, his face tight with misery.

Misery and grief. But Wednesday night

he'd slammed away from his desk, his face reddening with anger.

"Eric, why did you leave the newsroom Wednesday night?"

He was quiet for so long I thought he wasn't going to answer.

But finally, his voice deep and tight and thin, he said, "I was going to find Maggie. I went by her place. She wasn't there. Then I went to her class. I waited, but she didn't come. I didn't know where the hell she was. I looked everywhere. I drove all over town."

He buried his face in his hands, then slowly raised his head. "If she was screwing that bastard—everybody knows how he gets the girls. Shit, Kitty Brewster's been fucking him since she started work on *The Clarion*. You think she'd get the police beat any other way? She's got the brains of a gerbil, and she writes like English is a second language."

I shook my head. "Maggie had all the brains and talent and ability in the world. Why would she play Duffy's game?"

He rubbed the back of his hand roughly against his face. "She'd gone out with him a couple of times. Just drinks, she said. She promised me. But Duffy's wife seemed to know. And I was going to—" He drew in a ragged breath, shuddered.

"What were you going to do, Eric?"

"I was crazy. I was so mad—and now...now Maggie's dead and cold and gone forever." He buried his face in his hands—those big strong hands—and began to sob.

I left him then.
I knew two things.
Eric March loved Maggie.
He might have loved her enough to kill her.

seven

This room had a smell, too. Of sweat and never-washed trash cans and the embedded smoke from a thousand cigarettes. The bleak brown walls needed a paint job. A water leak had left an irregular, grainy stain on the north wall. The gray cement floors had been sloppily mopped, and there was a long sticky streak where some drink had spilled. Pebbled glass covered the windows, so the light had a milky hue like tears on porcelain cheeks. There might be a world out there, but you'd never know it from here.

Rita Duffy looked dumpy in the jail-issued orange coverall. Her thick blond hair still sprigged in an untidy mass. Her splotchy face still bore no makeup. But her pale blue eyes were no longer dazed. Instead, they glittered with fear.

"I'm scared. I'm scared to death." Her high voice trembled. "They think I killed that girl. I didn't do it. For God's sake, I didn't do it. And nobody will listen to me."

"I'll listen, Rita. Tell me about Wednesday. Tell me what happened." I scooted forward a little in my blue plastic chair.

Rita sat on the other side of a plain wooden table, its oak veneer scarred by cigarette burns and rings from sweaty pop cans.

"Wednesday..." One hand fingered the big metal zipper of her coverall. "I went out to the cemetery. I took a pumpkin, a great big one with a toothy grin."

A jack-o'-lantern?

"Carla would be fourteen now. Maybe she wouldn't even care that much about Halloween. But she loved it so much and we always had to keep our pumpkin on the porch all the way to Thanksgiving." A sweet smile curved Rita's pudgy lips, made them look lovely and loving. "November was her favorite month. I took leaves, pretty red and gold ones like she used to bring inside to me, running so fast to show me." Rita lifted her hands, cupped them, stretched them out toward me; then, reluctantly, as the memory in her mind dissolved, her hands fell apart, sank to the scarred table. "She was only eight that last summer. She got sick July fifth. She woke up with a sore throat. I thought maybe we'd let her stay up too late, that she'd gotten too excited over the fireworks."

She shook her head. Suddenly, she squeezed her eyes shut, fighting the tears.

"I'm sorry, Rita. I know."

Her eyes opened. Tears brimmed. She made no effort to wipe them away. It was as if she'd cried so much for so long that tears were as natural as breathing.

"You know." Her gaze was as open and

100

direct as a child's. "You do know, don't you?"

I knew. I told her about Bobby.

For a moment, we were two mothers sharing grief, sharing joy.

"...she giggled a lot. You know how little girls..."

"...he and his dad would order snails for hors d'oeuvres and they'd split them, Bobby taking the head and Richard..."

"...loved to play Monopoly. She always picked the little iron for her..."

"...even when he was really little, he'd pretend to write stories, carrying his paper and pencil..."

The dingy room receded and each of us flowered for a magical moment in a world that would never exist again.

That excursion made the real world both better and worse when we returned to it.

Better because love remembered is a balm for pain.

Worse because both Rita and I knew how much Wednesday meant to her.

The light seeped out of her face, leaving it heavy and sullen.

"I could have killed him." Now Rita's voice was heavy, too. "This time, this time, I think I would have. I had a gun with me this time."

My hands rested on my slacks. I could feel the thick ridges of the corduroy. That was real, but so was the anger pulsing in this room.

"A gun?"

"His gun." Rita's smile was sour. "Don't you love it, how men want to have guns around?"

Not Richard, I thought quickly. And not Jimmy.

"Big bad Dennis." Her voice oozed sarcasm. "Tough guy. Stud. Ready to screw any slut who'd give him five minutes. And I'd had it, had it up to here." Her hand jerked up to touch her chin. "I wasn't going to let him get away with it. Not again. And not that day. Not that day of all days."

"You got Dennis's gun—"

She nodded wearily.

"—and where did you go?"

"Her apartment. I got the address from the campus directory. The bitch's apartment." Rita's eyes blazed. "If I'd caught them there, I would have shot him. I would have. But nobody came to the door. I banged and banged. Some neighbors came out and then the manager. I asked her why she had a whore living there. She told me she was going to call the police. I told her to go to hell. I kept banging on the door, but she said the bitch wasn't there, that she was at school."

"Is that why you came to the campus?"

"I knew he was supposed to be at work. Sure, I've heard that one before. But I thought maybe he was still at the newsroom and she was there with him." Sudden awareness flickered in her eyes. "You were there, weren't you?"

I nodded. "I didn't see a gun."

"It was in my purse." Her expression curved into cunning. "I was saving the gun for him. That would have got me in a lot of trouble, waving a gun around. But the bastard wasn't there. Just you and some of the kids. So I thought maybe he was in his office with that girl. But nobody was in his office. I wonder how many of them he's screwed in there?"

"The offices have windows that look out on the newsroom." My voice was mild.

"If nobody's around, so what?" Her heavy shoulders shrugged. "Hell, he'd like that. Make it more fun."

I'd never heard the word *fun* sound uglier.

"Okay, Dennis wasn't there. Where did you go then?" I looked at her and felt unutterably sad.

Rita had stormed out of the newsroom around half past six. Early evening, that was when Lieutenant Urschel said Maggie was strangled. So this was the time that mattered.

Rita didn't hesitate. Her tone was unchanged, aching with resentment, surly with frustration. "I went down to the parking lot. His car wasn't there. So I got into my car. I drove around. God, I don't know where. Everywhere. By the motels first. But I didn't see his car anywhere. I went back to her apartment, looked over the parking lot. But Dennis's car wasn't there either. Then I went to the Green Owl. He loves the Green Owl. It lets him pretend he's young."

"When you were in the parking lot—by the J-School—did you see anyone?"

She pushed back a sagging swirl of hair. "It was dark. I didn't notice."

"Did you see Maggie's car?"

"I don't know her car."

"Are you saying you didn't find Dennis or Maggie at any time during the evening?"

"No. I don't know where they were. I couldn't find them." Her face crinkled in thought. "But," she said slowly, wearily, "I guess Dennis wasn't with her after all."

"Why not?"

Her eyes flared wide. "Somebody killed her! So Dennis *couldn't* have been with her."

I looked at her curiously. Dennis was a major slime in his wife's eyes. But not a killer! "Dennis could have killed her. He wasn't in his office. He says he was driving around." I deliberately made my voice skeptical.

"Dennis didn't strangle that girl. Not Dennis." She was sitting up straight, staring at me with outrage in her eyes. "Why would he?"

"I don't know, Rita. What if Dennis came on to Maggie, what if he wouldn't let it drop, what if she threatened to bring a grievance against him? These days the University wouldn't ignore that kind of charge."

Swiftly, emphatically, she shook her head. "No, you've got Dennis all wrong. He only went after the ones who wanted to play. He never leaned on anybody."

"How can *you* know that?"

"I know Dennis," she said simply.

"Maybe it was different this time." I didn't want to hurt Rita, but how could she be certain? And she didn't know Maggie.

Could I be sure I knew Maggie?

I thought back to our last meeting: Maggie,

so young and vital, good-looking, smart, quick, utterly confident.

Not the kind of woman to provide sexual favors for professors.

She didn't need to.

And also, quite frankly, not the kind of woman to tarnish her tough-gal image by whining about a crude-mouthed city editor.

Maggie wouldn't see that kind of confrontation as a plus in getting a job. The news business is still run, for the most part, by middle-aged white men. Maggie knew that, and nobody could ever call Maggie naive.

"None of it makes sense," I said irritably, thinking aloud. "I can't see Maggie having an affair with Dennis. Quite frankly, she didn't need to. And Dennis may have thought he was a coed's delight, but to Maggie he would have just been an old man on the make. Eric March was crazy about her. She told Eric she loved him. She was a senior, a top senior. Dennis couldn't have done anything, good or bad, that could have made a difference to her status on *The Clarion*. And to give him credit, I don't think he ever tried to sabotage a girl if she said no."

I suppose all along, ever since Rita had burst into the newsroom Wednesday night, I'd felt that the equation didn't compute. Dennis and Maggie?

Dennis had denied it, fervently.

But Dennis had admitted having an occasional drink with Maggie.

"Did Dennis use your car sometimes?" I asked Rita abruptly.

It was a question out of left field, but she was too upset to notice or wonder.

She nodded incuriously.

"But he had his car Wednesday night?"

Again, that indifferent nod.

Having a drink with a student and sleeping with one were two different matters. I doubted if it could ever be proved one way or the other.

Dennis denied an affair.

But Dennis would have to deny it, either to protect Rita or himself. Certainly he'd lie if he'd killed Maggie because she rejected him.

"Rita, what made you think Dennis was out with Maggie Wednesday night? Did you find a note, overhear—"

"The phone call. It was the phone call."

Now, finally, something concrete.

"Did you hear Dennis talking to Maggie?" I wanted to know if Rita had heard just his side of the conversation or if she'd picked up an extension. It could make a huge difference.

"Oh, no, no. Not Dennis." Those faded blue eyes stared past me. "I was looking at my scrapbooks. We went to Disneyland that last May. Carla loved it. There's a picture of her with Mickey...Then the phone rang. I almost didn't answer. But I thought it might be Dennis." She looked at me with bleak, misery-laden eyes. "I was holding the scrapbook and there was Carla laughing and so happy and I picked up the phone and this voice began to whisper, this breathy ugly whisper, and it said Dennis was going to fuck this girl and if I hurried I'd catch them. It said they were at her apartment or maybe in his office. Then the line went dead. It was hideous."

"Did you recognize the voice?"

She looked forbearing at my stupidity. She spoke very, very clearly. "It was a whisper. That's all. Just a whisper."

"A man? A woman?"

"I don't know." She gave an impatient shrug.

"The voice specifically mentioned Maggie?"

"Yes. Maggie Winslow." Rita enunciated every syllable.

"Do you have any idea who the caller was?"

"I don't know. Does it matter?"

"Oh yes, Rita. It matters. It matters very much indeed."

The silence on the other end of the line spoke volumes. Finally, his husky voice carefully polite, Lieutenant Urschel said, "That's real interesting, Mrs. Collins. I'll make a note of it."

Before he could hang up, I said urgently, "Lieutenant, please, give me a moment. I know this is secondhand information, but I think it's important. Rita Duffy was definitely set up."

It had been a long and draining morning. I licked my fingers for the last smear of Italian dressing from the hoagie I'd just finished. I don't like a lunch on the run, but I was in a hurry. Even though I didn't know where I was going. I opened my desk drawer and fished around for some chocolate. I needed more energy.

"Mrs. Collins, Rita Duffy's had quite a lot of time on her hands. Sounds to me like she's put it to good use..."

There was a brisk knock on my partially open door. "Delivery," a cheerful voice called.

"...given it some real thought. Now, I'll agree that this might be damn interesting—if it really happened. Funny thing, Mrs. Duffy didn't say a word about any phone call to us. You'd think she might have. Interesting she'd tell the press first." And he didn't like it one little bit.

A freckle-faced woman in her thirties shouldered my door wide. It took both hands to carry the flowers.

I motioned for her to come in and wondered how I could break through Urschel's resistance.

"Rita's scared," I told Urschel. "Lieutenant, she's scared to death. And she talked to me because her husband arranged it. It definitely wasn't an interview."

The delivery woman asked softly, "Mrs. Collins?"

At my nod, she placed the arrangement on a corner of my desk. She took a moment to regard it with pride.

I was impressed, too. I wondered how many carnations it had taken to create the single-engine airplane in blue and pink and white and red blossoms, nose high, taking off, a flight to fantasy. The woody perfume of the flowers wafted over me, sweet and refreshing as a kiss.

Urschel cleared his throat. "But you're going to do that series. Right?"

Dennis's creative use of my name in *The Clarion* might give me a little traction with Urschel. Not much, because cops don't cozy up to reporters. But some.

But maybe there was a better way. "Yes, Lieutenant, I'm doing the series. But I'm doing it for Maggie." I paused, then spaced out the words. "Not for any other reason."

Now his silence was considering.

I waited. I knew I didn't have to explain, not to a man who spent his life trying to catch killers.

"Yeah." He spoke so quietly, I might have imagined it. "Okay, Mrs. Collins..."

I signed the delivery slip for the flowers, still cradling the phone. "Thank you," I mouthed. The delivery woman gave me a parting smile as she ducked out the door.

I didn't reach for the card. I knew who'd sent this gorgeous bouquet. I was listening to the gravelly voice in my ear and I could have whooped with thanksgiving as Urschel continued, "...when did Mrs. Duffy say she got the call?"

Thank you, God. Urschel was willing to listen. He was going to give me—and Rita—a chance.

"A few minutes after six." I pulled my legal pad closer, marked an X on one side for the Duffys' home and drew a curving line. It touched a square that represented Maggie's apartment, then slanted to the campus and a triangle for the Journalism School.

"Six or so." Urschel's gruff voice was patient. "All right. The Duffy house is on Morrissey Avenue; the deceased's apartment is on Canterbury Lane. If Mrs. Duffy got this call at six and immediately left home, she could be at the Winslow apartment by six-ten, the Journalism School by six-thirty. That timing fits. Then out to the parking lot— where she could easily have found Maggie Winslow."

Urschel still saw Rita as the murderer, consigning the story of the phone call to the realm of make-believe. Or, if true, simply as the trigger to the night's violence.

But he was willing to think it through. "All right, Mrs. Collins. Let's look at it. There are two possibilities: Mrs. Duffy invented that phone call, or the phone call occurred. *If* the phone call is real, there are two further possibilities. It was simply a malicious anonymous call and the caller did it for no reason other than dislike of the Duffys. Or of Maggie Winslow."

That opened up a broad field.

"And it sent Rita Duffy out in search of Winslow and when she found her, she killed her. Or," he said thoughtfully, "the phone call came from the murderer with the definite intent, knowing Mrs. Duffy's explosive temper, of setting her off in two public forums, the apartment complex and the newsroom, with the result that when Maggie Winslow's body is found, Mrs. Duffy is suspect number one."

"Bingo," I said softly. "And if that is the case, Lieutenant, it tells us a very important fact."

"Yes, Mrs. Collins?"

"That Maggie was dead by six o'clock."

"According to the autopsy, that's possible," Urschel agreed. "She was last spotted about five-thirty—so far as we've been able to trace her—eating an early dinner in the Commons."

I added those helpful facts to my little hoard of information:

According to the autopsy, Maggie could have been dead by 6 P.M.

Maggie was last seen at the Commons.

Thank you, Lieutenant Urschel.

"Or," he thought aloud, "the call could mean the murderer planned to kill Maggie Winslow and knew it would occur soon."

"Quite a gamble, don't you think?" I crumpled a paper napkin in my hand, still trying to get rid of the stickiness on my fingers. I looked across my desk at the carnations and felt warm inside.

"It would mean the murderer had an appointment with Winslow."

I tossed the napkin in my wastebasket. "What if Maggie didn't show up?" I reached across the desk, felt a flowery wing tip.

"She was reliable, wasn't she?"

"That's too big a gamble. No, I think it was a done deal." I took a last sip from my bottle of cola. "And it gives us somewhere to start."

I heard a phone ringing in the background in his office and the rattle of papers and the squeak of a chair. Then Urschel said, and his voice wasn't unkind, "I'll tell you something, Mrs. Collins. I think you're wasting your time. But we'll look at what you find. Okay?"

"Thanks, Lieutenant." I hung up. It wasn't carte blanche. But it wasn't a stone wall either.

And I did have a place to start.

Six o'clock.

Where was Maggie Winslow—or her dead body—at six o'clock Wednesday evening? And why, oh why, had there been a delay in leaving her body in Lovers' Lane?

If I ever learned the answer to the first question, perhaps I would know the answer to the second.

I drove slowly around the apartment complex. It was designed like a motel—two-story, stucco, doors opening to the outside, stairways at either end. Windward Apartments catered to students. With the irregular hours common to students, there was no guarantee that I could approach Maggie's unit without being seen.

At the end of my second sweep around the complex, I pulled between a pickup truck and a van into a slot facing a ravine. My MG was effectively screened from view on three sides.

I picked up my mobile phone, once again rang Maggie's number. There had been no answer when I called from my office. There was no answer now.

I left my car unlocked. I might want to leave in a hurry.

Although it was early afternoon, the cloud cover made it dark as twilight.

If the temperature dropped another five degrees, sleet would be a reality. I liked that, and the raw, wet wind. I wore my trench coat, collar upturned, a navy scarf that obscured much of my face, and supple leather gloves—a costume quite unremarkable on a sullen, wintry afternoon and superbly suited for breaking and entering. In it, I was a swift-moving coated figure that offered nothing memorable for description.

Maggie's apartment was at the east end. No police tape marked the wooden gate to number 16.

I didn't hesitate. I lifted the latch, stepped into the enclosed patio, and drew the gate shut behind me. The six-foot fence afforded complete privacy.

Two candy-striped canvas chairs sagged forlornly on the small patio. A hibachi was tucked next to the back door.

I pulled open the screen. The back door was locked.

I lifted the flap on my shoulder bag and reached into the zippered compartment, digging past my checkbook, photos, receipts, assorted stuff. At the very bottom—and you'd have to know it was there to find it—rested a tool that I've found extremely useful through the years.

113

I want to be clear. I do not make it a habit to open locked doors illegally. Should anyone inquire, this useful implement is for that rare occasion when I accidentally lock myself out of my house. Certainly that can happen to anyone.

It's a very simple tool, really, an exceedingly narrow three-inch sliver of steel with a small wooden handle, making it easy to grip. Filament-thin pincers at the other end are magnetized. If I can work the blade between the door and the jamb, most locks are history.

As was this one.

I eased open the door and stepped into a small narrow kitchen, then paused. I stood quietly, scarcely breathing. I faced a closed swinging door. To my right, the length of the kitchen ended in another door. I tried it first and found a washer and dryer. There was no other exit from the washroom.

The kitchen smelled faintly piney. I spotted an air freshener cone sitting on the windowsill over the sink. On the green tile counter, pottery canisters were lined up next to a bread box. There were no dishes, clean or dirty, on the counter or the small white kitchen table.

All the while, I listened as if my life depended upon it.

Because it might.

It had occurred to me as I worked open the back door that if Rita was innocent, the murderer might be very interested indeed in Maggie's papers, the papers Dennis had so cavalierly (and publicly) announced I would be using to write the series.

Perhaps—and it was a comforting thought in that still, quiet, tense moment—the murderer had already been there.

Once again, I listened. There was no movement, no sound, other than an occasional faint plop from the dripping faucet over the sink.

I placed my gloved hand against the swinging door and pushed, paused, pushed, paused.

No light, no sound, no movement.

I peered through a six-inch wide opening. I could see perhaps a third of the combination living-dining room. On the windows to my left, the draperies were drawn. The light was murky, but good enough to see that Maggie kept her small apartment tidy. The gleaming oak dining table was bare.

So far, so good. I began to relax.

I still moved quietly, but I opened the door wide.

The living room was as silent as the kitchen.

I hesitated for a moment, looking back at the door to the patio. Should I leave it open behind me? If anyone stepped into the patio, the open door would be obvious.

The possibility of crossing paths with a murderer was perhaps remote. But the likelihood that someone from Maggie's family might arrive at any time was certainly not remote. I needed to make my clandestine search as fast as I could.

Swiftly, I stepped to the back door and closed it. It locked automatically.

I returned to the living room, stepping confidently now. My eyes scanned the bookcases, the coffee table. Novels, textbooks, CDs, cassettes. Nothing there to interest me.

I steeled myself not to reflect on the half-completed needlepoint—a golden surfboard rising out of a jade-green background—lying on the rumpled couch or the stack of letters on the sideboard, ready to be mailed, or the copy of *Editor and Publisher*, open to the employment ads.

I felt an instant's surprise at Maggie's bedroom. It was spartan, a single bed with a plain white cotton spread, a dressing table with comb, hairbrush, and a handful of cosmetics. The bed was made.

I took a deep breath, pressed my lips together as I looked at that simple bed and at the scruffy teddy bear propped on the pillow. It had only one eye. A worn blue cravat hung limply from his neck.

Oh, Maggie, Maggie, so grown up, yet clinging to that remnant of childhood.

No clothes were flung about. The wooden floor was bare of rugs. Maggie's bedroom was as plain as a barracks.

The focus of the room obviously was the elaborate computer setup along the wall.

A swivel chair was turned away from the computer toward a work area on the left with a legal pad, several folders, and an appointment book. Filing cabinets were to the right of the computer printer.

I sat in Maggie's chair. A square desk cal-

endar for November was covered with notations in small neat printing—appointments,
reminders, deadlines.

I looked at Tuesday, November 14. Four
notations:

Collins
Dennis
Campus cops—Wolf
Howard Rosen's brother

Wednesday, November 15. Four names
were jotted down:

President Tucker
Angela Chavez
Stuart Singletary
Dr. Abbott

That was all. There was no information by
any of these names. The first three I expected.
But why Dr. Abbott? Was he listed because he
was Singletary's father-in-law? Did that mean
Maggie was focusing on the young English
professor?

On Tuesday, Maggie had given me a sum-
mary of her series idea in the hallway, then gone
in to talk about it with Dennis.

She'd been scheduled and had duly come
for her independent-study session with me, so,
in effect we had a definite appointment.

I glanced at my watch, and dialed the newsroom.

"*The Clarion.*"

"City editor, please."

A click, a pause, and a voice answered. "Duffy."

"Dennis, on Tuesday when Maggie talked to you about her series, did she have an appointment with you?"

"No. She just dropped by. Listen, Henrie O—"

I broke in with, "Okay. Thanks," and hung up. I didn't have time to talk to Dennis now. I'd deal with him later.

Okay. Maggie listed people she intended to talk to, but it didn't necessarily indicate an appointment with them.

I knew she'd spoken to Stuart Singletary.

I would find out about President Tucker, Angela Chavez, and Dr. Abbott, ditto the campus cop and Rosen's brother.

But even as I glanced past the engagement calendar, I wondered if this was an exercise in futility.

In my heart, I hoped so.

If Rita Duffy killed Maggie, I was home free. My student's death would not have resulted from my insistence upon in-depth reporting.

And clearly Maggie's papers, including her engagement calendar, were untouched. Everything appeared to be in order—the folders neatly piled, the filing cabinets firmly closed. There was no evidence of a search.

But one thing appeared to be missing. I leaned back in thought. Yes, Maggie carried a small leather notebook.

I searched in earnest. I even went into the living room, checked the little butler's table by the door. No notebook.

It probably was in her purse or her car. Especially since she'd been working on the series that day.

I would check with Lieutenant Urschel. If he hadn't found the notebook, it should set off an alarm in his mind.

But this is the computer age. Maggie might not have current notes in her computer, but there should be something.

I booted up the computer. Maggie had Windows WordPerfect 6.0, the same system used at *The Clarion.*

It took only a moment to find her most recent files. I called them up one by one. The main file—INVST.SER—was saved at 2:47 P.M. Tuesday. It was the material she'd given to me on Tuesday morning, plus one page containing an informal record of ideas, fragments that would serve as pointers in her investigation. It included some information new to me and an excellent series of questions.

Good going, Maggie. You were truly trying, just as I asked you to.

I reached over, turned on the printer. I wanted a hard copy of this final page. Quickly I tore it off, tucked it in my purse, turned off the printer.

I'd found what she'd done to date on her series.

And it was still there, still in her computer.

Did that mean no one cared to see where she'd gone, what she'd learned?

Of course, in a computer age almost everyone knows that erasing a file destroys only the apparent existence of information. The words are still available in the computer's memory. But you'd have to be looking hard and be very expert to dredge through all the material erased from the file list, yet retained in the hard drive.

I took this as one more proof that no one else had surveyed Maggie's research and as yet another clear indication of Rita Duffy's guilt.

I shivered. I suddenly realized the apartment was very cold. Someone must have turned the heat off. Even in my coat, I was chilled.

I swiveled the chair to my left and the worktable. Three folders, three cases.

I checked the three folders. Maggie had searched *The Clarion* morgue files, just as I had, and printed out the stories with the most information.

She had included two items I had not found in my first survey.

In the Rosen-Voss file, she'd made the connection immediately that Stuart Singletary, now assistant professor of English, was also the roommate in 1988 of Howard Rosen.

Of course, it probably was obvious to her because she had a class this semester with Singletary.

So perhaps I owed her no kudos on that one.

In the Darryl Nugent file, she'd included an article on a student who'd fallen to his death from the Old Central bell tower the day the dean of students disappeared in 1976.

I nodded in admiration. Maggie had looked to see what else out of the ordinary was happening on the campus that day. Smart thinking.

All right, I'd follow her lead, see if there could be a connection.

But the remainder of the three files exactly corresponded to the papers now sitting on my office desk.

I closed the folders, replaced them precisely as I'd found them.

The cold in the apartment was seeping into my bones. I almost left then. I'd looked at everything.

But not quite.

Trying not to shiver, I got out of the chair and stepped to the three-drawer metal filing cabinet.

The top drawer held folders about classes in order of subjects: Economics, English, Geology, German, History, Journalism, Philosophy.

The second drawer held hard copies of all the stories she'd written for *The Clarion*.

The third drawer also held hard copies. There were six short-story manuscripts, and the beginnings of a novel. The opening paragraphs of the novel made me smile: short, swift, clever sentences, the protagonist a college senior—of course—the story line a raucous, hard-driving take on Generation X and its fumbling, funny, fractious efforts to comprehend a cyberforce world where gender is indistinct, history in flux, security elusive, and commitment—

There is no sound quite so distinct and unmistakable as breaking glass.

I heard it faintly.

Oh, Christ.

Yes, I was scared. I didn't process logical thought. I moved fast. I didn't even close the cabinet. Instantly, I grabbed my purse and was on my feet, darting around the end of Maggie's bed, the bathroom my goal.

Bathroom doors always lock on the inside. That was the fact I counted on to save my life.

I was certain that death was only a room away.

I plunged into the bathroom, shut the door, locked it.

Dennis, you bastard, you sorry, self-serving, myopic bastard!

Because I knew what had brought the murderer to Maggie's apartment: Dennis's interview in this morning's *Clarion*.

I leaned against the door, my heart thudding as if I'd run a long way. I looked desperately around the tiny antiseptic room. What could I use to reinforce the flimsy lock? I knew only too well how easy it is to open locked doors.

The intruder had broken glass in the kitchen to get in. That indicated no expertise in picking locks.

Still, I needed something. I turned, yanked the lid to the toilet, and wrenched free the metal arm holding the chain and stopper. It took only seconds to shove one end of the metal piece beneath the door, effectively jamming the door in place.

The wooden floor creaked in the bedroom.

The bathroom doorknob rattled.

I was already at the window. I unlocked it, pushed it up. The screen was hard to dislodge. When it finally screeched free, I pulled myself up on the sill and wriggled out. I landed heavily on the scraggly remnants of chrysanthemums in the flower bed below. My right ankle gave a sharp twinge, but I quickly righted myself and hurried down the sidewalk.

The weather had suddenly warmed, as it can do in November in Missouri. The result was a sudden and dense fog that turned the terrain a ghostly gray. I moved as quickly as I could, though my ankle flamed with pain.

A dog barked.

A gate banged.

Maggie's gate?

The intruder could have left her apartment as quickly as I had, desperate to escape without being seen.

I stood still. The parking lot was swathed in fog. I could see only a short distance. But that meant the intruder couldn't see either.

I had my keys in hand, which meant, of course, that I also held my Mace canister that serves as my key ring. I should be safe enough now. I hadn't glimpsed the intruder. If I had, I would have made my own death inevitable.

I reached the MG, checked to be certain it was empty, then slid in and locked the doors.

I shoved the key in the ignition. Now, locked inside the car, armed with Mace and a mobile phone, I was willing to take a chance.

The MG revved to life.

But when I drove past the back of the apartment house, I knew I was too late.

Maggie's gate stood open. The intruder was gone.

Stalemate.

I didn't know who had come. But I knew why, thanks to Dennis purveying me as Intrepid Investigative Reporter to every reader of this morning's *Clarion*. Maggie's killer had been afraid to risk the chance that I might find something—a hint, a clue, a giveaway—in Maggie's papers.

But I knew more.

I knew that Rita Duffy was innocent.

And I knew it was I who had pointed Maggie to her death.

eight

My ankle hurt like hell. The drive through the billowing fog to the campus was nightmarish. I've never found fog romantic, simply unpleasantly damp and dangerous.

I limped upstairs.

The newsroom throbbed with its usual late-afternoon deadline tension. I still find the quiet unsettling, even after a number of years in computerized newsrooms. The sense of excitement and eagerness and tension remains, but now there is no staccato of typewriters, no hurrying clatter of feet with reporters rushing sheets of yellow copy paper to the news desk. Everyone is absorbed, intent upon the task, acutely aware of the swift swing of the minute hand as deadline approaches.

Dennis looked up, saw me, and semaphored wildly.

I ignored him and stalked—as valiantly as I could with my painful ankle—to my office.

"Henrie O. Henrie O!" His chair scraped.

I unlocked my door, flipped on the light, shrugged out of my coat. As I tossed it on the coat tree, Dennis was at my elbow.

"Henrie O, somebody broke into Maggie's apartment! Just picked it up on the scanner. Kitty's checking it out."

I limped to my desk, wearily sat down, then glared at him. "I've read checkout-stand cheap sheets with more integrity than this morning's *Clarion*. You are a real piece of work, Duffy."

His gaze was a mixture of defiance and shame, but defiance had the edge. "Henrie O—" He took a deep breath. "I'd say I'm sorry, but I'm not. The whole damn town's buzzing. By God, they aren't going to railroad Rita! Not if I have anything to say about it."

I understand loyalty. My bleak anger began to drain away. I sighed. I can't camp on a holier-than-thou summit with any comfort. God knows my own faith in others has led me to a rash act or two in my past. "Okay, Dennis. We'll drop it. For now."

His face lightened at my change in tone. His eyes glinted with their old combativeness. "You can always tell me to fuck off."

"I know. And I may. In fact, I probably will. But, hey, Dennis, what's this about somebody trying to break into Maggie's place? That sounds good for Rita."

He nodded, his face pathetically eager. "It's terrific, isn't it? I called Rita's lawyer and told him. And listen, Henrie O, thanks. That's great stuff you got, about the phone call. That shows somebody wanted to make Rita mad, deliberately send her after Maggie."

I reached down, massaged my ankle. It was beginning to swell. "I think so, Dennis, yes. Look, I've got some work to do, so..."

Dennis didn't move. He stared down at the floor, clearly uncomfortable. "Have you picked up your messages yet?"

But he knew I hadn't.

He didn't look up, his eyes fixed on the shiny oak floor. His voice was unaccustomedly subdued. "Susan wants to talk to you."

Susan Dillon, the director of the J-School, was bright, smart, and a superb administrator. She had a great talent for always arranging everything to benefit one Susan Dillon. If she'd been on the *Titanic,* she would have reached a lifeboat. Count on it.

"Oh?"

"Yeah. So you might want to check your voice

mail." He jammed his hands into his pockets, eyes still downcast. "Or you might not want to."

"I see." I moved in my chair, trying to ease the pain in my ankle.

"Yeah. Well." His voice was tired. Finally, he looked at me, his eyes somber. "I told Susan that if you wrote Maggie's series, I'd run it. But you understand, no matter what was in the story this morning, I'm not *asking* you to do it. Or not to do it. You can tell me to go to hell."

"And what did Susan say about your running the series—that I may or may not write?"

Dennis's mouth twisted in a sour, tight grin. "Oh, it was all very roundabout and circuitous. You know how academics are, Henrie O."

"The bottom line? Spare me the gymnastics, Dennis."

He shrugged. "What the hell, Henrie O, who needs the stress of the city desk? And I'd probably enjoy teaching Reporting 101. I'd make the little bastards work. So, we'll see what happens. But it's not negotiable, and that's what I told Susan. I run the series—or she gets a new city editor for *The Clarion*." He turned away.

"Dennis!" He knew and I knew that tenure protects you only so far. Susan Dillon could take away the city desk, consign him to the lowest level of classes, load him up with the most boring committee work imaginable, insist he try for grant money—a full-blown industry within the academic community which requires paperwork worthy of a congressional subcommittee. "Why are you doing this?"

"Nobody tells me what stories to run. Or not to run. To hell with it." And he was out the door.

I watched through the plate glass as he strode toward his desk.

I hadn't intended to write the series. My goal was more basic than that. I wanted to determine why Maggie died and whether it came back to my insistence on her doing more than a simple rehash of the unsolved crimes.

Now I, too, had to make a decision.

I rubbed my temple. I was beginning to feel like the metal duck in a shooting gallery. There was no place to run, no way to dodge. I didn't need this. But it wasn't going to go away.

My phone rang.

I almost didn't answer. My ankle blazed with pain. My head ached. I needed a respite. But I also needed to face Susan and get it over with.

"Hello."

"Mrs. Collins."

I recognized Lieutenant Urschel's husky voice. I didn't peg his tone more than a degree above frost. So much for our earlier, almost-friendly accord.

"Been in your office all afternoon?"

Ping, ping, ping. Again I had a mental image of the battered little yellow metal duck in the shooting gallery.

"No."

Urschel waited.

I did, too.

"Any reason not to say where you've been this afternoon, Mrs. Collins?" Anger made his voice even raspier than usual.

"No." I opened my desk drawer, fished around for the bottle of ibuprofen. I shook out a tablet.

"So where have you been?" He was as relentless as cresting floodwater.

I added a second pill, poured some water into a cup from the pitcher I keep on a credenza.

It's always dangerous to lie. But I had no choice. "County jail. Then I timed the drive between Maggie Winslow's apartment and the J-School." I swallowed the tablets.

The silence between us bristled.

"Clever." But it wasn't said in admiration. "The apartment-house manager reported seeing an MG like yours. But I'll tell you something, Mrs. Collins, we've got your prints on record from that secretary's murder a few years ago. If I find your prints in Maggie Winslow's apartment, you're in trouble."

"You won't." Thank God for gloves. "I understand from the city editor that somebody broke into her apartment."

After a pause, he said without expression, "A pane in the window over the kitchen sink was smashed. Somebody climbed in. Knocked a deodorizer on the floor. The manager saw the gate swinging open about three o'clock, checked, and found the broken window. The back door was open."

129

The intruder had left in a hurry, just as I had. "Was anything taken? Or destroyed?"

"What do you have in mind?" It was as close to silky as I'd heard his rough voice come.

Tired as I was, I grinned, but Br'er Rabbit wasn't going to get caught in that brier patch. "Oh, I don't know. Let's see, Maggie worked on a computer, of course. Was it intact? How about her files? Had anyone been into them?"

"We haven't turned on the computer."

"Lieutenant, I hope you will check it out." I said it very pleasantly, my voice low-key, with no hint of criticism. I wanted to regroup with this man. There'd been a break in his aloof-cop demeanor once. If it happened once, it could happen again. I didn't blame him for being angry. If I were a cop, I'd despise smart-ass civilians who didn't follow the rules.

And, of course, I desperately wanted him to turn on that computer. If he did, it would reflect that a file had been called up this afternoon. That should get his attention.

"Maggie Winslow's computer files have nothing to do with Mrs. Duffy."

"But Mrs. Duffy couldn't have broken into the apartment, Lieutenant."

"Right." His tone was thoughtful. Then, abruptly, sharply, he demanded, "You swear you didn't break in there?"

I hadn't *broken in*. So my answer was quick, easy, and truthful. "I did not, Lieutenant."

"Hmm."

I liked this man. I liked him a lot. I could feel his mood changing. He was *thinking*.

"Nothing appeared to have been touched since I was there yesterday morning. Except the filing cabinets. One drawer was pulled out."

"Oh?"

"And somebody'd been in the bathroom. We had to get in through the window."

"Somebody locked the bathroom door from the inside?"

"It wouldn't open," he said dryly. He didn't intend to describe the rod jammed beneath the door.

And I, of course, knew nothing of that. "That seems very odd. But it certainly indicates something is going on—and, as I said before, Mrs. Duffy most certainly can't be involved, and what you've described doesn't sound like the work of a petty thief. So let's focus on what matters. Someone broke into Maggie's apartment. There has to be a reason."

"Maybe *somebody* is trying to divert attention from Mrs. Duffy." He wasn't altogether convinced of my innocence.

"No, Lieutenant." My answer was firm. And truthful. Then I asked briskly, "Was anything taken?" I sipped from my water. My throat and mouth were dry.

"Nothing, so far as we know. The obvious stuff—the TV, CD player, the computer—wasn't touched."

"How about Maggie's notebook? As I recall, she took notes in a small brown leather notebook. Was that in the apartment?"

There was a silence, a rustle of papers. "I don't have a record of a notebook."

"There should be a notebook, Lieutenant. Was it in her purse? Or her car?" Maggie's purse had lain forlornly beside her body. Her car had been found in the J-School lot.

Another pause, another rattle of paper. "It wasn't in either the purse or the car."

"Where is it? Lieutenant, that notebook's important."

"It could turn up."

I didn't answer that.

Now Urschel had to be concerned about the notebook—as I truly was concerned—and now, too, he couldn't be sure just what the break-in at Maggie's meant.

Yes, he might like to think I'd been nosing around there. But he couldn't be certain.

"If nothing valuable is missing—"

His interruption was swift. "As far as we know."

"I understand, Lieutenant, but the stuff a petty thief looks for wasn't touched. Right?"

"What's your point, Mrs. Collins?"

"Okay, that knocks out the idea of somebody reading about Maggie's murder and deciding to pull a spur-of-the-moment burglary. What does that leave?"

"You tell me."

"Maggie's murderer."

"Mrs. Collins, if somebody besides Mrs. Duffy killed that girl, all that person has to do is sit still, be cool. Why break into that apartment? We'd already looked it over. Any fool would know that's the first place we would check out. What possible reason—"

"The interview with Dennis Duffy in this morning's paper, Lieutenant. That's what stirred up the murderer. This killer has felt safe for a long time—maybe twenty years. Until Maggie found out something, and that's why she had to die. Now the murderer's scared there might be some hint of what she found in her apartment."

"No way, Mrs. Collins." He was supremely confident. "Winslow was strangled Wednesday night. Her purse was found with her body. Her car keys and key to her apartment were in it. The perp could easily have gone to her apartment sometime after he killed her, knowing nobody was there, and searched in absolute safety."

I looked through the plate glass across the newsroom at Dennis, hunched close to his computer. "But on Wednesday night the murderer felt confident the only person who was looking into the unsolved crimes would never look again. Lieutenant, I'm certain Maggie's notebook was taken by whoever killed her. And the murderer felt safe until this morning, when *The Clarion* ran that interview with Dennis, all about the earlier crimes and the articles that I'm going to write—using Maggie's notes."

"That's a fascinating theory, Mrs. Collins. You can share it with the defense."

I gently massaged my temple. God, how could I convince Urschel?

"Lieutenant, you must find Maggie's notebook."

"We'll look for it." A pause, then a brisk, "And I'll check out her computer."

"Thank you, Lieutenant." And I meant it.

"All right, Mrs. Collins—"

Before he could say good-bye, I said quickly, "One more thing, Lieutenant. I'd like to ask your help."

"The case is closed, Mrs. Collins." He was pleasant but firm.

"Yes, *this* case is closed. For now. But there are three famous Derry Hill crimes that have never been solved. I'm asking your help with those unsolved cases."

He answered carefully. "Information in open files is confidential."

"I know that. But I simply want some facts. My questions will in no way compromise your investigations."

I was startled when he gave a snort of amusement. "You're really something, lady. I bet they'll carve 'Never Give Up' on your tombstone."

I grinned. "Not, I hope, for a few more years. But, Lieutenant, I'd really appreciate—"

"Okay, okay. What do you want to know?"

I had my questions ready, three of them.

"I'll see what we can do." And he hung up.

The dial tone was one of the loneliest sounds I'd heard in a long time.

I was out there on a limb all by myself, and I could hear the screech of the saw blade and feel the quiver of the wood.

Susan Dillon looked up as I closed her office door behind me.

She didn't rise. She didn't smile. Susan

rarely smiles. Expressionless, she waved a glossily manicured hand toward the chair that faced her desk. Her chromosomes carried no genes for humor.

I limped across the shining parquet flooring, careful not to stumble on the Oriental throw rug. That's all my ankle would need. Or my ego.

Susan always reminded me of a highly bred Persian. Her round, firm, pink-cheeked face was elegantly framed by thick, shiny white hair. Her china-blue eyes were cool and remote and highly intelligent. She'd spent a major portion of her career in TV news in Los Angeles. After a second marriage to the head of the chemistry department at Thorndyke, she'd added a Ph.D. to an illustrious résumé. And when the directorship of the J-School opened up, she charmed the search committee. Susan was definitely a woman who preferred to be in charge.

"Henrie O, I appreciate your coming down." Susan rested her plump hands on her desk. The huge amethyst ring on her right hand matched the violet sheen of her silk shantung suit. More amethysts shone in a gold filigree pin on her lapel.

I wasn't in the mood for the intricate, measured wordplay so beloved of academics, with the nuances carefully shaded and meanings obliquely expressed. That was Susan's turf, not mine.

I sat down, met her cool gaze directly. "What did Tucker offer?"

135

I doubt that anyone had ever slammed a fist to the side of her head before. Or its verbal equivalent.

A faint flush stained her ivory-white cheeks. Her eyes glittered like sapphires in a rich cat's collar.

I tilted my head inquiringly. "Increased appropriation? Another tenured professorship? A Thorndyke journalism program abroad?" My ankle felt encircled by a band of fire. A reminder that I was no longer a young reporter, even if I persisted in acting like one.

Susan picked up a shiny silver letter opener with a carved jade handle, balanced it on the tips of her fingers. Her rose nails glistened in the lamplight almost as vividly as the silver. The flush had faded from her cheeks. "I do like to keep in touch with faculty." Her high, light voice was as metallic as a wind chime. "To be certain we focus on our mission. It's important that we work together as a team, Henrietta."

The use of my formal name indicated I was truly in deep shit.

Not that I gave a damn.

"It is certainly," Susan continued coldly, "obligatory for faculty members to remember that we must always function for the good of the whole."

One step forward, two steps back. My ankle hurt too much to join in this dance. But I definitely understood the beat. Susan would never admit it openly, but yes, President

Tucker had contacted her and she'd hastened to assure him that she would do everything she could to corral me.

Awkwardly, I struggled to my feet. I wanted to rest. I wanted to be left alone.

But Maggie Winslow would never write the words that had been in her heart and mind. And Maggie died because I told her to be a good reporter.

Could I be anything else?

"I'm going to write the series for *The Clarion*," I told Susan Dillon flatly.

I suppose that in my heart I'd always known that would be my decision, but I heard my own words with a tiny sense of shock. And yes, with regret. I'd come to feel at home here at Thorndyke. I enjoyed the students, treasured their eagerness, drew strength from their vitality. I'd made Derry Hills my home.

We gazed at each other, taking the measure of one another's convictions and weaknesses, then I turned away.

"We have valued your contributions, Henrietta." Her tone was cool and confident, with just a tiny curl of venom. "It would be a shame to lose your services."

She didn't have to wrap it with a bow. I understood.

But there was nothing more to say.

I closed my office door behind me. I needed to get home and put some ice on my ankle, but I took time to sit down. A small envelope dangled on a red ribbon from the tail of the carnation airplane that had arrived earlier today. I unlooped it, drew out the card.

There was no signature, but the message read: *Come fly away with me.*

I smiled. It felt odd on my face. It felt like a long time since I'd last smiled.

Slowly, mustering a reserve I wasn't sure I had, I got to my feet. I put on my coat, then gathered up the folders on the Rosen-Voss, Murdoch, and Nugent investigations. I had much to do, and I'd better work while I could. At least for the moment, I felt safe enough. Physically safe. For now, I doubted the murderer would make a move—a direct, physical move— against me. Had we come face-to-face in Maggie's apartment, there would have been no choice. But to kill me now would pose the terrible danger of suggesting to the police Maggie's death was indeed directly linked to the past.

But I knew the murderer was out there, dangerous and deadly.

I started toward the door, then came back to Jimmy's lovely bouquet.

One pink carnation nestled in my hand as I limped outside into the fog.

nine

I carried a mug of coffee into my study. I was walking with scarcely a limp. The ice pack had worked wonders. That and, of course, wrapping the ankle firmly this morning. As long as I took it easy and remembered the axiom embraced by the old and wily—every move a smooth one—I should be fine.

The early-morning sun slanted cheerfully across my desk. The single pink carnation poked jauntily out of a slim silver bud vase. I'd fixed it immediately when I got home last night.

Dear Jimmy, gallant and fun and always romantic. I liked him very much.

But was that enough?

I picked up one of my favorite photos of Richard. He stood next to a small plane, his hand on the wing. Wind ruffled his reddish-brown hair. His was a broad, blunt-featured, intelligent face with kind eyes and a generous mouth that spread in such an appealing, crooked grin. There was never anything mean or petty or small about Richard. He always tried to do his best. He was an honorable man in a world riddled with dishonor. I admired him without reserve, I respected him always, I loved him passionately.

I looked from the photo to the bud vase.

Richard was dead. Not all my tears or all my wishes would change that reality.

I could not expect Jimmy to take Richard's place, but there were sunrises yet to see.

I touched the carnation gently with my fingers. The vase sat next to the three folders that awaited me. But first I picked up the slick sheets mounding out of my fax machine. Ah, Lieutenant Urschel's response to my three questions. I owed Maggie for the first two questions. I was impressed that Lieutenant Urschel was at his office on a Saturday morning. I wondered if that was the time he devoted to niggling little housekeeping tasks. But I didn't care how much I irritated him, so long as I found out what I needed to know.

- -

To: Henrietta Collins
From: Derry Hills Police Department,
              Homicide Unit
              Lt. Larry Urschel
Date: Saturday, November 18
Message: Response to citizen request for
              information.
Question 1:   In re the Rosen-Voss murders,
              who is Joe Smith?

A thorough check of the DHPD files indicates there was no success in tracing "Joe Smith." The waitress at the Green Owl the night the students were killed heard them both refer several times in apparent good humor to "Joe Smith." At the time of the investigation, there were four Joseph Smiths (Joseph Alan Smith, Quincy Joseph Smith, Joseph Cornelius Smith, and Joseph John Smith) enrolled at Thorndyke University. So far as could be determined, none had any contact with either Rosen or Voss. No Joe Smiths were registered that night at any motel in Derry Hills. Eleven Joe Smiths were found in the Derry Hills telephone book. Exhaustive investigation provided no link to Rosen or Voss. Family members recalled no Joe Smiths in the pasts of either Rosen or Voss. Teletype inquiries in Missouri and surrounding states yielded no Joe Smiths on outstanding warrants. A Joe Smith was arrested three weeks later in a filling-station holdup in Springfield. On the night of the Rosen-Voss murders, that Joe Smith was in jail in Springfield on a DUI charge.

I sipped my coffee and watched dust motes whirling gently in the shaft of sunshine. Joe Smith. Who the hell *was* Joe Smith? The Derry Hills police obviously had gone at it every way they could. Carrying the fax sheets, I crossed to my desk. I flipped open the Rosen-Voss file. Hmm. Yes, there it was. The waitress at the Green Owl that long-ago night was Erin Malone. I circled her name in red.

I settled into my chair.

Question 2: Did the student who fell from the Old Central bell tower the day Dean Nugent disappeared have any connection with Nugent?

Leonard Cartwright's death is officially listed as an accident. There was no suggestion at the time that it was anything other than an accident. Cartwright's body was found in the early morning of March 15, 1976, at the base of the Old Central bell tower. He died from massive trauma, including severe head injuries and a broken neck. The injuries were consistent with having fallen from the north window of the tower. The window is seventy feet from the ground. Spiked iron bars reached to the middle of the windows on all four sides of the tower. Cartwright apparently climbed over the railing of the north window, then fell. The spikes snagged threads from his trousers. It was suggested at the time that Cartwright was engaged in a prank and was attempting to dislodge a gargoyle from its niche beneath the north window of the tower. Every year members of an engineering honor society placed a green plastic lei around the neck of the gargoyle. There was a long-standing rivalry between the engineering students and the architecture students, who tried to prevent the garlanding of the gargoyle. Cartwright was an architecture major. Campus authorities theorized that Cartwright lost his balance while pulling on the gargoyle. The statue came loose from the niche and plummeted to the ground, landing about ten feet from his body. Cartwright was a senior from Springfield. He was an outstanding student with a 3.79 grade average. He had served on the University Student Council, was a past secretary of his social fraternity, and played intramural volleyball. He had worked as a student assistant in Dean Nugent's office for two years.

- -

So Cartwright worked in the missing dean's office. I needed to talk to someone who had been in that office.

- -

Question 3:   Who was in the Murdoch house the night Curt Murdoch was shot?

Candace Murdoch, wife; Michael Murdoch, son; Jennifer Murdoch, daughter. Candace claimed to have been in the study talking on the telephone about a charity drive. Michael Murdoch was shooting pool by himself in the basement. Jennifer Murdoch was reading in bed.

- -

I slid the fax sheets together, put them next to the folders. But I didn't pick up a folder. Not yet. First things first.

I stood on the front steps of the Commons Building. At mid-morning on a lovely autumn Saturday, the campus was fairly quiet. Activity would pick up around noon as students and alumni began streaming toward the football stadium. But for now, there was only an occasional late breakfast seeker.

On Wednesday evening, the night Maggie met her death, it would have been quite dark. Of course, there were lamplights along the sidewalks. Nonetheless, it wasn't too surprising that no one had reported seeing Maggie after her early dinner in the cafeteria. She had walked out of the Commons and gone where?

She was on campus. She had a gap in time before her evening class with Stuart Singletary. She was working on the series assignment.

There were three obvious possibilities.

If she was concentrating on the Rosen-Voss homicides, she could have gone to see Singletary in his office in Evans Hall. Or—I

143

recalled the last name listed on her calendar—Dr. Abbott. He, too, would have an office in Evans Hall.

If she was working on the Murdoch murder, she could have set up an appointment with Angela Chavez, meeting her in the J-School office, which would have been virtually deserted at that hour.

Or had she gone to see President Tucker? I turned and looked across the gently rolling campus at Old Central, the building where President Tucker officed, the building where Dean Nugent was last seen, the building where young Leonard Cartwright fell to his death.

Each destination was only a few minutes from the Commons.

Stuart Singletary leaned on his rake. The breeze ruffled his glossy chestnut hair and stirred the pile of bronze and gold leaves. His two-story brick home, in Derry Hills's lovely historic district, was surrounded by massive oaks. A child's playhouse in the backyard was a charming miniature replica of the Tudor home. A little girl industriously wielded her play rake, making little mounds of leaves. Her narrow face was bright and happy and she darted me a shy glance out of velvety-brown eyes.

"Wednesday night?" His hand tightened on the rake. He tried to keep his voice casual. "Oh, I got back to my office around six. I usually go back an hour before class."

"Did you talk to anyone between six and seven?"

"No. I went straight to my office. I had some notes I wanted to review. Why?"

"I'm just sorting out where everyone was, Professor. Thanks." I walked away. Leaves crackled noisily underfoot. When I reached my car, I looked back.

Singletary was watching me. Maybe it was a trick of the light filtering through the bare tree branches, but his face looked like pieces of a jigsaw jumbled together. It wasn't an expression I could read.

Then I heard his little girl cry out, "Daddy, Daddy, what's wrong?"

Out of the mouths of little children...

President Tucker makes it a point to welcome well-heeled alums in town for football games. He headed the receiving line in the foyer of the Jackson Room at the Commons. The air was sweet with the brown-sugar smell of hickory sauce from the barbecue buffet.

The conversational level was exuberant, noisy.

When I reached Tucker, I leaned close and asked, "Where were you between five-thirty and six-thirty Wednesday night?"

For an instant, we stood in a tight pocket of silence, our faces inches apart. Little flecks of gold shimmered around the iris of his eyes, the fleshy folds beneath the sockets lapped down like lizard scales, his plump cheeks flamed with the red sheen of hypertension.

Then, his voice icy, he said, "That question is extraordinarily insulting, Mrs. Collins."

"Do you decline to answer?"

His massive shoulders lifted, fell. "I walked home about five-fifteen. I was there alone until I reached the Commons a few minutes before seven. I was in full view of several hundred people from seven o'clock until ten, Mrs. Collins. I spoke at the annual Phi Beta Kappa banquet."

Angel Chavez didn't invite me in. The J-School secretary stood squarely in the door of her apartment, arms folded across her chest.

"I was shopping at Wal-Mart." She didn't smile. Her dark brown eyes watched me warily.

"Did you see anyone you know?"

"No. Why should I?" She was defiant.

"It's a small town," I said pleasantly.

"I didn't." Her voice was harsh. "Then I grabbed a Wendy's and went to the parish hall. At seven. To play bingo. Do you want the names of some of the players?" It was a challenge.

"How long did you play?"

"Until ten." There were smudges of weariness under Angel's eyes. Not caused, I was willing to believe, by raucous evenings of bingo.

"No, thanks."

I was back at my desk by one o'clock after a light lunch. My foray hadn't simplified my search. Indeed, it was clear that Stuart Singletary, President Tucker, and Angel Chavez each had good reason to leave Maggie's body in a hiding place, then take it late at night to Lovers' Lane. Singletary had a class to teach, President Tucker was speaking at a banquet, and Angel was playing bingo. Unfortunately, not a single one had a rock-solid alibi between 6 and 7 P.M.

And they were only the three obvious suspects. I might well find others when I began to poke and prod into the past.

But first I wanted to look again at Maggie's plan, the single sheet I'd printed out of her computer the previous day and tucked into my purse. Its fragmentary notations were a tantalizing hint to the direction Maggie intended to take in her research:

Rosen-Voss

Find "J Smith"
Talk to Gail V's mother & brother
Did HR and GV often go to Lovers' Lane? Ask Prof. S
Talk to HR's brother

Curt Murdoch

Talk to Angel
Talk to Candace M
Talk to son & daughter
Could A. have been in Derry Hills that night?

Dean Nugent

Talk to wife
Talk to N's secretary
Who found student's body?
Campus files on dean's disappearance?

I put down the printout. It was quite a good plan of attack. I couldn't do better myself.

The important decision was where to start.

I knew only one certain fact: The murder of Maggie Winslow had drawn a tight, distinct circle around this town. That made my inquiries so much simpler than Maggie's had been. Maggie's murderer was in Derry Hills. So anyone involved in any of the three unsolved cases who was not in Derry Hills on Wednesday night was automatically cleared.

Rosen-Voss, Murdoch, or Nugent?

The murderer deliberately took Maggie's body to Lovers' Lane.

I pushed away the Rosen-Voss file.

Angel Chavez asked me to stop Maggie from writing about the old crimes, and Angel had been frantic to know if Maggie had started her articles.

I put my hand on the Murdoch file.

President Tucker used the power of his presidency to bring all the pressure possible to prevent my pursuing the series.

I pushed back the Murdoch file.

I picked up the Nugent file.

I wasn't sorry I'd insulted President Tucker.

I hoped I'd also worried him.

I opened the Nugent file. I jotted down several names. I wanted to know everything about the life and times of Dean Darryl Nugent, last seen late on a March afternoon in 1976.

The latest inside scoop was lifeblood to Helen Tracy, so she was quite willing to join me for coffee at the Commons.

"My dear, Dean Nugent's disappearance was a *sensation!*" Her voice quivered with delight. "Is *that* the case you're working on? I've been looking for you ever since I read yesterday morning's paper! You're harder to find than a Republican at a Labor Day rally." Helen wriggled in eagerness, her shaggy salt-and-pepper hair jouncing.

"I've been round and about. Listen, Helen, I really need your help." I cast my mind back to 1976. Watergate repercussions continued. John Erlichman went to jail. The Bicentennial. "That was the period just after Vietnam. Was there student unrest here? Could the dean have gotten into a problem there?"

The LifeStyle editor flapped her hands like a farm wife shooing hens. "Not *here*, sweetheart. Thorndyke came through those years pretty well. Tucker and Nugent stood between the kids and the Board of Governors. Oh, it got a little hairy a couple of times. The kids all started looking scruffy in the late sixties, you know, hair down their backs, couldn't tell the boys from the girls, and they looked dirty—old ragged jeans with holes, yes, and those *dreadfully* boring faded blue work shirts, everybody wore them—and the smell of marijuana absolutely *thick* in the library stacks; we had that kind of thing. But our kids were more worried about paying tuition than protesting corporate greed. We had a couple of marches, you know, in the early seventies, candles for the boys who died over there. And it was *dreadful* when Kent State happened." Helen's mobile face drooped, forlorn as a Piaf lament. She picked up her cup of tea, noisily gulped it half down. Then her mood abruptly shifted, and she beamed at me. "Darryl was wonderful then. Some students barricaded the cafeteria and said they wouldn't come out unless the University hired a black dean. Darryl talked and talked and talked to them and he finally persuaded them to name some leaders to be on outreach committees to broaden the faculty base. The governors *really* wanted the kids kicked out, but Darryl and David kept the lid on." She shook her wiry hair like a spaniel coming out of a pond. "But that was earlier. Nothing exciting was going on when Darryl disappeared. God, what a story! He was *so* good-looking. Have you ever seen his picture?"

She didn't wait for my answer.

"To *die* for, my dear. Golden hair and Cézanne-blue eyes, and one of those firm manly chins. He would have been a perfect veterinarian on a *Saturday Evening Post* cover. And when you saw him in shorts at the gym, you longed to go directly home and invite some man over. Any man. Darryl was what a baseball hero *should* look like, and not dribbling tobacco juice or scratching. And he was not only gorgeous, his wife was, too. Kathryn was one of those elegant women who made gingham look like mink. It didn't matter what she wore, the first thing you knew, *all* the other faculty wives had the very same look." Helen twisted the lid in her teapot; her voice dropped. "I see Kathryn every so often. She runs a nursery now. Plants, not kids. And she wears jeans and her hair is straight and *no* makeup. It's like she had a personality change. But I guess having your husband disappear and never resurface might be enough to change you. She dropped out of the social life like *this*." Helen snapped her fingers. "Be interesting to do a story on her..." She looked wistful. "But I'll bet she won't talk."

"What was Darryl Nugent like?" The coffee was strong and hot, a good antidote for the forlorn chill of disrupted lives.

Helen briefly pressed her fingers against her temples before replying. "Smart, nice, the kids liked him. I tell you, Henrie O, it was just the weirdest thing you've ever heard of. His secretary said good night to him, that was about five or so. And from that day to this, no one's ever seen him again!" She peered at me, her eyes wide. "Darryl always walked to and from his office, so he didn't have a car at school. I mean, that's the first thing you look for—where's the missing person's car? Well, his was right at home in his driveway. So, it was after five and usually he got home around five-thirty, maybe sometimes six. Now that was a wild day. You know about the student who fell out of the bell tower—"

"Fell?"

Helen's mobile face scrunched in dismay. "They think they can do *anything* at that age. It just made us all sick. That silly gargoyle. It was such a stupid prank, just to foil the engi-

151

neering students. What a waste...But back to Darryl, now this is really, really weird. Of course it was March and chilly. I think it was in the thirties the night before. So it figures people weren't lolling around on the campus. Another month and there would have been hardy sunbathers everywhere. *But* Old Central's right in the middle of the campus and people do walk around, on their way to the Commons or the library. Anyway, *nobody* ever saw Darryl come out of the building! The cops put out a call the next day. Maybe a dozen people surfaced who'd been in the area between five and seven, and there were maybe more than usual because some came by the bell tower to see where that student fell. But"—she gripped her teapot—"not a single person saw Darryl Nugent come out of that building." She stared at me earnestly.

"So the last person to see Nugent was his secretary, shortly after five?"

"Yes. They asked her if he was different that day. Well, of course he was *different!* Everybody was terribly upset over the student who'd died, and he was a favorite in the dean's office, a really, really sweet boy. So of course she said Nugent was just *sick* about it, and he was the one who had to call the boy's parents to tell them about it, and that was dreadful. But who wasn't upset? They'd all liked Leonard so much. But these kinds of things happen. The year before, three students were killed in a car crash. Alcohol, of course. And Darryl had to call their parents, too, so it's awful, but he'd dealt with that kind of thing before." Helen took the lid off her teapot, peered inside, frowned. "I probably drink too much of this stuff. Anyway, how Darryl acted the last day can't matter. Of course he wasn't himself that last day. Who was?"

"When was the alarm raised? About his disappearance?"

"Fairly soon, I think. Kathryn started looking for him around dinnertime. She called his office. When there was no answer, she sent their son over there. He didn't find anybody. But it was weird. The lights were on and Darryl's suit jacket was hanging on the coat tree. The boy went home and told his mom and she started calling friends. No one had heard from Darryl. Kathryn called the campus police about eight. The chief came by and it was beginning to look like something was wrong. He called in the town cops. And do you know, from that day to this, nobody's ever seen Darryl Nugent again."

Sometime after five o'clock on a bleak spring evening, the dean disappeared from his office.

Of course the weather was windy and cold, and no one was especially looking for Nugent. Obviously, if he disappeared on purpose, he'd managed to leave the building without being seen.

Did Darryl Nugent want to disappear?

"Good-looking guy," I said quietly.

"To *die* for." Helen was dreamily emphatic.

"Another woman?"

"Nobody else disappeared. I mean, if he ran away with a woman he didn't run away with anybody here in town. And don't think people didn't wonder. I mean, the *stories* that went around! Maybe he'd fallen for somebody he met at a conference. Actually"—she clapped her hands together—"this was the only tidbit they ever came up with. The weekend before, he'd told his wife he was going to a conference in St. Louis. Well-l-l, it turns out the conference he said he was going to wasn't scheduled until June! And they didn't find any registration for him at the hotel he'd said he was going to and they never found out where he was that weekend." Helen stopped for breath. "Everybody really thought this had to mean something." Her shoulders lifted and fell. "But whatever it was, wherever *he* was, it never came out. They thought maybe he met somebody—kind of like *Bridges of Madison County* but with a twist—and just slipped away the next week, leaving everything behind, giving his *all* for love and maybe he started a new life working in a gas station in some tiny Montana town and living in a cabin with some unknown woman. But his picture was all over the national tube and nobody called a hotline and said, 'Hey, I just saw this guy shopping for groceries in Butte.' So, I don't think so. Then, you had to wonder, did he lose his memory? You know, the old classic explanation. Well, if so, nobody spotted this good-looking, dazed guy anywhere. Oh, there were calls, from Seattle to Miami, but nothing ever checked out. And why would he leave? As far as everybody knew, he and Kathryn were happy. He didn't have any family problems, no kids with cancer or drug problems, just really nice, ordinary, everyday kids. He was a softball coach for his daughter's team, worked with his son's Scout troop. I mean, Henrie O, nothing figured for this guy to just disappear. No gambling debts. No drug or alcohol problem, and believe me, the word gets around about those. *Everybody* would have known. Sweetheart, if there's a reason, it's hidden so deep, nobody ever found it and they sniffed around his life like the Brit press after Prince Charles. Nada, nada, nada."

"What do you think happened?"

The animation drained from her face. Her shrewd eyes became thoughtful. "You want my take? I think he's dead. But I don't see how it happened. And more than that, why? They always say check out the family first. Well, Kathryn was at home with both her kids from five to six. Beyond that? Nobody was after Darryl's job. He wasn't crossways with anybody to amount to anything. No, nothing ever led anywhere, Henrie O. So why the hell? So maybe I'm wrong. Maybe he walked out of Old Central and started home and everybody was looking the other way. But if that happened, where did he go? And why?"

ten

Darryl Nugent was last seen two decades ago. People change jobs, leave town, die. It took most of the afternoon to trace some of those who had known either Dean Nugent or Leonard Cartwright, and that was simply finding them. Talking to them was going to take more time.

I worked in my office at the J-School. My files were in my study at home. At this point, I didn't need them. I'd pretty well memorized the general outline of each of the three cases, and I'd scribbled the important points and names in the notebook I carry in my purse. Nobody interrupted me. My phone rang once about four, but the line went dead when I answered.

The Clarion staff puts together most of the Sunday paper throughout the week. A skeleton crew handles late-breaking stories on Saturday, so the newsroom was even more hushed than usual.

About six, I studied my list of names:

Maude Galloway, Nugent's secretary, was now living in a retirement home in Saint Louis.

Buck McKay, chief of campus security when Nugent disappeared, died in 1985.

Emmett Wolf, then a campus patrolman, now owned a garage in Derry Hills.

Kathryn Nugent, the dean's wife, managed the Kensington Nursery. She lived not too far from me.

Cameron Rodgers, a member of Leonard's fraternity and also a senior in 1976, owned a photography studio in Derry Hills.

That last name required dogged effort, starting with the present fraternity president, leading to the alumni board, resulting in a half dozen names from the class of '76, winnowing down to Rodgers, who'd at one time roomed with Leonard.

Darryl Nugent and Leonard Cartwright.

Was I making a mistake to link the two?

At the time, apparently no one had done so.

Cartwright falls to his death. Nugent disappears.

Okay, nobody connected the two events. But maybe nobody had tried.

Except Maggie. Why else would she have Emmett Wolf's name on her calendar?

Maggie had told Eric March that "it made all the difference when you put everything in context."

Was this the context she meant?

It was dark by the time I pulled into my driveway. I always leave on the light in the front hall. My house was built in the thirties, a one-story brick bungalow on the edge of Derry Hills's historic district. My neighborhood isn't historic. It is plain, well-built, and has sidewalks, that reminder of another age. The houses have porches, another lovely relic. I like my neighborhood very much. A retired teacher lives on one side of me, a supermarket manager on the other. Actually, it isn't "my" house. I rent it. Considering my suddenly bleak prospects of continued employment at Thorndyke, that was fortunate. My furniture's been moved so often, I can decorate a living room in an hour—my favorite sofa where it will catch the winter sun, an easy chair by the fire, bookcases and more bookcases, a secretary, and an upright piano.

I'd canceled plans to go out to dinner with a friend from the history department, so I would have to microwave a frozen dinner or order pizza. I considered calling and reinstating dinner. I'd done as much as I could do this night, and it made no sense to brood. I'd debated whom to interview first. I chose the dean's secretary. Tomorrow I'd drive to Saint Louis and talk to Maude Galloway. She had agreed to see me and her voice, though frail, was quite bright and alert. But tonight—I unlocked the front door—I'd done enough. I hung up my coat and started for the kitchen.

Something moved in the dark living room to my left. There was a flash of gray and Malachai, my neighbor's Persian cat, streaked toward the kitchen.

I whirled and was out the front door and across the porch and down the steps and in my car, heart thudding, in only seconds. I locked the doors, turned on the engine, and punched the power on my mobile phone.

The young patrol officer and I stood in my kitchen, looking at the shards of glass sprinkled in the sink from the smashed window.

I waited while the officer searched the house. Malachai, meanwhile, had apparently exited as he'd entered, through the shattered window.

This intruder seemed partial to kitchen windows.

I turned down the patrolman's offer to call the robbery detail. No valuables had been taken.

When the officer left, I walked soberly into my study and looked at the folders on my desk.

I couldn't prove it, but I was sure they'd been moved.

I wondered who had thumbed through the notes I'd made about the unsolved cases.

It was unsettling to know that the hands which pulled the scarf tight around Maggie's neck had touched my desk, my chair, my work. I could pinpoint the time: four o'clock. That was when I answered my office phone and nobody was on the line. The searcher was making sure I was in my office and not at home.

It was easy for my unwelcome guest. This neighborhood is old enough that an alley runs behind the back fences. It would be simple to slip unnoticed up the alley to my gate.

I straightened the folders, checked the desk drawers. Nothing was missing.

But that wasn't the point. Somebody wanted to know what I was doing, what I had learned.

I taped stiff cardboard over the broken pane, then settled for a peanut-butter-and-jelly sandwich in the kitchen. I didn't have much of an appetite.

It was a bleak drive on Sunday to the outskirts of Saint Louis. An icy north wind buffeted winter-bare trees. Scudding clouds moved like ghostly pirate ships across the sullen pewter sky. I like my jaunty MG, but it is far from airtight and the heater is erratic. Even with gloves, my hands on the steering wheel were almost numb with cold.

Nothing lifted my spirits when I reached my destination. Oh, the retirement home was attractive enough, a low stucco structure with four wings radiating from a central entrance. But the cream walls and red-tiled roof damn sure didn't look indigenous, and I doubted if the fake-southwest aura thrilled anybody but visitors who would see what they wanted to see before driving home and leaving whatever resident they knew waiting to die there in a boxlike room.

That's the problem, of course, with any facility defined solely by age.

Welcome to the end of the line.

How about a game of canasta?

Oh yes, there's a beauty shop on the premises.

We have great Christmas parties, and the assistant director is the jolliest Santa Claus.

And it's better than living alone and everybody means well and I still don't want to end up in a dormitory for the ancient.

Call it a prejudice.

But Falcon's Retreat was a nice place. It smelled good, like wood fire and popcorn. Smells tell you all you need to know about retirement homes.

Maude Galloway was waiting for me in an alcove off the library. She sat in a wheelchair, a pink afghan over her knees. Her white cotton blouse was fresh and crisp. Heavily veined hands rested loosely in her lap.

"Miss Galloway?" I'd done my homework. She'd never married. She'd moved to Derry Hills in her mid-fifties to live with her widowed brother. The brother died nine years ago. He'd had no children. Maude Galloway had outlived everyone in her family. She was about ten years older than I. Her head turned toward me.

I looked into sightless blue eyes.

Her face might once have been plump. Her skin had the alabaster fairness of a strawberry blonde. Her hair now was a shining white. A pink sateen headband sat very precisely amid soft silvery curls. I had good thoughts about the staff at Falcon's Retreat.

"Yes. Mrs. Collins?" Her breathy voice had no resonance, no depth. It was as light and insubstantial as discarded paper rattled by the wind.

"Yes. I'm Henrietta Collins. From the University." I could still say that. For now.

Maude Galloway's lips curved into a welcoming smile. Her face was lovely, radiating kindness and warmth and a gentle serenity. "Please, come sit down."

161

I slipped out of my coat, settled in the uncomfortable brocaded chair close to her. "I appreciate your willingness to visit with me."

Her chuckle was lively. "Oh, my dear, to be honest, most of us would welcome a visit from a tax collector. Or a taxidermist. Or a taxi driver. Anyone but a doctor, though it's a very nice young woman, who takes good care of me. To break the routine, you know." She looked quite mischievous. "I do hope you won't think I'm impolite to say so."

I laughed too, and felt suddenly relaxed and a little bit ashamed. Maude Galloway and I weren't so far apart in age. I'd been guilty of approaching her as if she might be dotty or incompetent simply because she was frail.

"No, Miss Galloway. I don't think it's the least bit impolite. I think it's very honest."

"Now." Her sightless eyes looked toward me with uncanny accuracy. "Why have you come, Mrs. Collins? I've not been at Thorndyke for many years."

"You were Dean Nugent's secretary, Miss Galloway." I got out my notebook. She started to work at Thorndyke in November of 1975 and Nugent disappeared in March of 1976. She wouldn't have known the dean well. But she was the last person to admit seeing Darryl Nugent.

"Oh." Her voice was soft and sad. "That was such a heartbreaking thing. And so strange. So very strange."

"You remember the day he disappeared?"

"Of course, of course. It was such a difficult day. Do you know about Leonard?"

I nodded, then remembered she couldn't see me. "Yes, yes, I do."

"Leonard was such a gentle boy. Very quiet, very soft-spoken. I remember he often studied in a little back office when he wasn't working. He did filing, took messages, that sort of thing. I had just started with the University that fall and Leonard knew where everything was. He was very helpful to me. And I liked him because he reminded me a little of my brother Nate when he was young. Very tall and slim and dark. Such a handsome boy."

Maude Galloway's face was reflective, her sightless eyes half-closed in recollection. "It was such a dreadful shock to all of us, Leonard's fall. And you know, many people thought it must have been on purpose because he had to climb over those iron bars, and that wouldn't be easy to do. Now, I'm sure it's true that young people are very volatile, that their ups are so high and their downs so deep, but I *know* Leonard didn't jump." She shook her head firmly, her silver curls quivering. "Because the last time I saw Leonard was just before he left the office on Friday and he was so happy, so excited. And it was on Sunday night or early Monday morning that he died. So what could possibly have happened in such a short time? And he wasn't a moody boy. He was always pleasant and cheerful. But I'll never forget the last time I saw him. He showed me a paper he'd just gotten back—I think it was from an English course—and it was marked A-plus. I remember that the teacher had used red ink and made the A-plus so big, an inch big

163

at least. Leonard was so proud and excited. He said he was going to call his folks and tell them. So it must have been an accident, that silly gargoyle."

I was learning much here that I hadn't expected. I had come to find out about Darryl Nugent and I was discovering Leonard Cartwright. I had a sudden picture of the paper and the grade, the slim, darkly handsome boy, and the pleasure he'd shared and the poignancy of knowing, as young Leonard had not, that the sands were running so fast.

"I see." And I was having to recast my thoughts. I'd been so certain there had to be a link between the death and the disappearance. But this woman had been there, she'd seen Leonard on Friday afternoon, a happy, excited Leonard. "Did the police talk to you about Leonard?"

"Oh, yes." Her white head nodded. "I told them it *had* to be an accident! And, of course, as dreadful as it was about Leonard, everyone was simply distraught on Tuesday about Dean Nugent. There would have been a lot more talk about Leonard except for the dean being gone."

"What do you think happened to Dean Nugent?"

"I have absolutely no idea." Her voice rose in bewilderment. "It still seems impossible! I said good night to him. He was sitting at his desk, slumped in his chair, staring across the room. But not as if he were really seeing. He looked dreadful. Of course, he was extremely upset about Leonard. Why, they'd been such good friends, always laughing and having such a good time together."

"They were good friends?" I looked at her sharply.

But there was only kindness and gentleness in her face. "Oh, yes."

I didn't ask the question I was thinking. I felt certain I knew her answer, and I didn't want to upset her.

An attendant in a blue jumper stepped into the alcove and looked at us inquiringly. "Do you need anything, Maude?"

"Oh, no, Sandy. We're just fine." Maude Galloway's sweet smile was as cheering as a daffodil in early April.

When the attendant moved away, I tried a different tack. "Miss Galloway, what was Dean Nugent like?"

"Precise. Hardworking. And very charming. That's to be expected in the position he held. Of course, I didn't know him well, but I did enjoy working for him. It was such a good-humored office, everyone pleasant, and believe me, I've been in offices where that isn't the case." She pressed her lips together. "The next dean, well, he was a *very* difficult man and no one had a good time in *his* office. I found another position as soon as I could."

"Did Dean Nugent seem to be happily married?" I drew a series of question marks on my pad.

"I think so."

Was there just a hint of uncertainty in her voice? I leaned forward.

"Had he and his wife quarreled?"

"Oh, no, no, nothing like that. And you see, I never married, so I can't be sure. But my brother, Nate and his wife, when they were together I had a sense of delight, almost like a nimbus around them." A faint pink touched her cheeks. "But I know all marriages must be so different. The dean was very proud of his wife and his family and he had their pictures there on his desk, but when he talked to Mrs. Nugent on the phone, well, I never heard that sound—warm and eager and, oh, I don't know how to describe it, but his voice never sounded full of love, like Nate's used to when he talked to Sylvia." She pressed her hands to her cheeks. "Do you know what I mean?" she asked doubtfully.

"I know," I assured her.

"But the dean was very, very proud of his family. He was a very proud man."

"That last day, do you remember anything that you think could have had a bearing on the dean's disappearance?"

Her fragile hands clasped the edge of her afghan. "I've thought and thought over the years, and there's nothing. I said, 'Good night, Dean. You'll be going home soon, won't you?' I was worried about him. He'd had such a hard day, and I knew he was very tired, very upset. He looked toward me and nodded and said, 'Yes, Maude. Soon.' And I went out the door and I never saw him again."

I slipped my notebook back into my purse. There didn't seem to be anything more here.

And what had I expected or hoped for? The police, of course, must have talked to Maude Galloway many times over the course of the weeks after Dean Nugent's disappearance.

I stood.

With the acuity of the blind, her face lifted.

"Miss Galloway, I certainly appreciate your—"

"There's only one thing." She sounded uncertain.

"Yes. That last day?"

"No. It was the next day, Tuesday. But there was so much to be done and people asking questions, oh, so many people. Very nice men from the police, but so many questions. And they took photographs, the town police and our own campus police. Almost falling over each other. I tried to tell them, but they weren't interested. They said they would have pictures of everything." Her hands kneaded the pink wool of the afghan. "And later I tried to tell President Tucker—"

A bulldozer couldn't have budged me from that room. I listened, scarcely breathing.

"—but he said I must be mistaken. By then, of course, so many things had been moved out of the room, the things that belonged to Dean

Nugent, to make way for Dr. Pruitt's furnishings. Dr. Pruitt became acting dean."

"Yes?"

"But I'm just sure that when I went to the office on Tuesday morning, the morning after Dean Nugent disappeared, the rug in front of the fireplace was gone."

"The rug in front of the fireplace?"

Her laugh was embarrassed. "Of course, I know it doesn't matter. What difference could it make?"

"What size was the rug?"

"Oh, it wasn't very big. Perhaps eight feet long and three to four feet wide." Her blind eyes stared emptily at me. "All these years I've wondered who took that rug and why. Because"—her pleasant face looked unaccustomedly firm—"I know it was gone the next morning. Even if President Tucker didn't think so."

I met my Monday-morning classes, Advanced Feature Writing at 9 A.M., Editorial Writing at 10 A.M. Shortly before the close of each class, I announced: "If anyone knows anything about Maggie Winslow that might be helpful in investigating her death, I will be in my office at eleven A.M. today and will be glad to speak with you. Or you may make an appointment for another time." I posted the same announcement on the bulletin board outside *The Clarion* newsroom.

Buddy Neville was leaning against my office window when I arrived after my second class. I'd had Buddy in Reporting 101 two years ago.

He was small, dark, and always looked dirty. In part, that was because he was one of those men whose beard made a bluish stubble on his cheeks by midday. But his jeans were usually wrinkled and he habitually wore the same shirt, a dark-brown pullover jersey. Buddy didn't quite smell bad, but there's nothing attractive about breath sour with last night's beer and pizza and clothes that have absorbed both sweat and cheap talcum.

I try to be tolerant about the Buddy Nevilles of the world. But each time I saw him I felt a mixture of impatience and sadness. Impatience, because Buddy was bright and energetic, so why didn't he have the wit to figure out that cleanliness, if not next to godliness, was an essential in the workplace? Sadness, because I figured Buddy came from a slovenly background and I happened to know he held three part-time jobs to finance college and nobody'd ever encouraged him and he was probably bone-tired every day and the effort of clean clothes was just one effort too many.

"Hi, Buddy." I unlocked my office.

He managed a grunt and followed me inside. Unbidden, he immediately slumped in a chair.

"Coffee?"

He shook his head. I'd probably have scored if I'd offered cola. I still shudder at what some students choose for breakfast. But I reminded myself cola was caffeine, even if cold and fizzy.

He rubbed his stubbly cheek. "Mrs. Collins, listen, all that stuff about Maggie's a lie, that she was screwing Duffy."

I suppose my utter surprise must have been clear in my face. I distinctly remembered Buddy's cruel smile Wednesday night when Rita Duffy careened into the newsroom, clamoring for Maggie and Dennis.

A dull flush mounted his dark cheeks. "Yeah, I know. I thought it was funny when Duffy's wife blew in. Duffy's a jerk. Everybody knows he hustles the babes. But he didn't get to first base with Maggie. And I never figured anything weird would happen—I mean, that Mrs. Duffy would go psycho. I just figured it was super that Duffy's ass was going to be in a crack because he was leaning on Maggie, trying to make time. But it wasn't Maggie's fault. Listen—I knew her real well. We were in a writing group. She told me Duffy was after her and wouldn't take no for an answer."

"She told you?"

Buddy pushed back a strand of lank hair. His eyes flashed. "Yeah, I know. You don't think anybody as cool as Maggie could be friends with somebody like me. But we were in this writing group together. She was going to be a great writer." He glared at me as if I'd disagreed. "She thought I was good, too. Real good."

I've rarely felt more uncomfortable. Yes, I'd not expected the cool, cerebral, fashionable, arrogant Maggie to have a friend like Buddy.

I'd wronged both Maggie and Buddy.

I remembered his work. "Maggie was right. You are a very good writer, Buddy. And I know"—I picked my words carefully—"that there's a real bond between writers. But Maggie may not have told you everything about her and Duffy. She may have been putting a good face on it. She wouldn't have wanted you to know if she was fooling around with him. Would she?"

He leaned forward, planting his hands on his thighs. "Mrs. Collins, listen to me. Really *listen* to me. I tell you, Maggie and I were straight with each other. We showed each other what we wrote. She didn't even show Eric what she wrote. Not her book. So she didn't pretend with me. She didn't have to. And I'll tell you that Duffy was hot for her. She said she was going to tell him to back off, absolutely."

I played devil's advocate. "The thing is, Buddy, Maggie apparently went out with Dennis a couple of times—"

"Okay, so she had a drink with him at the Green Owl once or twice, but that didn't mean anything. Listen, Duffy knew she had a class Wednesday night. I think he left to go after her, one more time. She'd told him no and no. What if Maggie told him this time just to get lost? What if Duffy's the one who went psycho?"

What if Duffy's the one who went psycho?
I mulled Buddy's suggestion all the way across town. What, indeed?
The break-in of Maggie's apartment had convinced me that Rita was innocent and that Maggie's murder was somehow tied to one of

the unsolved crimes she was investigating. But if Dennis Duffy strangled Maggie, he, too, might have reason to be concerned about what was in her notes and papers, what she might have written down about his unwelcome advances.

Why, then, would Dennis encourage me to write the series?

Of course, he might not have expected me to make an unauthorized entry into Maggie's apartment. And he needed to make it clear that he believed his wife to be innocent.

And I shouldn't forget Maggie's boyfriend, Eric March. If Buddy was right, Eric had no reason for jealousy.

But Eric had slammed out of the newsroom that night, obviously in search of Maggie, and it didn't matter whether Rita Duffy's suspicions about her husband and Maggie were true; it only mattered that Eric thought they could be true. Jealousy is an irrational master. But Eric would have had no reason to break into Maggie's apartment—unless she kept a diary that might record they'd quarreled over her relationship with Duffy.

Circles within circles within circles.

I found Kathryn Nugent in a moist warm greenhouse. She held a plastic bottle. Mist sprayed over the ferns from the bottle's nozzle.

I smelled dark rich dirt and water and growing plants.

I studied her through the mist. Darryl

Nugent's once fashionable wife ignored the click of the closing door. Her faded ginger hair hung straight and unadorned around an oval face bare of makeup. And it wasn't simply the mist that obscured her face. This woman seemed carefully devoid of any scrap of color that would reveal her. She was slightly built, almost swallowed by her oversize man's flannel shirt. Her jeans, molding softly against bony legs, were so old they had a whitish hue. One knee was ragged. The laces of one muddy red sneaker trailed on the dirt floor.

It was hard to think mink.

"Mrs. Nugent?"

Slowly she turned to look at me. "Yes?" There was no welcome. Her voice was as unrevealing as her pale face.

I made a quick decision. "I'm going to ask you to help me solve a murder, Mrs. Nugent."

She put down the bottle, brushed back a strand of hair with her canvas-gloved hand. "I don't know anyone who's been murdered." She spoke dully, without a flicker of curiosity.

"The victim is a student of mine. She was looking into three famous unsolved crimes in Derry Hills. I'm Henrietta Collins and I teach journalism at the University." I walked closer and brushed against flowing ferns and felt an icy spritz of water.

Kathryn Nugent stood straight-legged and stiff. "That girl who wanted to know about Darryl?"

"Maggie talked to you?"

"No." She picked up a garden trowel. "I hung up on her."

A vent spewed a sluggish current of warm air. Despite the heat, my skin prickled.

"Why did you hang up?"

"There was nothing to talk about." She stared at me with empty, lonely eyes. I thought of a photograph I'd seen of her in *The Clarion* from long-ago happy days. What an enormous toll her husband's disappearance had taken. There was no trace here of a once vibrant and lovely woman.

A tabby cat jumped up on the table, nosed against her. She put down the trowel, slipped off her gloves. Her fingernails were cracked and stained. She picked up the cat, nuzzled her face against its striped back.

"Mrs. Nugent, Maggie was strangled by someone who didn't want her to write about those old crimes. I know it's hard for you, but please, help me."

The cat squirmed up on her shoulder. She said nothing and reached for the gloves.

I had a quick inspiration. "You have a daughter, don't you?" I asked.

Those blank pale eyes widened. It was the first spark of life I'd seen in her. "Yes. Why?"

"Maggie was someone's daughter."

She gave a little derisive snort. "Piranhas have parents, too. But who gives a damn?" She leaned forward until the cat jumped onto the plant table. As she straightened up, she glared at me. "I know who you are. It said in the paper last week. You're another one of *them*. Pulling

174

and sucking and tearing at people, never giving them any peace, any rest. Do you know what it was like, after Darryl disappeared? Call after call after call. Reporters slipping up to me in the grocery store, at the beauty shop, in the gym, at my daughter's recital, at my son's basketball games—'Had you quarreled, Mrs. Nugent?' 'Was he having an affair, Mrs. Nugent?' 'How was your sex life, Mrs. Nugent?' 'Has he called you, Mrs. Nugent?' 'Do you have insurance, Mrs. Nugent?'" She clutched the big earth-stained gloves against her chest.

"Mrs. Nugent, all I want to know is what kind of man your husband was. Won't you even talk to me about him?"

The animation drained out of her face, leaving it once again bleak and composed. She pulled on her canvas gloves. "I've got work to do."

"Mrs. Nugent—"

"Get out." Her voice was abruptly deep and harsh. "Leave me alone. Leave me *alone*."

eleven

I pulled into the graveled parking area in front of Acme Garage, Transmissions a Specialty. I found Emmett Wolf in the second bay, leaning beneath the open hood of a white Oldsmobile. A small space heater glowed brilliantly red. It did little to warm the cavernous, poorly lighted garage.

"The kid who fell out of the tower? Sure, I remember." Wolf wiped his hands on a rough red cloth. "When they rolled his body onto the gurney, it wobbled. Made me sick. The driver told me it meant the kid was all smashed up inside. And his head'd knocked into the wall and it was mashed and oozing blood. That's when I decided I didn't want to be a cop, and I went to work in a garage. Now I've got my own place." He thumped his fist against the fender of the sedan. "Damn sure better than fooling with people's broken-up bodies."

Wolf was mid-fortyish, with a skinny, wrinkled face, thinning brown hair, and oversize ears that sat square to his skull. His eyebrows drew down toward his nose, giving him a faintly worried look. A ragged orange muffler curled around his throat and disappeared into the neck of his stained green coveralls. He blinked at me owlishly. "You're the second one in a week wanting to talk about that kid. What's going on?"

"Do you read *The Clarion?*"

"Nah. Who cares?" He lifted his shoulders in disdain.

I'm always amazed when I find someone who neither reads newspapers nor watches newscasts. But these people exist.

I had to make a quick decision. If he was telling the truth, he didn't know what had happened to Maggie.

I didn't want to scare him.

"I work for the newspaper. The girl who came to talk to you—"

176

"Pretty." His grin was admiring.

"Yes. I'm working on that article, too. So, if you don't mind going over it again..."

Emmett Wolf glanced at the car.

It was a struggle between promised work and the pleasure of a break in routine.

"Well, I've got a few minutes..."

"So you saw Leonard Cartwright's body at the base of the bell tower?" Pernicious cold eddied up from the old, oil-stained concrete floor. I kept my hands in my coat pockets.

"Leonard Cartwright." Wolf drew out every syllable, as if his tongue were making acquaintance with the name. "Yeah. I'd forgotten his name. Like I told the girl. Forgot his name. Never forget his body." The mechanic sniffed, rubbed his nose with the back of a grubby hand, leaving a smudge of oil on his cheek. "Not at the *base* of the tower. Out some. Maybe ten feet. The guy who took them pictures said the kid must have flipped over as he fell. When his head whacked into the wall, that shoved him way out. He slammed into the ground so hard it left a print. Damnedest thing I'd ever seen."

"What time did you get there?"

He leaned against the fender, crossed his arms over his chest. "I'd just gone on duty. Maybe five minutes after six. I'd been a campus cop for about two months. It was a pretty good job. I had a dandy uniform, shirt and pants kind of a light blue. Even had this patch on my shirt sleeve, 'Thorndyke University Campus Patrol,' it said. I thought I was pretty hot stuff. The

177

chief was Old Man McKay. Was he tough! He'd been a Marine and he never thought civilians did anything right. He stood like they'd rammed"—brown eyes squinted at me—"he stood up straighter than a flagpole and walked with his chest poked out and his butt tucked in. But even the chief didn't look so starched when he saw the kid's body. I was the first one there, except for the guy who found him. Our headquarters was an office in the basement of the stadium. I'd just opened up my sack of doughnuts—you know, my breakfast—when the door burst open and this chemistry prof ran in, wild-eyed and about to puke. He was riding his bike to his office and he ran right over the kid's body. Knocked his bike over. He kept saying, 'There's blood on my bike. There's blood on my *bike!*' First thing I did was call the chief at home, then I went to the tower. The prof wouldn't even go with me. He was too shook up. It was still dark when I got there. Sun hadn't come up yet. I remember the light from the prof's bike showed the kid's hand. The chief got there real quick. Only time I ever saw the man that he wasn't spit-perfect. Always remembered he didn't have his shirt tucked in right. Hell of a day."

"What did you do first?"

"The chief called President Tucker and the town cops." He frowned. "And that was kind of funny." His face creased in thought.

"What was funny about that, Mr. Wolf?" I kept my voice casual, unassertive.

Wolf gave me his worried look. "Well,

Tucker was the president. A real big shot on campus. So I guess he figures he's in charge. And he lived practically right next door, so he got there before the town people. He walked all around and craned his neck and stared up at that tower, then he told the chief they'd better go up and take a look. The chief held back, but Tucker charged ahead, so the chief went after him. They hurried around the building and just left me there. You have to go in the main entrance and up to the third floor to get into the tower. I didn't like being down there by myself, just me and this dead kid. I kind of wandered around for a minute, then I decided to go after them. When I went inside the building, I couldn't see them. I ran up the main stairs. They were already on the tower stairs. I started up after them, and it was real spooky, like some old castle. I'd never been in there before. The stairs were made of stone, and the walls too. There wasn't much light, just these glass lamps screwed into the walls. I could hear the sound of their shoes on the steps. I didn't go all the way to the top. I started thinking maybe the chief'd be mad at me, and man, I didn't want that. That would be worse than being stuck down there alone with the body. So I turned around to go back down, but I could hear them. The chief says something like, 'Look at that.' Tucker says, 'I don't see a thing, Chief.' Then Tucker says in this real loud voice, 'Nothing of interest here.' There's a funny silence and all of sudden I hear steps coming down, so I hightail it out of there. I just made it outside before the chief got down. His face was red and his eyes had a glitter like a dog gone bad, but he didn't say a word to Tucker and then the town cops showed up and that's all there was to that."

"What do you think happened up there?"

Wolf pushed away from the car, stepped closer to the little heater. "Hell, I don't know. Maybe there was some pot and Tucker didn't want that to get in the papers. I don't know. I know the chief didn't like it. But he was the kind of guy who'd do what he was told, follow orders. And I guess it didn't matter. They seemed pretty sure the kid jumped. They put out a story he was fooling with that statue, but that was just to make it sound better."

"Why were they so certain he jumped?" I edged nearer the heater, too.

"His car. It was parked in the street close to the tower and it was crammed with his stuff, all jammed in there, books and clothes and everything. They figured he was upset and running away and then decided just to take a leap instead of drive off."

No one had mentioned Leonard's car. Why hadn't that been included in the police file? Was it because the University had taken advantage of the history of student pranks centering around the gargoyle and convinced the DHPD that Leonard's death was just an unfortunate accident?

The car stuffed with belongings certainly presented a different picture than Leonard's cheerful departure from the dean's office on Friday, his A-plus paper in hand.

What had happened between his good-bye to Maude Galloway and the moment that he tumbled from the bell-tower window?

"Did you ever tell anybody about Tucker and the chief going up in the tower?"

"Just the girl from University," Wolf said. "Last week was the first time anybody's asked me about it in a long time. Until you."

"You told her all about Cartwright's fall?"

"Sure. And she wanted to know about the dean who took a powder, too. He disappeared that night. See, the kid's fall was big stuff that day, but nobody ever talked about it much after that because the dean disappeared later the same day. The whole campus went crazy trying to figure out what happened to that guy." Remembered bewilderment permeated his voice. "The chief had search parties all over the place. Student volunteers put up posters and flyers with his picture in shopping centers and along the highways in and out of town. But nobody ever found a trace of him. Not to this day."

"What do you think happened to the dean?"

Wolf's lips curled in a knowing smile. "I always say when a guy takes a powder, look for the dame."

I doubted Wolf knew the phrase "Cherchez la femme," but it doesn't take knowledge of French to understand human nature.

No dame had surfaced in connection with the handsome dean, which ought to reflect a happy marriage. But Maude Galloway had recalled a man who was terribly proud of his family, yet not a man who seemed touched by love.

And Kathryn Nugent didn't want to talk about her missing husband.

Was it because Mrs. Nugent hated reporters? Or were there facts about Darryl Nugent that she didn't want to remember?

"What did Chief McKay think?"

Wolf folded his arms over his chest.

"He was ticked, I can tell you."

"About the dean?"

"Oh, no, ma'am. About the town cops taking over the case. So the chief just went right ahead and did his own investigation. Funny—he didn't figure it was a dame. He swore that guy was dead. I remember the look on the chief's face, kind of cold and calm. He says to me, 'Emmett, only a dead man's that quiet.'"

I had an hour before my appointment to have my portrait taken at Rodgers Studios, so I went back to my office.

I found a note pushed under my door. The handwriting was large and childlike:

Dear Mrs. Collins,

I MUST *talk to you soon and tell you the* TRUTH *about Maggie Winslow. It's terrible how people will lie.*

Sincerely,
Kitty Brewster

I wondered, recalling Eric March's harsh appraisal of *The Clarion*'s police reporter, just what Kitty would have to say.

I rang her extension in the newsroom.

"Kitty Brewster." Her voice was pitched low. I wondered if she watched old Lauren Bacall movies.

I asked her to come see me.

My first thought when she hurried into my office was: Dennis, you should be ashamed.

Kitty Brewster was apple-shaped, her clothes were cheap, and her huge brown eyes had the lost and vulnerable look of a child nobody had loved. Too much hair frizzed around a forlorn face liberally coated with unflattering orange-red makeup. The girl stumbled in her eagerness, bumping my desk, then floundered into the chair, her face flaming with embarrassment.

I suspect this child's face was often flushed.

Her eyes skidded away from mine, locked onto the carnation airplane.

Her mouth curved into an admiring bow. "Oh, Mrs. Collins, that's so clever! Where did you get it?" She leaned forward and smoothed a wing tip, her blunt fingers surprisingly gentle.

I'd crumbled an aspirin tablet and added water earlier. I'd not really looked closely, but now I did and I was surprised at the lift the elegant flower piece gave me, the sense of well-being and good humor.

"A friend," I said quietly. It was like pulling up an afghan on a snowy day.

Kitty's eyes eagerly absorbed every detail: bronze propellers, blue fuselage, white windows, pink wings and tail. Her nose wrinkled, seeking the dry, special scent of the carnations. "Oh, I love it." Her lips curved again and her soft smile gave her face a winsome charm. "And someone must love you."

Those lost, lonely eyes looked at me in surprise.

There was no bridge to span the gulf of years and experience that lay between us.

I simply smiled and picked up her note. "Kitty, what can you tell me about Maggie?"

The transformation of her face was startling, from softness and eagerness to sullen hatred. Her voice, too, grew venomous. "It's time somebody told you the *truth*. Everybody goes on and on about how wonderful Maggie was. Well, she wasn't wonderful. She was a slut— a jealous slut. And she was driving Eric crazy." She scooted the chair so close she pressed against my desk. "Mrs. Collins, I'm going to have to tell you something private so that you'll understand."

"Yes, Kitty." I knew what was coming. When this was over, I intended to have a talk with Dennis Duffy. But of course it was too late. Forever too late for this child.

Once again her face softened. "I know people might not understand." Her eyes beseeched me. "Sometimes when you fall in love, you have to be brave. Things can be awfully complicated. Mr. Duffy—Dennis—I don't know if you know, but his wife is *awful* to him." She paused, frowned. "But I guess everybody knows that, now that they've arrested her for what she did to Maggie. But anyway, Maggie was just *throwing* herself at Dennis and she was so jealous of me that she tried to act like he was coming after *her*. And she tried to break us up. She told me"—anger throbbed in her voice—"that he was a womanizer, that he'd screw anything in skirts." She stopped, swallowed convulsively, "Maggie said, 'The fatter, the better.'"

The vicious words hung in the air.

I'd suspected Maggie could be cruel. Maggie was so sure of herself, so dismissive of those who couldn't match her talents or brains or looks. And Maggie would be quick to confront anyone, anyone at all. I doubted she'd realized how much pain she had caused this desperately lonely girl.

Or cared.

I had to wonder where Kitty Brewster had been the night Maggie died.

Kitty pressed trembling hands to her once-again flaming cheeks, then clasped them convulsively in her lap. "I thought you ought to know what she was like."

"I appreciate your coming to see me, Kitty. Yes, I'm trying to find out everything I can about Maggie."

And who was the real Maggie: my brilliant and ambitious student, Eric's passionate lover, Buddy's comrade in words, Kitty's cruel slut? Which Maggie was murdered?

I folded Kitty's note. "And I'm trying to find

out more about Wednesday night. I didn't see you in the newsroom."

Now the anger was gone, leaving her vulnerable face limp and bereft. "Wednesday night? Oh"—she moved uncomfortably—"I just kind of hung around."

Maybe it was intuitive. Maybe it was the forlorn timbre of her voice. "Were you waiting for Dennis?"

Kitty's lips quivered. She tried to speak, couldn't. She came to her feet, a hand pressed against her mouth, and blundered toward the door.

In the newsroom, Dennis Duffy hunched at his computer. He didn't even notice as Kitty bobbed her way clumsily past his desk.

I blinked against the sharp white flash of the strobe.

"Turn a little to your left, Mrs. Collins. And if you would lift your chin just a fraction...that's good, ver-y-y good. Now, just a few more shots..."

I'd had no luck engaging Leonard Cartwright's one-time roommate, Cameron Rodgers, in a coherent conversation. The photographer's smooth patter was impervious to interruption, a nonstop monologue designed to entertain and relax his subjects. "...now you don't want people to confuse this picture with a shot of West Point cadets marching! Come now, let's have a little smile, then a big smile, then, hey, what's the problem, have the teeth police been by here? Oh, now, that's good, that's better, that's..."

Rodgers was fortyish, balding, with a cherubic smile and aloof gray eyes. He bounced around the studio with surprising agility for his bulk. He was under six feet and must have weighed two hundred pounds.

We had the large studio to ourselves. Banks of lights, assorted backdrops, and several cameras on tripods crowded the big room.

"That's it. We got some good ones." He gave me a final bright smile. "Mrs. Collins, you can pick up your proofs next Wednesday. I'm sure you'll find some perfect shots for your family." He turned to lead the way out of the studio.

I didn't move. "Mr. Rodgers, if you have a moment, I'd like to talk to you about your years at the University. And about your fraternity."

Slowly he turned to face me. "My years..." His face was abruptly wooden. "Collins." He looked at me sharply. "Collins," he said again. His face flattened, the professional charm vanishing. "You're the reporter, the one they had the story about on Friday. On page one."

Duffy would be pleased to know how carefully *The Clarion* was read.

"Yes, and I'm here because I want to know what happened to Leonard Cartwright the night before he died."

The color seeped out of his face. "I don't want to talk to you." He said it firmly, his voice grim. "That's what I told that girl, and that's what I'm telling you. Look, I've taken the shots. We're finished. If you want to come and get your proofs, fine. If not—"

"Mr. Rodgers, do you have any children?"

He scowled. "Why? What the hell does that have to do with anything?" His voice rose angrily.

"Life. Death. Justice. Maybe you don't care, Mr. Rodgers, but Maggie Winslow was young, just getting started. Maggie had a brilliant career ahead of her and someone killed her because she wanted to write about those people, those unsolved cases. Maybe you don't have any children, maybe it doesn't mean anything to you that Maggie died, but I'm asking you to help me find her killer."

Rodgers turned away from me. He walked heavily to a chair beyond a bank of lights and flung himself into it.

I stood motionless, waiting and watching.

Finally he looked up.

It took me a moment to realize that the shine in his eyes was the glitter of tears.

"Funny you asked if I had a kid." Roughly he swabbed the back of his hands against his eyes.

I stepped a little nearer.

"My boy. Cameron Junior." Rodgers looked up at me defiantly, as if I had challenged him. "He's a good kid. He's a hell of a kid."

I didn't reply.

There was no sound in that big, quiet, shadowy room.

Rodgers slumped in the seat, misery in

every line of his stocky body. "And he's gay." His face twisted. "And I know what's going to happen to him, I know how he'll be treated. Sometimes I think it's God's way of getting even, making me pay for—Leonard."

"What happened to Leonard, Mr. Rodgers?"

"Oh, Christ, if we'd only thought...If we'd only *thought!*" He pushed up from the chair, walked toward me.

He stopped a few inches away, folded his arms tightly over his chest. "You don't know brutal"—each word was as slow and heavy as a dirt clod striking a coffin lid—"until you've lived in a fraternity house. Any guy who doesn't cut it, everybody makes his life miserable, makes it hell." His voice was as harsh as the clatter of metal in a salvage yard. "And all the guys, they have to fit in. Everybody's macho, you know, making girls, scoring, getting drunk, raising hell. Leonard was already considered kind of a drip. He didn't drink very much, and he never dated. But nobody thought he was gay."

"How did you find out?"

"A bunch of us, we decided to spend the weekend in Saint Louis. Just for the hell of it. Do some bars. Pick up some girls. We ended up at a motel on the outskirts of town."

And now I knew why there was a weekend unaccounted for in the life of Darryl Nugent. "You saw Dean Nugent and Leonard."

"How'd you know?" He didn't wait for me to answer. He didn't care. It didn't really matter. "Yeah, yeah, we saw them. And we thought about breaking in on them. We were so fucking mad about it. How could Leonard do this to us, make us all look bad? But we were kind of scared of the dean. So we planned it. On Sunday night, when Leonard got back, a bunch of us would go to his room, we'd find out what the hell was going on. So we did. Five of us."

He stared past me, his mouth trembling. "Like a pack of dogs. Like a mob. And once—oh God, I'll never forget it—when the guys were yelling at him, Lenny looked at me, we'd been roommates once, but I didn't want the guys to think I could be like that, so I just yelled at him too, like he was some kind of scum. I'll never forget the look in his eyes. The *hurt*. We took all his stuff and threw it out on the lawn and then we threw him out. The last time I saw him, it was about midnight and he was trying to cram everything in his car and we were yelling and swearing at him. And..." His voice shook. "Lenny...was crying." Rodgers buried his face in his hands.

I reached out and touched his shoulder. "I'm sorry," I whispered.

But it was no help.

Nothing would ever help.

Dusk was falling when I got back to the campus. And so was the temperature. It was going to get down below freezing tonight.

I crossed the street from the J-School to Old Central.

The wooden blinds were closed in the president's office, but light filtered through the cracks. No light shone from the southwest corner of the second floor, the office of the dean of students. More had changed in twenty years than just the occupant. Now some schools and departments were headed by women. Not many. Middle-aged white men still rule academia. But the present dean of students, Charlotte Abney, was both a woman and black.

I looked at President Tucker's office again. It was one floor below Charlotte's office and what had been Darryl Nugent's office. Then I circled around the building.

The bell tower rose into the darkening sky on the back side of Old Central. Lights glowed on all four sides.

An eagle spread stone wings in the niche beneath the north window. No gargoyle.

I didn't remember reading whether the gargoyle had been smashed in its fall. I don't suppose it was surprising the gargoyle had never been replaced.

I completed my circle, then walked up the broad shallow stairs, pushed in one of the heavy oak doors. The building featured a central open marble lobby. Wide corridors led east and west. Ornate, heavily carved stairs led to the second and third floors. A skylight with green glass roofed over the third floor. On a sunny day, the lobby glowed as richly, as serenely green as shallow water in the Bahamas. At dusk, it was as murky as the dark depths of a pond.

I had never been up in the bell tower. My

steps echoed loudly in the hushed cathedral-like silence. I wondered if anyone else was in the building. Most office workers are well ready to leave their posts at five.

It was this time of day when Dean Nugent was last seen in his office. Nugent must have been in an agony of distress—and apprehension. I doubted very much that Leonard had called, told him of the awful events at the fraternity house.

Nugent and his youthful lover had parted in Saint Louis on Sunday. Leonard's body was found Monday morning.

The dean must have been stunned, bewildered. And frightened. What had happened to Leonard? And why?

I reached the third floor and the door to the bell-tower stairs.

I gripped the handle. The door opened.

I was a little surprised at this easy access. Had there been discussion, wrangling by the Board of Governors? Views always diverge. Ask anyone who's ever tried to run any endeavor.

I could imagine the positions, sharply and angrily espoused:

The bell tower must be closed to prevent future accidents.

Closing the tower would be an admission of University culpability in Cartwright's death.

The bell tower was a campus landmark that alumni and students should be able to visit at will.

A single tragic accident shouldn't prevent the Thorndyke family from enjoying a treasured retreat.

I started up gritty sandstone steps. Wall sconces provided a soft golden glow as I climbed.

I found the answer to my question when I reached the square tower level.

Iron bars stretched from the top to the bottom of the openings. No one ever again could fall—or jump—from these windows.

I walked to the north window. The cold, damp air smelled fresh after the close, musty stairwell.

I pressed close to the bars. A seventy-foot drop. When the window was barred only halfway, it would have been an extremely dangerous maneuver to climb over the bars and drape the green plastic lei over the gargoyle. The effort would require a student with no fear of heights and a gymnastic athleticism.

I stepped back from the window. I knew now, of course, that Leonard Cartwright certainly had not been involved in a prank that went terribly wrong.

No, Leonard had driven away from his fraternity house in tears and despair, his car jammed with his possessions, with no place to go, no one to take him in.

I didn't know what his family situation had been.

Obviously, the idea of driving home, telling whoever waited there what had happened—and why—had been unendurable.

I would never know where his odyssey led that night. I only knew that hours passed and toward dawn he finally came this way. Or had he come straight to the bell tower, spent his final hours pacing this high, bleak square, or huddled miserably against a cold wall?

But, sooner or later, he'd come to this building where he'd worked, where he'd been happy, and walked up these stairs, passing the dean's office, continuing his climb to the bell tower. He must have been exhausted, defeated, hopeless.

There is no agony in life that is not at its worst in the hours before dawn. At a few minutes before six in the morning, he'd jumped. His body had not lain there long because blood still oozed from his crushed skull when Emmett Wolf arrived.

Leonard jumped, but he had left something behind in this gray, square tower. Something that David Tucker found—and took.

I looked around the flagstoned floor.

A note? A last good-bye to his parents? Or to Dean Nugent?

What else would Tucker have snatched up, taken to keep?

It had been 1976, so I understood why Emmett Wolf thought of drugs. But Wolf didn't know what had happened to Leonard that night.

Yes, Leonard could have left a note—

That's when I heard footsteps coming up the stone stairs.

The shadow came first, wavering, huge and distorted, in the golden glow of the wall sconce.

David Tucker was a big man.

He looked enormous as we faced one another.

Tucker's rounded head with its sparse tufts of gray hair seemed perched on massive shoulders, his throat hidden by a white silk muffler. He wore a navy cashmere coat. He stood with his gloved hands loose at his sides.

He stood between me and the stairs.

But the windows were barred. There could be no more "accidents" from the tower.

He took a step toward me.

I had trouble pulling my eyes away from his gloved hands. He was too big and too strong for me to elude. Should he move quickly, should those powerful hands seize my throat, I wouldn't have time to get to my keys and the canister of Mace in my shoulder bag.

My hand dropped to my purse and its catch.

"What brings you up here, Mrs. Collins?" His tone was casual. His eyes were not.

"I might ask the same of you, Dr. Tucker." Yes, my voice was thin and tight. Without looking down, I unlatched the flap of my bag, eased it up and slipped my hand inside.

"I saw you go up the stairs, Mrs. Collins. It seemed an odd time to visit the bell tower, when it's dark and there is no one about."

There was nothing threatening in the words or tone, but the measured emphasis started my heart pounding.

Yes, it was dark and quiet and no one would hear me if I cried out.

Tucker's mouth stretched in a sudden smirk of satisfaction.

He knew I was afraid.

My fear amused him.

That made me mad, and suddenly I wasn't scared.

"What did you take from the tower the morning Leonard Cartwright died, Dr. Tucker?"

His eyes flared in shock.

I added swiftly, "He left a letter, didn't he?"

"Leonard Cartwright died in a very sad accident."

"It was no accident."

"You can't prove that." It was as close to an admission as he would ever make.

"Don't count on it."

"In any event"—now his eyes watched me intently—"what purpose would be served by making this kind of charge now? It would do nothing but bring unhappiness to Leonard's family."

"And to the family of Dean Nugent."

He expelled a heavy breath of air.

"You see, Dr. Tucker, someone always knows something. That's what Maggie Winslow told me. And she was right."

He rocked back on his heels, jammed his hands in his coat pockets. "I suppose you're pleased with what you're doing, Mrs. Collins. Obviously"—he paused, then picked his words carefully—"if there is any truth to the gossip you seem to have dredged up, it would appear there was a reason for Dean Nugent to disappear. I have no personal knowledge of this, of course."

"Oh, of course not, Dr. Tucker."

I yanked my hand out of my purse. I held the Mace canister with my thumb on the button. I raised it until it was quite visible to him.

He stared at the canister, inclined his massive head in a tiny nod. His eyes met mine. Byzantine eyes. For an instant, a chill smile touched his lips. "It's been a pleasure talking with you, Mrs. Collins."

He turned away.

I raised my voice. "What did Leonard's suicide note say, Dr. Tucker?"

He didn't pause or look back.

"Did he tell about his relationship with Darryl Nugent?"

My only answer was the heavy thud of his footsteps, descending the stone stairs.

I waited until the sound was gone.

When I walked down the steps, I still held the Mace canister.

Damn Tucker. What did he know? That he knew much more I didn't doubt.

As I crossed the darkened campus, listening uneasily for footsteps, I was aware that I didn't know where to look next. I might be sure of what happened to Leonard Cartwright, but I still had no idea where Darryl Nugent went that March evening so many years ago.

twelve

I have no Tuesday classes, but I got to my office shortly before eight. I had plenty on my mind. And I was coldly angry. David Tucker hadn't quite made me look a fool, but he had intimidated me. When he'd turned away from me last night in the bell tower, it was as arrogant a dismissal as I'd ever received.

I wasn't through with David Tucker.

I put my three folders, folders that were now getting dog-eared, on my desk; the Darryl Nugent file on top, the Murdoch file second, the Rosen-Voss file third.

At precisely 8 A.M., I picked up my phone and punched numbers I was getting to know.

"Office of the President."

Baker, that was his secretary's name, Bernice Baker. "Bernice, this is Henrietta Collins in the Journalism School. As you will recall, I visited with Dr. Tucker last week. I just wanted to double-check. What time was it on Wednesday that he saw my student, Maggie Winslow?"

"Oh, just a moment, Mrs. Collins. Let me look at his appointments..." A pause, then her smooth, muted, efficient voice continued, "At four o'clock, Mrs. Collins. Is that what you needed?"

"Yes, Bernice, thanks."

I nodded in satisfaction as I hung up. It wasn't enough to order handcuffs, it wasn't enough to interest Lieutenant Urschel, but it definitely proved Maggie had talked to Tucker.

I flipped to a clean sheet in my legal pad and wrote:

Cartwright—suicide.
Note?
Rug missing from Nugent's office?
How could Nugent have left the building without being seen? If he got out, where did he go?
What does Tucker know???

I took the legal pad with me and hurried to *The Clarion* morgue. I lugged the heavy volume of bound newspapers for March 1976 to a table at the back of the room.

Leonard Cartwright's accident was the lead head on Tuesday morning, March 16:

SPRINGFIELD SENIOR
DIES IN TOWER FALL

But I'd already read these stories. My objective now was photos.

A grainy two-column photo at the bottom of page 1 showed a stone gargoyle on the grass. The caption read:

Student Prank Turns Deadly—Old Central's famous gargoyle lies on the lawn, a mute reminder of Leonard Cartwright's fatal effort early Monday to dislodge the statue, long the center of rivalry between engineering and architecture students.

In the photograph, the gargoyle appeared to be undamaged. I had assumed, when I saw the stone eagle in that niche, that the gargoyle had been smashed in its fall. Apparently not. Perhaps the University (And who would that be? Tucker? The Board of Governors?) had thought it inappropriate to return the gargoyle to its place even though no future accidents could occur with the window completely barred.

I wondered idly what had happened to the gargoyle.

There was no mention of the disappearance of Dean Nugent in the Tuesday-morning paper. The desk obviously had decided the story wasn't yet certain enough by the Monday-evening deadline.

Beginning Wednesday, however, the focus shifted to the missing dean. Within the next week, I found photos of Old Central with an arrow pointing to Dean Nugent's office, a front view of the main steps into Old Central, Nugent in his cap and gown in the previous year's commencement procession, Nugent and his family at an Arts and Sciences picnic, and even a picture of the door to his office.

But that was as close as I got to what I wanted.

I was ready to shelve the volume when I decided to scan it quickly one more time.

That's when I found a small story on page 19 three days after Leonard's death and the dean's disappearance:

GARGOYLE TAKEN; RETURN REQUESTED

University maintenance chief H. L. Thomas has issued a plea for the return of the Old Central gargoyle, which apparently was taken from the basement of Old Central.

Thomas explained that the gargoyle was placed in the basement of Old Central after it fell from the side of the tower in the Monday-morning accident which claimed the life of Thorndyke senior Leonard Cartwright.

It was discovered Wednesday that the statue had been removed from the basement. The granite statue weighs approximately forty-five pounds.

The University's Media Information Bureau declined to comment.

It took half an hour to skim six months' issues of *The Clarion*. The missing gargoyle was never mentioned again.

I added the missing gargoyle to my collection of little mysteries involving the missing dean. But no matter what had happened in that deadly sequence of days twenty years ago, I could count on it that the dean hadn't taken the forty-five-pound gargoyle with him when he vanished from Old Central. He hadn't even bothered to take his own suit coat.

College students have a taste for the macabre. The gargoyle could have ended up in a fraternity rec room.

I shook my head. No. Word would definitely have gotten out.

I shrugged. I doubted that now, two decades later, I'd solve the Mystery of the Missing Gargoyle.

And it didn't matter as much as another puzzle: the Mystery of Maude's Missing Rug.

Was Nugent's secretary right and was an Oriental rug absent from its place in front of the fireplace on Tuesday morning?

Or was President Tucker correct and the rug was among the dean's personal possessions that were removed later in the week by his family?

I'd hoped for a photograph of the interior of the dean's office. It would have been a natural with a caption: "Dean Last Seen Here." Obviously, *The Clarion* either had bowed to the dictates of taste, always doubtful, or to pressure from the University.

But there was another possibility.

All evidence, reports, or testimony which have been part of a court proceeding are, as a matter of law, part of the public record and, as such, are available for any reporter to see.

But of course in cases which have not been solved, the information gathered by the police is not open to the public.

However, these fine points are not always

known to everyone working in a law-enforcement agency. I knew better than to try and be clever with the Derry Hills PD. I recalled Lieutenant Urschel's steady, intelligent gaze with respect. The campus patrol was, in my mind, another matter entirely. Once again *The Clarion* morgue was very useful. I found a feature written the previous year, when a new director, Roland Steele, took over. Steele was in his forties, another retired military cop.

I looked up Steele's number in the University directory. And if it took a little dissembling to gain my objective, I was quite willing to do it.

"Chief Steele, this is Henrietta Collins in the Journalism School. I'm working on some exercises for my students in covering crime news. I'd like to do some surveys in your old files, oh, say, in the seventies, so it wouldn't be anything current, to gather some materials. Would it be convenient for your office if I dropped by in a few minutes?"

Chief Steele was pleased to be of service. In fact, he was quite genial and obliging. "Come by anytime, Mrs. Collins."

The campus force was still housed in the basement of the stadium. My shoes echoed against the concrete runway.

Chief Steele had already given instructions to the cheerful student who was a part-time aide. She led me to a small, dingy backroom.

"Our old files are in these cabinets." She waved toward a bank of very old-fashioned wooden cabinets.

"Thanks so much. I'll be quick."

"Do you need—"

"No. I'm fine. I needn't take up your time."

And I had the room to myself.

It didn't take long. The files were kept by year. Within that section, the Nugent case filled two accordion-sized folders. Each folder had a table of contents. Chief McKay, by God, had been master of his own domain.

The first folder contained what I was looking for: photographs from every angle that provided a complete record of everything visible in the office of Darryl Nugent. The photos were dated the day after his disappearance.

Thank you, Chief McKay.

There was a large—at least nine-by-twelve-foot—Oriental rug directly in front of his desk.

That was the only rug visible in the entire room.

No rug lay in front of the fireplace.

But I wanted to be sure.

There were twenty-four photos. I looked at each one slowly, carefully, thoroughly. There was one rug in the dean's office, and only one, the morning after his disappearance. The pictured rug was much too large to be the one Maude Galloway had described.

But the photos revealed more than that.

Family photographs took pride of place on Nugent's desk. I counted eight. The desktop was bare of papers. A lovely old conference table sat in one corner of the room. Roses filled an elegant cut-glass vase. The blooms drooped.

On the west side of the room, a circular iron staircase rose to a narrow balcony. Filing cabinets filled the balcony. The dean's suit jacket hung from a coat tree tucked between the spiral staircase and a glass-fronted bookcase. Huge casement windows, eight to ten feet tall, were in the west and south walls. Heavy draperies were looped to each side of the windows.

Except for one window.

In the west window nearest the circular staircase, the draperies hung straight. I glanced from that window to the next one. Yes, those draperies were looped, held in place with long braided ties.

I found the photo of the south wall and saw four casement windows with draperies looped to each side. I estimated each tie to be at least four feet in length, more likely six. Two ties knotted together would afford a piece of cord eight to twelve feet in length.

Then I studied the photo of the balcony. It was an old-fashioned balcony enclosed by a balustrade.

One of the photos showed that corner of the room. The floor was parquet.

It was a floor I wanted to see.

Charlotte Abney rose to greet me. "Henrie O, what a pleasure to see you!"

Charlotte and I often played tennis together, but I'd never dropped by her office unannounced.

"What can I do for you?" There was the faintest hint of reserve in her tone.

"Actually, Charlotte, will you permit me to roam around your office for a few minutes?"

Charlotte is slim and attractive, with a vibrant face that mirrors her enthusiasms. This morning, however, she looked aloof and thoughtful. There was an instant's hesitation before she replied, "Certainly."

I walked to the windows. The draperies were a stiff red brocade, the ties gold cords with two-inch tassels at the ends. I unlooped a tie. A chair scraped. Charlotte joined me at the window. "I've heard some gossip." Her voice was crisp.

I held the cord up. Yes, it was fully six feet long. "I'll bet you have." I pressed the braided cord between my fingers. It felt strong.

"Henrie O, they say you're in trouble." Her tone was distant.

I relooped the tie, pulling the stiff drapery back in its customary place. "My husband always insisted that trouble was my middle name."

Charlotte leaned against the mantel, her arms crossed. She looked especially striking, her crimson blazer crisp, her black skirt short and fashionable. She also looked wary.

I patted her shoulder as I turned toward the corner of the room and the winding stairs. "Don't be worried on my account, Charlotte. I'll survive, one way or another. Here, or somewhere else."

I looked up at the balcony. It ran the length of the room, which I estimated to be about thirty feet. The staircase was in the northwest corner. The police photographs showed Nugent's desk to be midway between the staircase and the east wall.

I walked to a spot halfway between the staircase and where Nugent's desk had sat. The floor was bare of carpet now, as it had been then.

Charlotte followed me.

I knelt and began to study the parquet flooring.

Charlotte stood with her hands on her hips. "Henrie O, what in the world are you doing?"

But her words seemed to come from a long distance. I traced the long scar that had at one time—but I knew when—been gouged into the wood.

I looked up. The balcony was directly above me. I stood, glanced around, pulled a Windsor chair to that spot.

I could see two ways the chair could have scored the wood.

In a struggle, a chair could have been violently shoved. That was one way.

Or—I stepped up onto the seat. I looked at the balustrade above. Then I looked thoughtfully at the draperies.

Charlotte drew her breath in sharply. She stared at me with shocked eyes. "Jesus Christ, Henrie O!"

I didn't yet know exactly what had happened between five and six o'clock on the evening of March 15, 1976, but I knew enough to have a very interesting talk with President

207

Tucker. However, I didn't go to his office.

Instead, I nosed around the rear of Old Central's ornate main lobby. An inconspicuous door opened onto steep narrow stairs.

The basement was painted gray and was a repository of folded tables, stacked chairs, and discarded furniture. There were several even more subterranean rooms, but I was interested in the dark and shadowy north side, where a huge unused coal furnace sat. The modern heating system, all gleaming metal and softly humming machinery, was along the east wall.

At the very far end of the basement, past the unused furnace, I found a wide wooden overhead door. I stood on tiptoe, peered out of dirt-crusted windows and saw the sloping concrete drive of the service entrance.

It would have been easy for someone who knew the building well to move the gargoyle, temporarily placed here, out of the basement and into a waiting car—the gargoyle and anything else that required disposal.

Why the gargoyle?

So far I could imagine, but no farther.

I walked out of Old Central, circled around the building.

Yes, a car had been essential.

But what then?

I stood on the lawn that sloped from Old Central to the street. The J-School was directly across from me. The street then curved to the right to pass Frost Library.

Beyond the library, Frost Lane plunged into the wooded preserve, becoming, in popular idiom, Lovers' Lane, and leading to the amphitheater and the lake.

The lake. Oh God, of *course*.

Suddenly I understood why the gargoyle was taken, the absolute necessity of the gargoyle.

I crossed the street, hurried up to my office and picked up my tape recorder. It is an excellent little machine. I tucked it in my purse. If I put my purse down and opened the flap, I'd get a good recording.

I definitely wanted a record of what Tucker said.

I reached for the telephone.

Bernice Baker was, as always, polite. "Just a moment, Mrs. Collins. I'll see if the president is free." I would have loved to see her expression if she listened when I spoke to her boss. Even the perfect secretary might be startled.

While I waited on the line, I got up and retrieved my water pitcher. I poured water into my flower arrangement. Some of the carnations on the top were browning. I needed to call Jimmy. He would be leaving for Mexico on Friday. The fact that I was teaching this semester hadn't stopped him from asking me to come, and come now.

Yes, someone else could take my classes. Obviously, next fall someone else would be teaching in my place. I didn't doubt that. But I'd committed for this academic year.

Yet, there was something incredibly appealing at the prospect of doing what one wanted to do without regard for consequences. I put down the pitcher, touched a blue propeller.

A click. Tucker's voice was brusque. "Yes?"

I wasn't surprised he'd taken my call. I supposed he'd half expected it to come.

"Dr. Tucker, please meet me in half an hour at the end of the pier on Boone Lake. It is, as you are well aware, an exceedingly private place. We can talk freely. We have a great deal to discuss, including the rug that was missing from Dean Nugent's office the day after he disappeared, what use was made of two drapery ties, and what happened to the gargoyle that was stolen from the basement of Old Central. I think you'll agree that I'm making progress on a definitive story about Dean Nugent and Leonard Cartwright. Whether I write that story will depend upon your response."

I hung up without waiting for a reply.

I had the same feeling you get the last instant before you plunge off the high dive. Only worse, because pools don't have uncharted, potentially deadly currents.

But I damn sure wasn't going to jump without a life preserver.

I looked through my window into the newsroom. My choices for backup were slim to none. Only one person owed me big time.

Dennis Duffy sagged in his chair, looking as lumpy as a potato sack. Even across the room, I could see the greenish tinge of his once-handsome face. Nursing a hangover, I was willing to bet. I was also willing to bet that Dennis was soon—in the next few seconds, in fact—going to feel a lot lousier.

I opened my door and started toward the city desk.

I might have laughed—if I hadn't been quite so tense.

I turned up the collar of my coat. The wind off the lake came from the north, carrying the bite of winter as well as the bone-chilling damp of the water. Moisture beaded the wooden pilings, making the planks underfoot slick and treacherous. The water and sky flowed together, the color of dull pewter. Whitecaps bristled as harsh and glittery as chunks of broken pop bottles.

My yellow MG had the graveled lot to itself. I'd dropped Dennis short of the lot while we were still in the protective cover of the firs. Sullen, swearing, shivering, he'd hefted my mobile phone and a pair of binoculars from the sports editor's desk and skulked into the woods.

No, it wasn't on a par with having a SWAT team at the ready. But even a hung-over Dennis should be able to punch 911 if the need arose. And Dennis should by now be crouching in the pine grove that grew almost to the tip of the point.

I leaned against a piling, wrapped my arms tightly together, and tried not to shiver. I watched the parking lot.

My first warning was a bump against the pier. The wooden ladder creaked.

I jerked around to face the choppy water.

Tucker's massive head rose above the edge

of the pier. Gloved hands reached for the stanchion, looped the rope around it. Thorndyke's president heaved himself over the side with surprising agility for a man of his bulk. He wore a dark stocking cap, dark turtleneck sweater, and wool trousers tucked into gum boots.

I suppose my surprise was evident.

"I often row, Mrs. Collins. I keep a boat in the University boathouse." He nodded toward the east shore.

"So you've always been familiar with Lake Boone. Even in the early days of your presidency."

There was grudging admiration in his eyes. "Oh, yes." A bleak smile. "I'd enjoy giving you a closer look at the lake. If you'll come this way—"

"Thanks so much, but I'd rather stay here."

He glanced around at the end of the pier. "Quite an interesting spot you've chosen for our meeting, Mrs. Collins. And I suspect it may have all the electronic capabilities of a well-equipped office. But if you wish to talk with me at any length about the subject you mentioned in your call, I would much prefer a sojourn on the water. There we can indeed speak freely. As you promised."

I was dealing with a highly intelligent man who was quite well aware that any rendezvous, no matter how apparently remote or rustic, can be wired for recording.

First score to David Tucker.

But the game wasn't over.

"I see. I understand your concern. I'd be delighted to take a row with you, Dr. Tucker."

"Good. I'll go down first and hold the boat steady."

The ladder was slick, too, but I took my time and stepped safely into the rowboat, with Tucker's hand firmly on my elbow.

He could have tossed me into the water.

He didn't.

I remained wary.

And I hoped to God Duffy was paying close attention.

When I was seated, Tucker stepped past me and took his place. He shifted the oars and we eased away from the pier. He was strong and a superior oarsman. We glided about twenty yards from the pier. He brought us around until my back was to the wind. Quite the gentleman.

The waves slapped against the stern. The little boat bobbed up and down.

Tucker's moon face was fairly pink with exertion. His cold eyes regarded me stonily. "You mentioned information you are gathering for a story, and whether you might or might not actually write that story."

"That is up to you, Dr. Tucker." My purse was in my lap. I opened it, fumbled for a moment to reach my notebook. I also turned on my tape recorder. I drew out my notebook, leaving the flap of my purse tucked back. I flipped several pages, then said, "I'd like to read from an interview—"

He was such a large man, it was an easy reach for him to grab my purse. He pulled it smoothly, swiftly away from me. In an instant, he held the recorder in his hand. His gloved thumb pushed the power off. He tucked the recorder back in my purse, closed the flap and handed the purse to me.

"If you wish to proceed—without electronic aids—please do so, Mrs. Collins."

I didn't need the notebook, of course. I spoke crisply, my eyes never leaving him. "You found Leonard Cartwright's suicide note, you suppressed it, you made certain his death was attributed to a 'prank.' I don't know exactly what happened next. But I'm sure Darryl Nugent is dead, and his body is in this lake."

Tucker sat very still, a huge, brooding presence. The boat bobbed up and down. He studied me, his eyes taking on the deathly gray hue of the water. "What do you want, Mrs. Collins?" He shifted on the seat, used one oar to steady the boat.

I watched that oar, watched it intently. If he lifted it, I could be out of the boat in an instant. I was a good swimmer. And Dennis would call for help. So it didn't take great courage to meet Tucker's cold, calculating gaze.

"I want the truth," I told him bluntly. "What happened to Darryl Nugent? Either he committed suicide, or you killed him."

Whitecaps slapped against the hull. Waves gurgled mournfully among the rocks along the shore.

Tucker's voice was quiet. It betrayed nothing. "I will tell you, Mrs. Collins, but only on one condition."

214

"And that is?" I knew, of course, what was coming.

"You will not reveal—ever—what passes between us."

"I make no promises, Dr. Tucker."

We stared at each other with mutual animosity and determination.

The wind had risen and the little boat was running toward the rocks. He shifted the oars, began to row toward the pier. "Then we have met for no purpose."

"But if you do not tell me what happened to Dean Nugent that night"—I lifted my voice above the creak of the oarlocks—"I will write a story laying out the possibilities I've described. I would imagine this might pose some problems for you."

He dipped one oar, swinging the little boat about.

I spoke rapidly. "Nugent's disappearance was big news. A suggestion that his remains are in Lake Boone would result in a thorough search. I doubt, Dr. Tucker, that the results would please you."

Tucker stopped rowing. "If I tell you, what then? Will you simply have the information to provide an even more titillating story for the masses?" His voice was heavy with anger and disgust.

"If you convince me, Dr. Tucker, that the secret you've held for so many years did not lead to Maggie Winslow's death, then I will have no reason to write about Dean Nugent."

There was an instant of naked surprise on

his face. He leaned forward, his eyes search-
ing mine. "I begin to understand, Mrs. Collins.
At least, I think I do—if you are not lying to
me."

There was not a great deal of trust between
the two of us.

"I assure you, Dr. Tucker, I have no inter-
est at all in hurting either the Nugent or the
Cartwright families unless those terribly sad
events are connected with Maggie's murder.
That's what I'm looking for—the truth about
Maggie Winslow."

The wet, cold air ruffled my hair, sent chills
through my body.

"Mrs. Collins, I solemnly swear"—the
cadence was measured, the words spoken
with great dignity—"that I did not kill Maggie
Winslow to prevent her from writing about
Darryl Nugent."

"Then you can tell me about the dean with
no worry about my revealing what you say."
I met his gaze directly.

Tucker's face was bland, revealing nothing
of his thoughts. I wondered if he was a chess
player. Only his eyes were alive, calculating,
processing, judging.

Finally, he asked bluntly, "Are you an honorable woman, Mrs. Collins?"

"I try to be." My tone was weary. "Often,
Dr. Tucker, it is difficult to know where
honor lies."

His gloved hands closed on the oars. He once
again jockeyed the boat until the stern faced
north. He looked past me, out onto the chop-

py waters. "I found the envelope left by Leonard Cartwright." His eyes were bleak. "It was addressed to Dean Nugent. Yes, I took it. But I didn't even look at it until late that afternoon. As you can well imagine, there was much to be attended to. I debated opening it, but I wanted to know the contents. I wanted to know what had caused this tragedy. I felt it was my duty to know." His face was as somber as this gray November day. "Thank God"—his voice was suddenly harsh—"I opened it. Thank God."

The boat rocked in the swells.

He swung his massive head toward me. "Do you have any idea, Mrs. Collins, how destructive it would have been for the University if it were publicly known that our dean of students was involved in an affair with a student who worked in his office, and that, moreover, the affair led that student to such despair that he committed suicide?"

Yes, I well knew what kind of havoc that story would have caused.

He twisted to look at the opposite shore. Through the trees, we could see the sprawling redbrick complex of the library.

"I have had one love in my life, Mrs. Collins, and that is Thorndyke University." There were no defenses in his deep voice now. "I will admit that my first thought that day was not for Leonard Cartwright, not for his family, not for Darryl Nugent. My first thought was how to protect the University." His big head swiveled back toward me. "And what is the

217

University? It is the students first, the faculty second. So beyond my desire to keep scandal from damaging the University, I had to think about my responsibility to those entrusted to my stewardship. One fact was unequivocally certain: Dean Nugent had to resign."

I hadn't looked past Tucker's discovery of the note. I should have expected that raw emotion scalded everyone involved that day.

"I had a short, bitter talk with Darryl on the phone. At first, he resisted. Darryl claimed it was all a horrible mistake, that Leonard obviously had been unbalanced. But I made it clear that Leonard's letter was explicit, that I would, if need be, obtain the services of a private detective, that I had no doubt as to the truth of Leonard's assertions."

Tucker bowed his head for a moment. Then, taking a deep breath, he lifted his head and met my waiting gaze, his eyes dark with anguish. "I told Darryl that I would come to his office about five-thirty. I promised to give him Leonard's letter in exchange for his letter of resignation."

The oars squeaked in the oarlocks. Jerkily, Tucker pulled us away from shore. We had drifted into the shallows.

"I arrived at his office at twenty minutes past five. I knocked. There was no answer. I opened the door. Darryl was hanging from the balcony." Tucker looked profoundly weary. "You said at the outset that either Darryl committed suicide or I killed him. I'm afraid, Mrs. Collins, that both are correct. Darryl Nugent was an extremely proud man. His family was very important to him. His reputation was important to him. His position was important to him. I should have known he was distraught. I should not have attacked him so angrily. I'm an administrator. I know that every problem must be solved both in terms of facts and in terms of emotions. At a critical juncture, I failed to remember that I was dealing not only with the University—but with a man's life." There was no apology in his tone. There was only grim acceptance.

"But, no matter what happens, it is always the University that comes first," I said softly.

His face was stubbornly, passionately defiant. "Yes. Yes. What would you have done? If I called in the police, the scandal would have been enormous. There would have been no way to hide it. The police would immediately have questioned the circumstances of Leonard's death. And the Pierce family was considering a multimillion-dollar gift to the University. We would have lost it. I know that. Because I know the Pierces. And do you want to know how I felt as I stood there, looking up at Darryl? I was furious. I was enraged at his stupidity. At his selfishness! I think it was that fury which carried me through the rest of the day. I had to work fast. The cleaning crew starts at the top of the building and goes down. I picked up the chair—"

Oh, yes, the Windsor chair, knocked over by Nugent's final desperate kick, scarring the floor.

"—and stood up and braced his body to take the pressure off the cord, then I worked the cord loose and let him fall. I rolled his body in the rug from the fireplace and tied it with the cord he'd used. I went out and checked where the custodians were, then I carried the rolled-up rug down to the basement. I hid it in one of the storerooms that's never opened. About midnight I returned and got his body and the gargoyle. I drove to the boathouse. I unrolled the rug, shoved in the gargoyle, tied it all up firmly with a rope from my garden shed. When I'd rowed out to the middle of the lake, I heaved it all over."

The rowboat had once again drifted into the shallows. David Tucker lifted the oars. He rowed furiously, his head bent. When the boat bumped up against the pier, he held it steady as I climbed out.

When I stood on the pier, Thorndyke's president looked up and gave me a terse nod. "Now, Mrs. Collins, it's your turn to make judgments."

thirteen

Judgments, they never come easy.

Tucker knew that.

But I needed to remember that David Tucker was a man accustomed to gauging the effect of his words, even if he claimed that on one traumatic day he had not done so.

Judgments.

My steps echoed hollowly on the pier.

Dennis Duffy was waiting at the MG. "Shit, Henrie O, I'm colder than a witch's tit in Siberia." He hunkered on the running board, his arms wrapped tight against his body, shivering uncontrollably.

"You're in lousy shape, Dennis. Come on, let's go."

But I was glad, too, as we sped along Lovers' Lane, to leave behind the lake's bone-chilling miasma, damp and cold and elegiac as a grave.

"So what's the deal?" Dennis groused. "Why, for God's sake, did you and Big Butt tête-à-tête in the middle of that damn lake? And why did I have to serve as a frozen audience of one? What the hell's the lake—" Dennis blinked, jerked his head toward me. "Wait a minute, wait a *minute*. Christ." An unholy light flickered in Dennis's pale eyes. "Nugent."

Nobody ever said Dennis was slow.

"Pretend this morning didn't happen." The MG curved in front of the library.

Dennis twisted in the small seat. He hadn't bothered with a seat belt. "Goddamn, *what* a story!"

"No."

"No? Forget that, Henrie O. Goddamn. Hey, I can—"

I jolted to a stop in the J-School lot and faced Dennis. "No way. You're going to follow my lead, Dennis. I'm trying to find out the truth about Maggie. As far as I'm concerned and"— I measured the words—"as far as you are concerned, the past is past—if Tucker told me the truth."

"Henrie O." There was real anguish in his voice. "What a *hell* of a story."

"I gave my word."

"He's a golden-tongued bastard."

"I know that."

We slammed out of the car. Dennis was close at my elbow.

I walked fast. "He didn't toss me in the lake, Dennis. He could have."

"Yeah." Dennis opened the back door. "But it was broad daylight."

"Nobody around."

"He's not a man to take chances."

The warm, stuffy air of the J-School felt like a plunge into a spa.

At the newsroom, Duffy grabbed my arm. "Goddamn, Henrie O. Please..."

I shook my head. "Sometimes, sweetheart, people are more important than stories."

It didn't play with Dennis.

I held out a sliver of hope. Because it might be fatal to underestimate David Tucker. "Okay, Dennis, let's put it like this: If I should die suddenly and questionably, get the cops to drag Lake Boone, with special attention to the central portion."

I left Dennis staring after me.

I hoped I knew what I was doing.

Although it would be of no comfort to me, should Lake Boone be dragged in the eventuality I'd described, the truth would finally be known.

I wondered if David Tucker had an appreciation for the forensic capabilities of today's police. It would take only a portion of the backbone in the neck or the skull to determine whether Darryl Nugent died from hanging or, for example, from a savage blow to the head.

Time would tell.

I was ravenously hungry. I wolfed a cheeseburger and chocolate malt at the Green Owl. The unceasing noise—voices, dishes, music—was a welcome antidote to that bleak meeting at the lake. I was back in my office by a few minutes before noon. I took time to type up a complete report of my talk with Tucker. Since it would only see light of day should something happen to me, I felt this was fair enough. Otherwise, I intended to keep my mouth shut, although I was in no hurry to share this decision with Tucker.

There was, of course, the question of Kathryn Nugent. Didn't she have the right finally to learn the circumstances of why her husband vanished?

I would think about that later.

Upon application to the court, a missing person can be declared dead. I assumed she had followed that procedure, for insurance and estate purposes.

But there was still the open-ended loss of her husband. What was decent? What was right?

I might still write about either the Murdoch or the Rosen-Voss case. Whether I did or not, I was determined that neither Thorndyke's president nor the director of the J-School should ever think I'd succumbed to their pressure. But I couldn't see anything positive to be gained by a late revelation about either Nugent or his young lover, Leonard Cartwright. Let them rest in peace.

If Tucker was telling the truth.

At this point, he was still on my list of those who might have killed Maggie, but he no longer got top billing.

That left me with Maggie's personal circle— Dennis Duffy, Eric March, Kitty Brewster— and with the Rosen-Voss and Murdoch cases.

If Maggie's killer came from her personal circle, it was quite an extraordinary coincidence she'd just begun to investigate the most famous unsolved crimes in Derry Hills. Moreover, I didn't see any reason for a search of her apartment by anyone within that circle except, perhaps, Dennis.

I put coincidences right on a level with magic tricks. I don't believe in magic. I understand there's more than meets the eye, and that, if you know where to look, you can beat the man in the cape every time.

So—Rosen-Voss or Murdoch; Murdoch or Rosen-Voss?

It had to be a toss-up.

Maggie was last seen dining in the Commons, close to both the J-School and Evans Hall. Angel Chavez, that surprise witness in the Murdoch case, worked in the J-School. Stuart Singletary, Howard Rosen's roommate, taught in Evans Hall. I knew that Maggie had talked with both of them.

Singletary had no apparent motive for his roommate's murder in 1988. Lieutenant Urschel obviously had found nothing to suggest Singletary might be guilty.

So why did it spook Singletary when I'd gone to see him? He seemed uncomfortable about the way he and Howard met. Singletary was dating Cheryl Abbott then. Cheryl had introduced Stuart and Howard. Was Cheryl somehow involved?

Singletary definitely was spooked.

But Angel Chavez was worried. She wanted to know if Maggie had written anything yet about the Murdoch case.

Once again I imagined Maggie leaving the Commons Wednesday evening, walking out into the dark.

Stuart Singletary could have waited in the shadows near Evans Hall. He knew Maggie would be in his evening class.

But Angel had access to the student files in the Journalism School, including class registrations. She could easily have determined where Maggie might be found that night. And Angel desperately didn't want the investigative series to be written.

I picked up the Murdoch file.

"The scene of the crime," Michael Murdoch proclaimed airily. He pointed at a marble bench near the reflecting pool.

In summer, it would be an idyllic spot. Now, a sodden newspaper floated in the murky water. Scudding leaves mounded against the bench. Leafless tree limbs rattled like loose teeth in a bleached skull.

Murdoch's paint-spattered smock hung from his scrawny frame. The smock flapped open in front, revealing a purple velour jumpsuit. He stood with his arm outstretched, holding the pose, but he looked at me, his faunlike eyes sly and unwinking.

"That's where your father was shot?"

"Yeah. Right in the kisser." His arm fell and now he did look at the bench, his thin face suddenly malevolent. He bunched the smock back behind his arms and jammed his hands into the pockets of the jumpsuit.

"It must have been quite a shock." I kept my voice level.

"Surprised the hell out of me. I never thought she'd have the guts." Sheer admiration lifted his voice.

"She?"

Michael gave a high whinny of laughter. "My pinup gal of the year, my favorite dumb broad, good old Candy."

I suppose I must have looked blank.

He stood straight, put his right arm in front, his left arm in back and gave a half-bow.

"More formally, madam, my esteemed step-mother, Candace."

"She was acquitted."

"Yeah. Makes you believe there's a God after all. That, or Candy sure had something on that gal who alibied her." Once again his tone was admiring.

"Do you think that's what happened? Do you think the witness was lying?"

He rocked back on his heels, eyed me quizzically. There was a sardonic glint in his eyes. "Lady, how many four-leaf clovers have you ever picked up?"

"Is this the way you always discuss your father's murder?"

"I don't"—his tone was abruptly mincing—"discuss my father's murder." Then he looked thoughtful. "Funny thing is, you're the first person to ever come right out and ask me about it. People get skittish when you've been involved in a murder. So how come you want to know about the old bastard's bloody end?"

"Mr. Murdoch—"

"Michael. Please." He gave a swift small smile that was oddly endearing.

"Michael, will you be serious for a moment? I need your help."

"Serious?" His gaunt face was suddenly stern and old far beyond his years. "You want serious? You want to hear how many ways a man can be a bastard? Would you like that? Do you want to hear how he hurt my mother, made her cry? When I was a little kid, I'd lie in my bed and jam the pillow over my head so I wouldn't hear her scream. She tried not to scream. Because of me and Jennifer, but he hurt her so bad, and the screams were awful—like an animal caught in a trap."

Michael's long thin fingers bunched into tight fists. "Serious? You want to know what he did to Jennifer?" Sudden bright tears glistened in his dark eyes. "My little sister. The last I heard she was drugged out in Chicago. I begged her to come home. Do you know what she told me? She said it was too late."

He strode to the bench, glared down at it. Suddenly, he was on his knees, his fingers scrabbling at one of the flagstones in the path that curved around hedges to lead to the terrace and the house, the very substantial house in one of Derry Hills's finest neighborhoods, a house too far from its neighbors for cries to be heard.

Michael was breathing raggedly as the stone worked loose. He grabbed it, stood, and flung it down with all his might. The stone splintered on the marble bench, leaving a thin white streak. Like a scar.

"I see."

His chest heaving, he stared at me wildly, then, slowly, gradually, he began to calm. "No, lady, you *don't* see. Just like you don't understand why I like that bench. I can walk out here and look at it and I know the bastard's dead. If you go close"—he took swift running steps, and pointed down—"and look really hard, you can see where blood seeped into the pores of the marble. He's dead, dead, dead."

The branches creaked in the wind.

"Did he abuse your stepmother, too?"

"Oh, yeah." But the emotion was spent. "Yeah. But he finally went too far. That day, he killed her damn bird. Funny, after all the things he'd done through the years to Mom and Jennifer and me, and then to Candy"— his mouth slipped sideways in a peculiar smile—"Candy shot him because he killed her parakeet. It was vintage bastard. He took the bird and he broke its stupid neck and he put it on her plate at dinner. She came in and saw it and she dropped the platter—it was fried chicken—and she started to scream."

"None of this came out at the trial."

"Jesus, you think we were going to tell the cops? All Jennifer and I ever said was that we didn't hear the shots, we didn't have any idea what happened; no, we didn't think Candy would have shot him, why would she?"

"But if he abused your stepmother—"

"Jeez, you find four-leaf clovers and you live in a cloister. How many abused women get off? Give me a break." There was nothing endearing about his scathing look of disgust.

"But how can you be so sure Candy shot him?"

"Okay, okay, let me show you." He came up beside me, pointed toward the evergreens that screened the bench and the pool from the terrace. "You can't see the house, not even now, in November. In the summer, it's thick, really thick. So this place is really private. He—"

I realized that Michael always called his

father "he" or "the bastard," never by name.

"—came down here every night to smoke a cigar. He was shot by somebody standing right in front of him with *his* gun from *his* study. I was in the basement. Jennifer was in her room. There was nobody else around. They found Candy's fingerprints on the gun. Her dress had pine needles in it. And she comes up with this nutty story that she's talking on the phone with some woman who'd just called to ask her to put some stuff out on the front porch for some charity drive and Candy doesn't remember the woman's name or the charity. I mean, Candy's so damn dumb you can't believe it. She told this story and that's all she ever said, over and over and over again."

"Angela Chavez testified that she did make that call, that she was on the telephone with your stepmother at the precise time the shots were heard by your next-door neighbor."

Michael's smile was pitying. "Sure, she testified to it. And I know the cops couldn't find any connection between her and Candy, but, lady, believe me, it's there."

"If it isn't there, if Angela told the truth, it means someone else shot your father."

His eyes narrowed. "Like me? Or Jennifer?" Slowly, he shook his head. "You know something, if I'd killed the bastard, I'd have said so—because I would have been proud of it. But I didn't. It was like I was frozen. I couldn't do anything about him. I couldn't." His voice ached with pain. "Don't you think I would have saved my mom if I could have?"

230

He looked so young, so forlorn, so bereft.

"All right, Michael. Not you. Not Jennifer. But is there anyone else who might have hated your father, someone he worked with, someone he'd quarreled with?"

"No." Michael's voice was thin and high. "That's almost the worst part. Everybody thought he was such a great guy. A *great* guy. And he was the hell of a businessman. Made money like it was cotton candy and he owned the machine. Oh no, everybody at the club thought he was wonderful. Great sportsman. Had a six handicap in golf. And when Mom died—she had cancer—everybody was so goddamn sorry for *him*. Because nobody knew what he was like. Just us. And nobody would've believed us—because he was such a great guy. No, it was all here at home. So now when I meet people, I wonder, 'What are you really like? How do you act at home?' I don't know what's real. I don't think I'll ever know."

"So there's no one you know about who would have had a reason to shoot your father?"

"No. Besides, it was *his* gun. From *his* study. How did the helpful stranger get his gun?"

I didn't answer.

"Nope. It starts here. It ends here. Candy did the good deed and your Angel saved her ass."

"I'd like to talk to Candy, Michael. Could you tell me how to get in touch with her?" I'd had no luck finding Candace Murdoch in the directory.

"Sure. She lives in Vegas. She took her part of the loot and got the hell out. Last I heard, she was having a great time."

"So you don't think she could have been in Derry Hills last Wednesday night?"

"I'd think that's about as likely as my visiting the old bastard's grave. But come on in, I'll get you her number."

We followed the winding path around the shrubs and through the trees to the house. Michael held open the back door for me.

In the study, he found an address book, copied a number, handed it to me.

He pointed to the open desk drawer. "The famous murder weapon was taken from that drawer." His tone was flippant.

"And your sister's address..."

He shook his head. "My last letter came back, 'Addressee Unknown.'" Now his voice was empty.

No matter where Jennifer Murdoch had been last week, I didn't think she'd been contacted by Maggie Winslow.

Michael Murdoch was apparently the only member of that unhappy family who had been in Derry Hills when Maggie died.

"Michael, could you tell me where you were last Wednesday night, say between six and seven?"

He didn't even bother to ask why. "Sure. I work at the Battered Women's Shelter on Wednesday nights. I was serving dinner."

I would check it out, but this alibi was too simple, too open to be anything other than true.

I took the front entrance to the J-School. Instead of going directly up the stairs to the newsroom and my office, I walked down the hall to the main office.

Angel was working at the copy machine, sorting a multi-page document as sheets slid onto different levels.

I came up behind her. "Hi, Angel."

She stiffened. It broke her rhythm. She scrambled to catch up as the sheets continued to click into place. Her elbow caught a stack of sorted documents and they toppled to the floor, fluttering in every direction.

"Oh, I'm so sorry. I didn't mean to startle you." I bent down and began to gather up the sheets. "Here, I'll help you get these in order—"

She clicked off the machine, bent down, and hurriedly scooped up papers. "No, no, that's all right." Her hands trembled. She kept her eyes on the spilled sheets.

I knelt beside her. "Oh, this won't take long. We can visit while we work."

"No, please—"

I didn't give her time. "I could really use some help. You told me the other day that you grew up here in Derry Hills and I'm thinking about buying a house and I wanted to ask you about neighborhoods."

Her face swung toward me. Her relief was so complete, so palpable that I almost felt ashamed. Until I thought of Maggie.

Michael Murdoch was quite correct. You can never be sure of the face you see. But Angel didn't have Michael's painfully achieved wisdom.

By the time we had the sheets sorted, Angel was relaxed and cheerful and I heard all about the Linwood neighborhood where she'd grown up and Brookhaven, the lovely street where her Aunt Delores lived, and how she missed living in a real house, but her apartment was awfully nice.

It was easier than shagging balls at a driving range and sometimes, yes, when necessary, I can dissemble with the skill of an actress, the guile of a politician, and the coldness of a reptile.

I dressed appropriately, of course: a navy silk suit, a red-and-navy lattice print silk blouse. I wore a small diamond-burst pin on my lapel. And dark hose to hide the angry purple bruise on my ankle.

I was smiling as the door opened. I held a notepad prominently in my hand. I introduced myself as a reporter for a new publication that would be launched in the spring and I was gathering material about this wonderful old section of Derry Hills, and if Mrs. Simpson could spare a few minutes...

Mrs. Simpson wore a red tam over a fringe of gauze-thin orange hair. She'd learned eye makeup from Theda Bara. Three streaks of green bracketed each eye. Twin spots of rouge rode high on her plump cheeks and matched the bright crimson of her checked gingham apron. She dried her hands on a dishtowel and said shyly, "I'm in the middle of baking, but if you don't mind talking in the kitchen..."

I didn't mind.

She brought her mixing bowl to the table.

As she stirred the batter, she said, "Is your magazine the same one the young lady worked for?"

"Maggie?" I felt as if I'd pulled the lever and quarters were gushing out, bright, shiny, and jingling.

"Yes, that was her name. She was interested in the neighborhood, too." Her face puckered in distress. "That was so awful, what happened to her."

"Yes, yes, it was."

"Tell me, is it true that she was involved with that woman's husband?" Mrs. Simpson paused, her wooden spoon suspended above the bowl, her eyes avid.

"There's some question about that. Apparently, he often had affairs, but he claims not in this instance."

The spoon moved again, rhythmically, thumping against the sides of the bowl. "Well, of course he would say that."

Of course he would.

I put my notepad on the table. "I hadn't realized Maggie had already talked to you. But this is such a lovely old neighborhood. I hate to ask you to go over it all again..."

"Oh, I don't mind," she said happily. "It's fun for me to remember."

I recorded pages of information about Simpsons, of course, while drinking several cups of strong black tea. She popped up once to lift out a steaming pan of gingerbread. I ate two pieces. We worked our way through the histories of her next-door neighbors, the Willoughbys to the east and the Jacobsons to the west, as she dropped dough on shiny aluminum.

"And, let me see, that lovely house across the street..."

"Oh, yes, the young lady was very interested in the Chavez family. That's the kind of family she wanted to write about. The people who've lived there since, the Mabrys and then the Cokers, everybody worked, and it wasn't the kind of family she wanted to know about." Mrs. Simpson set a timer as she slid two cookie sheets into the oven. She returned to the table, her eyes sparkling. "...such nice people, Louisa and Carlos. Carlos taught Spanish in the high school. He and Louisa had Paul and Angela, and theirs was a real old-fashioned kind of family." Mrs. Simpson stirred her tea. "They went to church every Sunday and Louisa was a homeroom mother and helped take the kids on field trips, and Carlos was a Scout leader. And he worked so hard, had a second job at Carstairs Grocery." She looked at me earnestly. "You know how hard it is to get along on a teacher's salary, but he wanted Louisa to be home with the kids and I think that's wonderful. But everything turned upside down when Carlos died. Here one day, gone the next. They sent a senior from the school to get Louisa. They took him to the hospital in an ambulance and we were all so worried. I went over to stay with Paul and

Angela. But when I called the hospital, it sounded okay. It was his appendix. They did the operation, but the next day he got peritonitis and he died three days later. Well," Mrs. Simpson heaved a sigh, "the good years were over. Paul got a job after school. Angela was still too little. Louisa went to work in the school cafeteria. She had to sell the house and they moved to a tiny little apartment. Then, when Angela was in high school, Louisa got cancer. After Louisa died, Angela moved in with her aunt and her cousin, Loretta. I know how much they meant to her. Angela just adored Loretta. And that was the saddest thing."

"What happened to Loretta?" I'd stopped taking notes. I supposed I was following behind Maggie, but if she'd found something here, she was cleverer than I. What possible difference could it make about Angela's cousin Loretta?

"Cancer, again," Mrs. Simpson said mournfully, her eyes dark with the fear that all women know. She tossed her head. "But I think she would have lived if she'd had good care. It's just dreadful what can happen to you now."

I was puzzled. "What, Mrs. Simpson?"

Her voice rose indignantly. "Loretta'd worked there for ten years. But nobody cares about that anymore. When she got sick and they found out it was cancer, they fired her, so she lost her health insurance." Mrs. Simpson reached up, her hand clutched the bib of her apron. She looked at me with anxious eyes. "Do you think that's going to happen to Medicare? Do you think they're going to take it away? People like me, we don't have any money. If we don't have insurance..." Her voice trailed away.

"No, Mrs. Simpson, I don't think they'll take away Medicare." Although I would hate to stake my life on it.

Her old, frail hand squeezed the gingham. "Poor Loretta. Her doctor wouldn't keep her, so she had to go to the public hospital. But you wait and wait and wait there and the doctors aren't so good. Or maybe they're just so busy...so many sick."

Abruptly she pushed back her chair. "Let me show you..." She darted down the hall, but returned in just a moment. "Here, this is a neighborhood picnic when our kids were little." She pointed out faces to me in the moment captured on a brilliant summer afternoon when life and health must have seemed forever secure. I recognized Angela in the smiling face of a little girl roasting marshmallows on a stick. "And that's Paul. And that's my son, Robbie"—an arthritic finger gently smoothed the snapshot—"and my daughter, Beth. And there's Louisa and Carlos. See, he was pushing her in the swing. And there, next to the tree, that's Loretta."

Loretta was laughing as she looked up at a stocky teenage boy. Sun slanted through tree limbs, catching her in a nimbus of light.

"Where did Loretta work, Mrs. Simpson?"

Slowly, the happiness seeped out of her face.

"Do you remember?"

"Oh, yes. I've never forgotten. She worked for the big cement company. She was in the office of the president. She worked for Mr. Murdoch."

Oh, yes. For the bastard.

Good going, Maggie.

In the cross directory, I found a listing for a Delores Hernandez at 2103 Brookhaven, so, Loretta Hernandez. Once again in *The Clarion* morgue, I pulled up an obituary for Loretta Hernandez on June 11, 1982:

LORETTA HERNANDEZ

Funeral for Loretta Hernandez, 31, of Derry Hills, will be at 10 A.M. Saturday in St. John's Catholic Church, with the Reverend Albert Kroft officiating.

Miss Hernandez died Thursday in a local hospital following a lengthy illness.

Rosary will be at 7 P.M. today in the Sandstrom Funeral Home Chapel. Burial will be at Resurrection Cemetery in Derry Hills.

Miss Hernandez was born January 3, 1951, in Derry Hills. She graduated from Derry Hills High School in 1969. She attended the Bittle Business College and was employed as a secretary with Murdoch Construction from 1971 to 1981. She was a member of St. John's Catholic Church, where she sang in the choir and had served as treasurer of the Altar Society. She had been a member of the Derry Hills Community Chorus.

She is survived by her mother, Delores Hernandez, of the home.

Memorial gifts may be made to Hospice of Derry Hills, 129 Swallowtail Road.

Loretta Hernandez died in June of 1982.
Curt Murdoch was shot on July 21, 1982.
And Angel had adored her cousin.

Temple Harris was in the coffee shop in the basement of the courthouse. Temple was one of Derry Hills's most successful trial lawyers. He had been an assistant prosecutor when the Murdoch murder case was tried. He was also active in the Nature Conservancy, and that was where I'd become acquainted with him.

"Hello, Temple, do you have a minute?"

He rose with a smile. He was tall and courtly, with silver-streaked black hair and a flowing silver mustache. "I always have time for lovely ladies." He pulled out a chair for me.

I'd barely begun when he grabbed the conversation and galloped. "Of course I remember, Henrie O. God, we were hacked. Talk about a surprise witness! But the judge overruled our objections about lack of notice because the defense was clearly astonished and announced it also lacked prior notice and hadn't known of Chavez's involvement in the case until the morning that she testified. That was a real Perry Mason appearance. I still can't believe it."

He frowned, his eyes glinting. "I know it was a conspiracy."

"Did you investigate that possibility?"

"You bet we did." He cradled his coffee cup in big gnarled hands. "We asked the police to investigate Chavez to see if she could be charged with either false testimony or conspiracy." He blew out a spurt of outrage and his mustache quivered. "They went after her like hound dogs after a rabbit, but they couldn't find a single solitary point of connection between Chavez and the Murdoch woman."

I wasn't surprised. And who could fault them? I doubt that the prosecutor's office examined Angel's family tree. And why should any investigator have troubled to discover the job history of Angela's dead cousin?

"Yeah." Temple's voice was thoughtful. "I was the one who kept after them. The night of Murdoch's murder, Chavez was baby-sitting across the hall in her apartment house." He squinted at the ceiling. "I even remember the parents' name. Dorman. They wouldn't budge on their story. They got home ten minutes before Curt Murdoch was shot and they saw Chavez walk into her apartment. And she couldn't have gotten across town unless she flew. She sure as hell didn't jog. She'd just had some foot surgery and was still all bandaged up. Oh yeah, it was a solid story—and I know damn well she was lying in her teeth. But I don't know why. Oh, I don't think she shot Murdoch. No, that was little Miss Candy.

Chavez was in her apartment, but I'll never believe she was on the phone with Candace Murdoch when that gun went off. Hell, they could give me an affidavit from the Pope, and I still wouldn't believe it. Chavez is lying. But nobody will ever prove it, Henrie O."

I had to agree with that.

I got back to the J-School about four. There was only one file left now. I settled into rereading my notes about Howard Rosen and Gail Voss. But I kept my eye on the time. At five to five, I hurried downstairs. I was waiting for Angela when she came down the side steps.

"Angel."

She looked up with her usual equable smile. "Hi, Henrie O. Have you made any progress in your house hunt?"

"Yes." I reached out, patted her arm. "I'm sorry about your cousin Loretta."

Her face congealed in shock. Then, like shutters closing, her expression smoothed into a stolid blankness. She ducked her head, began to walk swiftly toward the parking lot.

I kept pace. "I know what happened." I spoke gently. "Your cousin died because of Curt Murdoch. At least, that's what you believe."

For an instant her walk checked, then she picked up speed again.

I can move fast, too. "Angel, you went off to L.A. to visit a friend. You left the morning after Murdoch was killed. But I'm sure your aunt kept you informed. There were no tears in Mudville over his death, not from anyone

242

in your family. I imagine your aunt told you when Candace was arrested and maybe even sent you clippings about the murder investigation, so you knew Candace had put out a plea for the woman who called that night to come forward. Then you came back to town—"

We reached a green Honda. Angel yanked her car keys out of her purse.

"—and the trial was underway and everyone laughed about Candace's silly little story; wasn't it just like her to come up with such a dumb alibi. But you make calls for several charities—Habitat for Humanity and the Hospice of Derry Hills—and you saw what you could do—and you did it."

Angel opened her door, slid behind the wheel, slammed the door.

When she looked up at me, she was no longer the kind and thoughtful woman I'd come to know. She looked angry and fiercely determined and utterly satisfied. "Henrie O, it's just like I told Maggie; you'll never prove it."

The motor roared to life.

I stepped back and the Honda squealed into reverse, jolted into the lot, then bucked forward.

I watched the dust whirl.

Yes, I expected that was precisely what Angel had told Maggie.

I wondered if Angel had heard the hint of admiration in my voice.

Justice?

Who can say? Certainly not I.

I turned and walked back toward the J-School.

And the Rosen-Voss file.

fourteen

❀

At seven o'clock, I pushed back my office chair, stretched, and realized I was hungry. In the newsroom, Duffy fished french fries out of a sack from the Green Owl. Eric March was back in his place as deputy city editor. The glow from the monitor cast an eerie pall over his somber face. Buddy Neville, no longer at the helm, lounged in his chair reading *G.Q.*, his sneakered feet on his desk.

I'd put in some good work. Every time you study a mass of material, you pick up something new. This time I'd paid particular attention to the feature stories. Like a crow salvaging bright objects, I was adding to my store of interesting (and sometimes poignant) facts about the 1988 murders in Lovers' Lane:

The night of the murders, Stuart Singletary invited his girlfriend—Cheryl Abbott—over for pizza. Singletary took Cheryl home about eleven.

Howard Rosen and Gail Voss were at the Green Owl from eight to almost eleven. They had pizza—and champagne. They'd brought their own bottle to the café.

244

Eleven, eleven. Numerals glistened in my mind like neon dice.

The contents of Rosen's car, after it was returned to his family, included an ice bucket, a half-full fifth of champagne, two plastic champagne glasses, and pink paper streamers.

Across the years I could almost hear laughter and the fizz of champagne. I wondered if Howard and Gail got engaged that night. I checked again the contents of the car. No mention of a ring.

Gail Voss had knitted a sweater for Howard's birthday. It was a soft blue. Singletary said Howard thought it was kind of girly, but he wore it to please her. He had it on the night they died.

Gail was a Green Peace volunteer. She collected rabbits, all kinds, made out of ceramic or china or silver, even cardboard. Big plush bunnies, rabbit pictures, rabbit puzzles. Her favorite piece of jewelry was a silver charm bracelet, all rabbits. Her family placed it in her casket.

Howard Rosen was always the life of the party. You could hear him all the way across the newsroom in an ordinary conversation. When he really got going, his voice rose to a shout. He clowned around constantly. But he didn't seem to have a single close friend. Just Gail. The two of them spent every minute together they could.

The English department awarded the first

annual Howard Rosen Writing Award in 1989 to Sylvia Maguire. The award, funded by the Rosen family, was presented by Dr. Thomas Abbott, chair of the English department.

I tucked the file under my arm, grabbed my coat and locked my office.

Duffy studiously ignored me.

That was fine. I suppose he was afraid I might ask him to serve sentry duty in a graveyard next.

I stashed the file in my car and headed for the Green Owl. As I hurried toward the restaurant, I was sharply aware of geography.

Maggie had eaten dinner in the Commons. She walked out into the dusk and met her killer. The possibilities, people who were in the area at that time and might have had reason to strangle her, included:

Rita Duffy, the angry wife.

Dennis Duffy, the philandering city editor.

Eric March, Maggie's boyfriend.

Kitty Brewster, the object of Maggie's disdainful cruelty.

Angela Chavez, the mystery witness in the Murdoch trial.

David Tucker, Thorndyke's president when the dean of students disappeared.

Stuart Singletary, Howard's roommate.

I knocked Rita off the list because she could not have searched either Maggie's apartment or my house.

Dennis, Eric, and Kitty, so far as I knew, would have had no reason to search Maggie's files and should not have cared at all about

Maggie's research into the unsolved crimes. However, it *was* possible that any one of the three might have been concerned that Maggie could have recorded some kind of quarrel or disagreement.

Angel Chavez might well have had reason to fear Maggie's revelations. But what could Maggie do with her suspicions? Why shouldn't Angel simply respond, as she had to me and as she claimed she had to Maggie, "You'll never prove it." Was Angel willing to kill to avoid public embarrassment?

Tucker was still a dark horse. If his story was true, he was out of it. But if he had lied...

And then there was Stuart Singletary.

Stuart Singletary, who was in Evans Hall, where Maggie was supposed to go.

Stuart Singletary, who had radiated uneasiness when I talked to him about Maggie.

Stuart Singletary, who took his girlfriend home "about eleven" the night his roommate died.

But why would Stuart Singletary have killed either Howard or Gail?

The question burned in my mind as I opened the door to the Green Owl. It was cheerful to step inside, escaping the dank November night, even though I carried with me a ghostly picture of two happy college students sitting in a back booth, sharing champagne and laughter.

As always, the Green Owl hummed with activity. I spotted Helen Tracy, looking quite satisfied and happy, in a nearby booth. And with her was the object of her interest, Dr. Tom Abbott. They were deep in conversation. Abbott gestured emphatically, his freckled face intent.

Helen hadn't seen me.

I was tempted to foist myself upon them. I definitely wanted to talk to Dr. Abbott about his son-in-law.

But I had a strong sense that Helen wouldn't welcome an interruption. She was flashing a vivacious smile and bouncing a little in her eagerness to entertain.

Then I saw another familiar face.

As Helen had said, if you came to the Green Owl often enough, you'd see everyone you knew.

Larry Urschel wasn't looking my way. His face was somber in repose. A man at the end of a long, tough day.

If I were after a story, I wouldn't choose to approach a man at the end of his workday, a man staring into his beer. I wondered what he saw, what he was remembering.

But I wasn't after a story.

I was after a killer.

I'd spent a lifetime asking people questions they didn't want to answer. I could do it one more time.

Urschel's head jerked up when I stopped beside his table. For an instant I thought he didn't recognize me, then I realized I had indeed caught him with his thoughts far away. He blinked. His gaze sharpened. Abruptly, a wry smile tugged at his mouth. "Still after it?"

"Yes, Lieutenant. May I join you?"

He shrugged. "Sure."

I slipped into the chair next to his.

We gazed at each other for a moment.

I wondered if I looked as tired as he did.

Urschel's crew cut looked more gray than brown tonight and his skin had a sallow tinge. Deep lines grooved his face. He looked like a man who'd seen it all and found no pleasure.

His eyes flicked to the diamond-burst pin on the lapel of my navy suit.

Not a man to miss anything.

"Thanks for the background stuff on the old cases."

"Sure."

The waitress brought me water and I jerked my head at Urschel's mug. "Same, please."

Urschel lifted his mug, drank deeply. And waited. He didn't owe me polite conversation.

"I've been talking to a lot of people," I said quietly.

"No law against it." His voice was weary.

"And now I'd like to talk to you, really talk to you—"

He held up his hand. "Mrs. Collins, I've done what I can do for you. Like I told you earlier, those cases are still open and—"

"You know anything about guilt, Lieutenant?"

His eyes met mine, old eyes in a middle-aged man's face.

"Because that's why I'm here, Lieutenant. I'm guilty of sending a young woman to her death. Oh, I didn't intend it, of course. And

249

that's the easy answer, isn't it? To say, *Nothing you can do about it now. Don't blame yourself.* And yes, she was arrogant. But so was I, Lieutenant. I told her what kind of stories I would accept. I told her she had to find new facts. *I told her, Lieutenant.* So that's why I'm pushing and pressing and scratching. It isn't for a story. It's for atonement."

He drank his beer, wiped his hand against his mouth. His eyes still met mine.

"I know you're a good cop. You'd never reveal anything that would compromise an investigation. But, Lieutenant, I swear before God— if you'll talk about the past, talk as if no one can hear you—that I'll never betray you."

He put down the mug, then turned it around and around between his hands.

My beer came. I took a deep, refreshing draft, and waited.

Finally, reluctantly, he lifted his eyes. "So what've you got in mind?"

"Death in Lovers' Lane. And Stuart Singletary."

"The Rosen-Voss kill." His voice was reflective. "Yeah. Anybody—" He carefully, intentionally didn't look toward me. He was a man talking to himself, reminiscing over a beer. "—who thinks that setup was cockeyed is right on. Lovers' Lane was fishy as hell. Park and pet, that was the fifties. My big sister used to come in late with her angora sweater misbuttoned and I thought she was a wild woman. In the eighties, they started screwing in grade school."

He looked across the room, his face bleak.

Without being told, I knew he was staring at the booth where Howard and Gail had spent their final evening. "Yeah, I looked at Stuart Singletary. He and Rosen shared an apartment. But they weren't big-time buddies. They'd only met that fall. I thought of every motive on the books—sex, jealousy, drugs. Maybe Singletary offed the guy because he had something on Singletary. But that came up zero, zero, zero. Maybe Singletary wanted to steal Rosen's thesis. Grad students'll do anything to score. Couple of years ago a grad student in chemistry went nuts and started stalking his adviser. But Rosen and Singletary weren't doing the same kind of work. Rosen's thesis was some nonfiction thing. And Singletary did something on poetry. But I was desperate at that point. I asked to see Singletary's notes. Very neat notes, wouldn't you know. Yeah, the harder I looked, the more I found out about Singletary, the weirder it got. He's the original Mr. Perfect. Won every scholarship he ever applied for. Top grades, every prof's favorite student." Urschel downed the rest of his beer. "Yeah, I looked at him hard. I'm still looking. I get that goddamn file out every year and try again. But I never find anything that opens this case up. As for Singletary, that man's got good karma. Slid through a murder investigation like a greased eel, graduated with top honors, landed a job here at Thorndyke. Then he married his girlfriend and her old man's loaded and now Singletary gets to live like a prince."

I felt a quiver of excitement. "Maybe that's

it! Maybe it comes down to money. Maybe Cheryl was interested in Howard Rosen, and Singletary was determined to marry her."

"Not unless everybody's lying." Urschel tugged at one ear. "Of course, people lie a lot. But as far as I was able to find out, Rosen was crazy about Voss; Voss was crazy about Rosen. Nobody ever told me anything different. And besides, the Abbott money didn't come until later, when the old man's book hit it big. No, it all comes down to karma." His mouth twisted as he spoke.

I wondered about Larry Urschel's karma. He didn't wear a wedding ring. And he was eating dinner by himself on a Tuesday night. No one to go home to? And his eyes held shadows and a sense of pain. I'd figured correctly that he was a man who understood about guilt. There are so many kinds of guilt. A marriage goes sour and everybody feels guilty.

"All I can tell you"—now he looked at me directly—"I think Stuart Singletary's a lucky bastard. But I don't know whether he got away with murder." Urschel picked up his check and pushed back his chair, "If you do find something, Mrs. Collins, don't play it the way Maggie Winslow did. Come and get me, Mrs. Collins."

I watched him walk across the room.

No swagger.

No heroics.

Yes, I'd be glad to call on Larry Urschel. Anytime.

When I got home there were two messages on my voice mail:

MESSAGE 1—8:23 P.M.

Henrie O, this is Dennis. (The words slurred just a little.) Listen, I got a source in the prosecutor's office who told me on the sly that the cops found a lipstick with Rita's fingerprints on it underneath Maggie's body. Christ, this is crazy! Anybody ought to be able to see it's a plant. But the prosecution's acting like it's gonna set Rita up for a one-way ticket to the big house. But I know it's a plant. It has to be. The cops think it fell out of Rita's purse or her pocket or something when she dumped Maggie's body in Lovers' lane. Anyway, they've got the goddamn lipstick. So how did it get there? I thought—God, I don't know what to think—but once I brought Kitty Brewster over here. To the house. Rita was out of town. I know, that sucks. But the house is never locked. Kitty said something about it when we got here. So she could have called Rita, sent her out on a rampage. It wouldn't take Kitty a minute to slip inside and grab a lipstick. Hell, Rita's got a half dozen on her dresser, a basket of 'em in the bathroom. Oh God, Henrie O, what am I going to do?

Message 2—8:52 P.M.

Sweetheart, you didn't see me tonight. I was at the Green Owl with—you'll never guess—Tom Abbott! I'd like to think it was my Marlene Dietrich appeal. But, alas, I think he was trying to pump me. However, I was so-o-o charming, he's asked me out for next weekend. Just a chamber music concert, but, hell, it's a start. Maybe I will be the second Mrs. Abbott. Actually, I'd settle for being a kept woman. You know—furs, fripperies, fandangos. Don't know what the hell they are, but they sound great. Anyway, had a super evening. But Abbott's definitely spooked about his son-in-law. Reason I know, he kept insisting Stuart was fine, just fine, thank you, and had really enjoyed visiting with Mrs. Collins. But Tom tried, with all the tact of a bishop seated by an evangelical at an ecumenical lunch, to figure out if you were on Stuart's trail. And I want you to know Tom's eyes matched our coffee saucers when you and the grim Lieutenant Urschel put your heads together. And what, my dear, was that all about? I'll be reading romantic prose at least until midnight—you know, to get in the proper frame of mind for my weekend. Give me a call.

I erased both messages.

I had no intention of calling Dennis. Some lower life forms are better ignored. Moreover, though he'd talked fast and long, his speech was definitely blurry. He was probably deep in an alcoholic slumber by now.

But I couldn't ignore the fact that physical evidence—unmistakable, unexplainable physical evidence—linked Rita to Lovers' Lane. No wonder Urschel had moved so fast. No wonder he felt confident of his case.

But if the whispered call occurred, sending an enraged Rita off into the dwindling daylight to search for her husband and his supposed paramour, Dennis was definitely right that the lipstick could have been taken.

So I wasn't ready yet to throw in the towel for Rita. I took a quick shower, slipped into soft sweats, brewed a pot of decaffeinated coffee, and returned to the telephone.

Helen Tracy's good humor burbled over the wire. "Henrie O, I'm not a downy duck when it comes to men. Actually"—her tone was droll—"as they wrote in a less sophisticated age, 'Therein lies a tale!' But you know, I've always found that perception suspect. Whenever was there an unsophisticated age? I'm sure a Cro-Magnon would be right at home in a boardroom. And bedroom. But anyway, I did not just roll into town on the turnip truck, so I know better than to be swept off my feet—metaphorically speaking as yet, unfortunately—but Tom Abbott is definitely the sexiest man on campus. Oh, there's that new wrestling coach, but I'm nothing if not a realist and he—the coach—is only twenty-seven." A regretful sigh.

Before she could launch again, I flung out my net. "You said Dr. Abbott was mesmerized when Urschel and I—"

But Helen was as uncontrollable as any school of fish. "Oh, my dear, *what* was going on? You and Urschel *deep* in conversation. Will wonders never cease!"

I was after information, not in a hurry to divulge any. "Urschel's quite reasonable if you deal with him politely. But, Helen, how does

Tom Abbott know Urschel?" Even as I asked, I had a quick flash of understanding. And disappointment. "Or did you tell him?"

"Not I. Of *course* Tom is acquainted with the grim lieutenant, sweetheart. Urschel interviewed *everybody* who knew Howard and Gail. You have to remember that Tom's daughter was at Stuart and Howard's apartment that night! And you can bet Poppa was on the scene when Lieutenant Urschel came by to talk about that! I mean, Poppa's never very far away from his girl. Which might not be one of the jollier aspects of being the second Mrs. Abbott. Though I could probably cope. And, of course, Tom is head of the English department and he actually had both Howard and Stuart at his house a number of times. And Tom chaired Howard's thesis committee. And Stuart's, too, I'm pretty sure. Oh, it's all *heavily* intertwined. Tom said he talked with Urschel several times, but there wasn't anything at all in Howard's school life that seemed relevant. Tom said Howard was an excellent student, though perhaps a little slapdash. Tom's really worried about the effect of all this..."

I had talked to so many people at this point, absorbed so much information, so many nuances. I tried now above the continuing flood of Helen's commentary to pinpoint the exact source of Stuart Singletary's uneasiness when I'd interviewed him in his small, luxurious office.

There was something about the way he'd met Howard Rosen at the Abbott house.

Did it involve Cheryl Abbott?

That meeting, that introduction, what was the story there?

"...on the kids, as he calls Cheryl and Stuart. I think they're a bit long in the tooth for that designation, but I'm just a fast-talking floozie hot for Poppa's body. Howsoever, it seems Cheryl's been telling Daddy that it's just so awful to have the whole thing dredged up again."

I needed to know more about the Abbotts. I took a deep drink of my coffee. And pulled Helen's string and hoped my ear wouldn't wilt.

"...well, I don't think the way Tom showers money and gifts and treats on Cheryl is *Freudian*. I mean, Cheryl is a really, really sweet girl. It all comes down to sheer spite. Perhaps another little indicator that I'm in over my head, but what the hey, it's more fun than sitting home watching Macaulay Culkin on the tube. You see, Tom's never really gotten over the divorce. And it galled him, right down to the quick, all those years when Myra—that's Mrs. A number one and Cheryl's mom—could buy Cheryl anything at all her heart desired and all Tom had was an English professor's salary. Myra married big bucks! A guy she met on a flight to Denver. Myra and Tom always flew separately, you know, that spooky deal of not wanting to go down together. Well, that blew Tom's marriage out of the water. Myra and this guy—Harrison, I think's his name—were seatmates and they clicked. Myra got a quickie divorce and married Harrison. He's an

257

international financier, and ever since Myra's spent money like the Atlanta Braves on a roll..."

Helen's obsession with Tom Abbott's marital status was the price I had to pay to gather a few crumbs of information about Cheryl and, indirectly, Stuart Singletary.

"...and so, of course, Cheryl's been indulged from the get-go. Myra thinks up something special—a spa weekend in Carmel—Tom tops it with a shopping spree in Paris. It's a wonder Cheryl's half as nice as she is."

"Somebody told me Cheryl had a crush on Howard." I wandered over to the fireplace. The logs were in place. I turned on the gas, lit the flame.

"Really? I hadn't heard that—and I don't think it's so. I mean, Cheryl knew Howard, of course. But I never thought..." Helen came to a full stop.

For an instant, silence filled the line. It was a nice change.

"Is that what you're thinking, Henrie O? Hmm. Actually, I can't see it. Stuart's just not— well, can you see him shooting people over a girl? I mean, really."

"Sex and money, Helen. In my experience, one or the other is behind most murders. So yes, maybe Stuart wanted Cheryl that much."

"My dear, he does woodworking and he made a plaque for Cheryl, the Browning poem, of course. And he's the one who got up at night with..."

I listened patiently for another fifteen minutes.

If there was wheat among the chaff, I didn't winnow it.

Maybe it was getting too late.

I finally said good night to Helen, who was as chipper as at the start of our conversation.

I wasn't. But I went to my computer. I was driven, compelled, determined to link Stuart Singletary to Maggie's murder. He was the answer, I was sure of it.

Modems are the twentieth-century equivalent of Aladdin's magic lamp. If you have one, you can go anywhere. I stayed at my computer until almost midnight that night, calling up every reference I could find to Stuart Shelton Singletary. Most I skimmed. I printed out a couple. Every word reinforced Urschel's description of Stuart Singletary. From a modest working-class background, he'd excelled all the way through public schools, won a scholarship to Thorndyke. And he'd been on easy street ever since Tom Abbott's novel became a runaway best-seller. As Helen Tracy had told me, Abbott showered Cheryl and her husband with luxuries—summers at Oxford, a vacation home at Eureka Springs, a cabin cruiser on Beaver Lake. Singletary and his young wife were social lions in Derry Hills, entertaining at small dinner parties two or three times a month. The social notes also carried news of their travels. They'd spent last summer in Ireland with her father. Cheryl Singletary played tennis and was active in several Derry Hills charities. Usually as social chairwoman.

I hoped Singletary liked his father-in-law as well as he liked being married to the daughter of a rich man.

Cheryl Singletary. I definitely wanted to talk with her.

When I went to bed, my mind teeming with minutiae about a man I'd never met until a week ago, I was discouraged.

What possible motive could Singletary have had to murder Howard Rosen and Gail Voss?

And how the hell had Maggie figured it out?

fifteen

As always, I scanned *The Clarion* at breakfast. No big stories had broken locally. There was a small story on page 6 about Maggie Winslow's funeral yesterday in her hometown of Saint Louis. The inset thumbnail photo of Maggie had reproduced poorly and the young face looked pallid, uninteresting, without a trace of her beauty and vitality. Nothing more was likely to run until Rita Duffy's preliminary hearing in December.

Today's *Clarion* was the same old, same old. Trouble was brewing in the Middle East. The stock exchange had plummeted seventy-five points the previous day. Today's weather forecast called for a high of fifty-five and sunny in Derry Hills. November made palatable.

I checked the weather in L.A. for today—sunny and seventy-two degrees. I wished it weren't two hours earlier there. I'd like to talk to Jimmy.

But I couldn't talk to him until I decided what my answer would be.

Mrs. Jameson Porter Lennox, Jr.

I looked down at the simple gold band I'd worn for so many years. Many widows switch rings to their right hand. I had not done so.

But it was too early to call Jimmy, even if I were ready to do so. And I wasn't.

Instead, I called Helen Tracy and asked her to take my nine- and ten-o'clock classes. Her curiosity quivered between us. Then Helen asked silkily, "If I do, can I have an exclusive on How-I-Tracked-My-Student's-Murderer?"

I grinned. Old reporters may die, but they never stop trying for a story. "Sure, Helen."

"Happy sleuthing, Henrie O."

I hung up and riffed through my file until I found the printout from Maggie's computer. It was important to remember that Maggie's plan of attack had led her into danger. My best bet was to follow her lead. Cautiously, of course.

The first item on Maggie's list: Find "J Smith."

"Honey, no. Please don't eat the Play-Doh."

The little boy squirmed and wriggled as his mother tried to edge the gooey red ribbon out of his mouth.

A baby's wail rose from the back of the apartment.

The pretty, plump young mother plunged two fingers into the toddler's mouth, expertly retrieved the slippery mass, then jumped to her feet.

The boy's face turned red, and he wailed furiously.

His mother gave me an apologetic look. "I'll be right back."

I fished a small squeezable plastic flashlight from my purse and held it out to the complaining toddler. I pressed it; the light on the end came on. His mouth remained open, but he was abruptly quiet as he watched the light blink. Then he grabbed the plastic tube, plopped down on the floor and began to pump it.

The young mother returned with a tiny baby cradled in the crook of her arm. "Oh, how nice. Johnny, did you say thank you?"

He looked at me, his eyes shining, muttered something that sounded reasonably like thank you, then concentrated totally on the flashlight.

I knew I'd better work fast. "I appreciate your willingness to see me. I know this isn't a pleasant memory."

"It brought it all back to me—when the girl from *The Clarion* came to see me. And now she's dead, too." Erin Malone Howell nestled the infant against her as she sat down across from me in the small, cheerful living room. Toys were scattered about, but the room was almost painfully clean. She looked at me with stricken eyes. "Do you think..."

She didn't have to finish.

I nodded.

"Oh, God," she said huskily. "It's all so *awful*. That means the murderer's here in town. I had nightmares for years. They were so happy that night. Gail and Howard. Pretty names. They were handsome together. He left me a twenty-dollar tip. I ran after them and he said, 'No mistake. It's from Joe Smith.'" Erin patted the baby gently. "You know, it's tough being a waitress. I worked my way through Thorndyke waiting tables at the Green Owl. That was the best night I ever had in tips, and then, when they were killed and we all knew it must have happened right after they left, it made me sick. I've never trusted life since then. I almost broke up with Ronnie. He said I was crazy, just because some psycho killed people we didn't even know. But I felt like I couldn't trust anything, like a pretty day is a lie because you know that all these evil things are happening around you and you don't even know about them. It took me a long, long time to get over that feeling. And really, I don't think I've ever gotten past that night. I still dream about Lovers' Lane and a car splashed with blood. And now, with my babies, I think of them growing up and I wish I could take them someplace safe." She looked at me forlornly. "But no place is safe, not if something like that can happen here in Derry Hills. And that reporter, she was trying to find out what hap-

263

pened and now someone's killed her! So, if I can help you"—her young voice was firm—"I will."

"Joe Smith. What did Howard and Gail say about him?"

Erin Howell reached out and smoothed her son's rumpled shirt, then leaned back and rhythmically patted the baby, who made tiny satisfied mewing sounds. "You know, I've thought and thought about that. It was funny. They were so high." She added swiftly, "Not drugs. They were excited, thrilled. And like I told the police, every so often I'd be at their table, you know, with their salads, then with the pizza. I wasn't paying close attention, but I heard snatches of their talk and I was noticing because they'd brought some champagne with them, and they were toasting each other. Once they held up their glasses, and he said, 'Here's to Joe Smith. I didn't really believe in him,' and she said something like, 'I did.' Then the girl—Gail—paused and said, 'I love Joe Smith,' and the way she said it made me feel so good inside, and he looked at her real soft and said, 'I know you do.' And then I was taking a big order, a bunch of guys at a table behind them, and it got real noisy. But the next day I thought about it, all that kidding about Joe Smith, and then she got real serious and said she loved him. I could tell she meant it. So it wasn't a joke. But in the paper, it said the two of them planned to get married. So who was this Joe Smith guy? All I know is, I'm sure she meant it. I swear to you, she loved Joe Smith. I never did figure it out."

I found Frank Voss out in the hall at the county courthouse, waiting for his case to be called. I saw no resemblance to his dead sister. Where Gail Voss had been blond and slightly built, Frank Voss was tall, stocky, and dark-haired. Reddish cheeks bulged in a heavy face. He had John L. Lewis eyebrows and pale green eyes which possessed all the charm of pond algae.

Over the shuffle of footsteps in the marble-floored hall and the rumble of deep (primarily male) voices, Voss boomed, "Why dredge it all up? What can be done now?"

"I've received some new information, Mr. Voss. But I need a clearer picture of your sister and Howard Rosen. I'll be very brief," I promised. I kept my notepad in my purse.

He shrugged bulky shoulders in an expensive but ill-fitting black pinstripe suit. "I can give you a clear picture of Howard. He was a blowhard. All the personality of an anthill. All noise, no substance. What the hell Gail saw in him—" He broke off abruptly, pressed his lips together. "Goddamn, if she hadn't been out with him, she'd be alive today." Voss glared at me.

"Why are you so sure?"

The transformation was startling. The red faded from his face. His eyes softened. And he spoke quietly, all the bluster gone. "Nobody would have wanted to kill Gail. She was gentle, so gentle. She deserved a wonderful guy to love her. Instead"—and his face hardened—"she fell for this creep."

"Why did you dislike Howard so much?"

Voss's full lips curled in disgust. "He was a bumptious, pushy loudmouth."

"Then why did your sister fall in love with him?"

"I don't know." His bewilderment was clear. "The last time I talked to Gail, we quarreled. Over the creep. She kept telling me I didn't know Howard, that he wasn't at all the way he seemed. So I said if he wasn't, why did he act that way and she said it was a defense. I thought that was a lot of psychological crap. I told her so. She hung up on me." He took a deep breath. "The next day she was dead." His voice was dull, empty, inconsolable.

"Mr. Voss, I talked to the waitress who served your sister and Howard that last night. The waitress overheard Gail say, 'I love Joe Smith.' Yet, everyone agrees she was very much in love with Howard. Do you have any explanation?"

"Oh"—his mouth turned down in disgust—"it had to be some stupid joke Howard made up. The guy was always making noise about something."

I could have told him that Erin Malone Howell was certain Gail meant every word of it.

But there wasn't any point in that.

I was certain of only one fact from Frank Voss: He had utterly despised his sister's boyfriend.

There was a flurry as lawyers began to stream toward the courtroom.

Voss looked toward the doorway.

I spoke quickly. "One more point, Mr. Voss. Have you talked to anyone recently about the case?"

"Yeah. A reporter from *The Clarion*. That girl who was strangled." He stared at me, his pale eyes startled. "My God, do you think that's connected to Gail and Howard?"

"Yes."

"I'll be damned. Look, they're calling the docket. I've got to go." He moved toward the courtroom. "But keep me informed. Please."

I hurried to keep up. "Mr. Voss, where were you last week on Wednesday night?"

"Wednesday night? The night that girl died?" He frowned and gave me a sharp, probing look. "I play poker on Wednesday nights." He hesitated, shrugged, gave me the address.

It wasn't far from the campus.

Then he plunged into the courtroom.

"Daughters, of course, don't tell their mothers everything." Maureen Voss refilled my coffee cup. She was as thin as a mannequin, her once lovely face haggard and gaunt. When she was young, I imagined she'd looked very much like the pictures of her daughter—tall, slender, blond, with an air of gentility and grace.

Mrs. Voss's voice was soft and gracious, but I heard the undertone of pain. "I can tell you without any doubt whatsoever that Gail was terribly happy. She was filled with excitement that last day. I knew her well enough—"

Oh yes, mothers can read children's hearts without ever a word being exchanged.

"—to know something special had happened. Afterward, I tried and tried to think what it could have been. It wasn't their engagement. Gail expected to receive a ring on her birthday, that's what Howard had planned." Her composure wavered. "She would have been twenty-one on July 12."

"But something grand had happened, something they were celebrating." I thought of the champagne and the pink streamers.

Mrs. Voss nodded. Her faded blue eyes filled with tears.

She put down her cup, drew a lace handkerchief from her pocket, pressed it to her face.

"I'm sorry." I hated this moment, wished I did not have to witness this sorrow.

Her hand fell away. She looked at me and now her eyes glittered with bitter anger. "No, I'm glad you've come, Mrs. Collins. I want more than anything to know what happened, and why. I want the person who took her away from me—from us—to be punished."

"Will you tell me about Gail and Howard? What were they like?"

Her description of her daughter was what I expected. "...Gail was kind and generous. She was never silly. She was very earnest about life, about what she enjoyed, what she admired."

I put down my coffee cup. "Mrs. Voss, this is what everyone has told me about Gail. And I find it puzzling. It seems absolutely at odds with her interest in Howard Rosen. What do you think attracted Gail to Howard?"

The grieving mother looked across the room. I followed her glance to a full-length oil portrait of Gail in a soft white summer dress. The girl had looked straight at the artist, quite pleasantly, but there was a definite reserve, an unmistakable formality.

"I don't know," Mrs. Voss answered quietly, "that it could matter now to anyone, but, for what it's worth, I'm quite sure that Howard must have been, beneath that loud, boisterous exterior, a very serious young man." She looked at me directly. "I know my daughter. To be quite honest with you, Gail really didn't ever see anything as funny. I think she looked beyond the Howard that the world knew to a Howard that she loved."

"You're sure she loved Howard?"

"Oh, yes. Gail loved Howard." Her lips quivered.

"Then, Mrs. Voss, I have another puzzle. The waitress who served them that night heard Gail say, 'I love Joe Smith.' Did you ever hear Gail talk about Joe Smith?"

Her headshake was immediate, decisive. "The waitress must have misunderstood. The police asked us about Joe Smith. Lieutenant Urschel said that Gail and Howard discussed someone of that name. But none of us in the family ever heard her talk about a Joe Smith. Mrs. Collins, there was no Joe Smith."

In my office, I scoured the Rosen-Voss file again. I realized that I had the names of several girls who had been close friends of Gail's.

I didn't have a similar list for Howard.

Howard, the lone wolf.

Howard, the loudmouth.

Howard, the man Gail Voss dearly loved.

I placed a half dozen calls. Howard's parents were on vacation in Africa and their itinerary showed them on safari in Kenya. Then I started the search for Howard's older brother. Benjamin Rosen was a highly successful Chicago surgeon. I finally located him, via his mobile phone, on a mountainside in Colorado.

Our connection wasn't the best.

"...who'd you say you are?" His voice was brusque.

I didn't answer directly. "I'm investigating the murder of your brother, Dr. Rosen. I believe it's connected to a murder that occurred here in Derry Hills last week. You can help me catch your brother's murderer."

"You really mean that?" It was a harsh, grating demand.

"Yes. I mean it."

"And who're you?"

"Henrietta Collins. I teach at Thorndyke. It was a student of mine who was killed last week."

"I see." Although he clearly didn't. A pause,

then, crisply, "All right, I'll do what I can. Although I don't see how I can help you. I hadn't seen Howard since he was home that December. And I hadn't talked to him in a couple of weeks before he died. That's what I told a reporter last week."

"That reporter was my student. That reporter was strangled last Wednesday night."

Static crackled in the silence. "I talked to her on Wednesday. All right." Abruptly, the irritation was gone. "What do you want to know?"

"No one could know Howard as well as you. Why was Howard so loud? Why was he always joking?"

The silence was so long this time, I was almost afraid I'd lost him. But, finally, I heard his sigh. "You don't know my father."

"No."

"Aaron Rosen is one of the most successful dealmakers in the history of Chicago. He's brilliant. Nobody can match him. More than that"—Benjamin's voice softened—"he's absolutely scrupulous. If Aaron says it's a certain way, that's the way it is. Dad's charming, intense, voluble, creative. He's a big, strapping, handsome man. He's a champion tennis player. You name it, Dad excels. So what do you think it's like to be his sons?"

"Difficult."

"You got it. I worked my butt off. Howard clowned. That was his way of dealing with Dad. And Howard *was* funny. Everybody loved being around him. You know the only person who ever worried?"

"Your mother."

"Yes. She was afraid that the clowning around was crippling Howard. Yet there was nothing you could point to, complain about. Howard made great grades. He was a good kid. But nobody knew him, least of all my dad. Howard was secretive. I think maybe I'm the only one, besides Mom, who sensed there was another Howard, a sensitive, retiring, quiet guy. Howard read everything he could lay his hands on. He worked on the school paper. He kept notebooks. He never showed any of us the stuff in his notebooks. You know"—the faraway voice was pensive—"I think someday Howard would have surprised everybody. He would have become one of those columnists everybody reads. The girl thought so, too, the one who called last week."

Yes, I was sure Maggie felt a kinship with Howard. Maggie, too, had notebooks and stories and dreams for her future. She'd found a link to the dead young man that must have made his callous death especially harrowing for her.

"You say you hadn't talked to Howard for a couple of weeks before he died, so I don't suppose you have any idea what he and Gail were celebrating the night they were shot?"

"No. But I heard they were happy. I'm glad."

"Did Howard ever mention a Joe Smith?"

"No, the police asked us that. Maybe it was one of Howard's jokes."

"Jokes?"

"Sometimes he'd pretend he was somebody else. I think it was another way of escaping the pressure of trying to live up to Dad. When we were in high school, Howard would convince girls his name was Sylvester Kaplan and he was captain of the football team. Or he'd say he had a twin brother, Harold, and he'd act like a completely different guy, really suave and cool and laid-back." Benjamin Rosen laughed. "God, he was so much fun."

I put the phone down with finality. I was ready to give up my search for the elusive Joe Smith. No one close to either Howard or Gail could identify him.

But I wondered if Lieutenant Urschel had pursued the question of Joe Smith with those less closely linked to the dead students.

In any event, I'd been wanting to talk to Tom Abbott about Howard. Actually, my intention was to pump him about his daughter and her husband. I decided Joe Smith would make a nice beginning.

I called Abbott's University number.

"English Department."

"This is Henrietta Collins in the Journalism School. May I speak to Dr. Abbott, please?"

"Dr. Abbott isn't in his office during the day on Wednesdays. He holds office hours from seven to nine Wednesday evenings."

"Thanks. I'll call back."

I checked Abbott's home address.

Somehow it did not come as an overwhelming surprise to find that he lived next door to his daughter and son-in-law.

I knew the way from my visit on Saturday, when I'd found Stuart Singletary and his little daughter raking leaves. This morning no one stirred outside the Singletary home.

Abbott Père's house was even more imposing than his son-in-law's, a three-story sandstone Greek Revival mansion with immense white columns.

The lion's-head brass knocker on the oversize front door glistened brightly.

A uniformed maid answered the door.

"I'm here to see Dr. Abbott." I delivered this announcement with confidence and a cheerful smile. "Please give him my card." I've always been partial to provocative statements. On my card, I'd written: "Do you know Joe Smith?"

The maid showed me into a living room that was both lovely and comfortable, filled with antiques and plenty of softly upholstered couches.

I remained standing. My eyes were drawn immediately to the lovely oil painting over the Adam fireplace. Homage to yet another daughter. Cheryl Abbott and Gail Voss had little in common. Where Gail had looked out so seriously from her portrait, Cheryl's freckled face, framed by luxuriant, vividly red curls, exuded a vibrant, pixieish, spirited charm. This young lady obviously was quite willing to be the center of attention, indeed would always seek and expect that center.

"Gorgeous, isn't she?" Tom Abbott beamed at me from the doorway. He was, in a very mas-

274

culine fashion, equally as attractive as his daughter: red curls tight to a leonine head, a broad, brash, freckled face.

I understood Helen's sexual interest. He was trim and fit and undeniably appealing in a fashionable cashmere sweater, pleated khakis and sockless loafers. He would have looked equally at home in the pages of *Architectural Digest* or the *Thorndyke Alumni* magazine. He was pleased with himself, his world, the day, and, apparently, his unexpected guest. He strode forward, smiling warmly, hand outstretched. "Helen Tracy tells me you're a wonder. I'm delighted you've come by."

He held up his left hand, my card in his palm. "But what's this all about?" He had an actor's voice, as do many excellent professors. It was deep and full and would carry to the highest row, the farthest seat.

"The name Joe Smith doesn't mean anything to you?"

His face crinkled in dismay. "Should it?" He swiped a hand against his temple. "Damn, I remember less every year. A former student? Someone we've both known in the past?" He gave me a charming, faintly embarrassed smile. "You'll have to give me some help here."

"The Rosen-Voss murders, Dr. Abbott."

"Tom," he said briskly. "I feel I know you very well, Henrie O. And Helen told me you were trying to find out more about that terrible crime." His mobile face shifted from remembered sadness to sudden bewilder-

275

ment. "Though I'm confused about what it could have to do with the young lady's murder. That seems to be pretty clear-cut. Poor Rita. Such a temper. But I'll be glad to help you if I can. Let's sit down." He waited until I sank into an overstuffed chair, then settled opposite me, his tasseled loafers crossed. "But who's Joe Smith? I don't recall that name."

Perhaps that wasn't surprising. There had not been extensive mention of Joe Smith in *The Clarion* coverage. "The mystery man of that evening, Dr. Abbott."

He flashed a friendly smile. "Tom, please."

"Howard and Gail talked about Joe Smith at the Green Owl. Actually, the waitress said they toasted him."

Abbott's face reflected sudden comprehension. "Oh, yes, of course. I'd forgotten all about that. But do you know, Henrie O, I've always thought the waitress must have misheard, misunderstood. Stuart and I talked about it at the time. He didn't know anybody named Joe Smith—and he was living with Howard. No, I don't know why you're looking at that, but I don't think it's relevant."

"What do you think is relevant?"

A Persian cat with thick fur the shade of sea mist wandered into the room, his claws clicking against the highly polished oak floor.

"Here, Rudyard, kitty, kitty."

The cat turned his magnificent head, coolly observed Abbott, then daintily walked past him and jumped up on a rosewood table next to his owner. The cat stared at me with piercing blue eyes. Balefully.

"Relevant," Abbott mused as he stroked Rudyard's glistening fur. "Relevancy implies order and reason. I think that's impossible in the circumstances. Howard and Gail were in the wrong place at the wrong time. A drifter came upon them. Killed them. There was no rhyme or reason involved."

I'd heard this theory before.

From his son-in-law.

Such a convenient theory. It excluded the possibility of motive.

Rudyard's throaty rumble of a purr sounded oddly cheerful.

Despite the somber subject of our conversation, there was a general sense of relaxation and mutual accord. Pale November sunshine flowed through the French windows, turned the oak flooring the shiny color of butter. Cut roses in a tall Dresden pitcher scented the air.

I decided it was time to roil the water. "What had Stuart and Howard quarreled about?"

The rhythmic petting of the cat stopped. Abbott's pleasant, freckled face was abruptly blank. "Quarrel? There was no quarrel between them. Where did you hear that?"

"I'm not at liberty to say." A nice cover for invention. "Was it over Cheryl?"

"Absolutely not. Mrs. Collins"—ah, so much for our bonhomie—"my daughter was simply friends with Howard Rosen. She knew him solely because he was a graduate student and she served as my hostess when I entertained for the department."

"Was Howard in your home often?"

"Once or twice." Abbott's fair skin handled anger poorly. His cheeks flamed.

"But Howard met Stuart here?" I tried to watch his whole demeanor, his eyes, his mouth, his hands. But if there was a subtle response, I missed it.

"Not here." It was clipped. "At our old house."

"Do you remember the occasion?" Why did mention of that introduction make Stuart Singletary nervous? If I knew the answer...

"Of course not." Abbott's deep voice was majestic in its disdain. "I am supportive of all the graduate students, but I certainly don't focus on their social lives. I did know Howard and Stuart quite well because I chaired their thesis committees. But I certainly didn't see a great deal of either of them. Of course, when Stuart and Cheryl began dating, that was a different matter. And let me tell you, Mrs. Collins, my son-in-law is a fine young man. A fine young man. And your harassment of him is not only absurd, it is beyond the bounds of civilized conduct." Abbott stood so abruptly, the cat hissed and jumped from the table, skidding on the wood floor as he landed.

I stood, too, of course. A sudden thought occurred to me. "You chaired both Howard and Stuart's thesis committees?"

"Yes. But what possible relevance does that have, Mrs. Collins?" Abbott's voice bristled with anger.

"What were their subjects?" Was it possible I was close to the truth? Could Stuart have stolen from Howard—an idea, part of his thesis? All of it?

Abbott glared at me, his voice rich with disgust. "Stuart wrote about a minor American poet. Howard was in the creative-writing curriculum and his topic was student unrest here at Thorndyke during the early seventies, a nonfiction work. Now, I hope you find that information quite fascinating. But I want to be clear, Mrs. Collins. You must stop this attack on my son-in-law. It is unconscionable."

So much for brilliant flashes of insight. Just to be sure, I'd check the library for a copy of Singletary's thesis. If it turned out to be the life and work of a minor American poet, I didn't have to check further. That wouldn't be Howard Rosen's choice of research. I knew him well enough now to be certain of that.

I was beginning to feel I knew Howard Rosen and Gail Voss very well indeed.

Howard, loud, sensitive, brilliant, abrasive, playful.

Gail, serious, intense, sweet, loving.

Abbott's eyes glittered with cold, implacable hostility. Nice man—unless his precious daughter was threatened. Even indirectly.

But I felt I had the last word as I walked toward the door.

"I don't know all the strictures of civilized conduct, Dr. Abbott. But murder isn't genteel."

279

I had lunch in the Commons, a more healthy choice today, vegetable soup and corn bread.

I'd scratched over the ground that Lieutenant Urschel had covered so thoroughly over the years, and I was quick to realize I hadn't come up with anything. Even Joe Smith no longer seemed an important focus. Was it just a way for Howard to kid, a special joke he and Gail shared? If so, that couldn't have anything to do with their deaths. I was stymied.

I was taking a last bite of corn bread when Helen Tracy appeared at my table. "Join you?"

"Of course."

Helen plopped down her tray, removing the heaping plate of macaroni and cheese, with a side dish of brussels sprouts. She was talking a mile a minute. "...left you a message on your desk, but I'm glad I found you. Cissy Randolph came by your nine-o'clock. She'd heard you were interested in stuff about Maggie. She wants to see you as soon as possible."

I went directly to the J-School library. The library is not synonymous with *The Clarion* morgue, but is truly the library, containing books, reference materials, CD-roms, and, of course, computer stations. It has the hushed atmosphere typical of all libraries. The marvelous smell of books, old and new, mingled with the faint acrid scent of electronics.

Cissy looked up as I stepped inside. She rose from behind the checkout counter, gave quiet instructions to a student aide, then gestured for me to come into her office at the end of the reading room.

Her office was a mélange of muted desert tones—sepia prints on the walls, a crocheted pink-and-beige throw over a couch, amber frames on family photographs. It was as tranquilly welcoming as a Grandma Moses painting.

"I understand you are seeking information about Maggie Winslow." Cissy sat behind her desk and her fine-boned, chocolate-hued face was troubled. Cissy is a tall, slender, elegant woman with a retiring personality and an incredible memory for detail.

I took the chair nearest the desk. "Yes. I don't believe Rita Duffy is guilty of Maggie's murder."

Cissy regarded me soberly. "I'm uncomfortable about what I'm going to tell you. But I don't feel I can remain silent...Wednesday afternoon I overheard an extremely heated exchange between Angel Chavez and Maggie. They were in the rose garden—"

The rose garden is a sunken area surrounded by evergreens behind the J-School. There are metal tables and chairs among the plantings. It is a favorite spot for both students and staff to grab a few minutes' break in the sun.

"—and they didn't realize I was walking up the path on the other side of the trees. I didn't hear very much because I hurried to get past. I realized it was a very personal, very intense"— Cissy paused, frowned—"actually, I'd have to call it a confrontation. Maggie's voice was loud,

281

overbearing, I would almost say obnoxious. She said something like, 'I know all about your cousin, and I'm going to write about your cousin's death and everybody will know you lied, so you might as well tell me.' And then Angel burst out of the clearing. She didn't see me. She was running and...she was crying."

Cissy stared at me imploringly. "Henrie O, I hate telling this. I hate it. Angel is a friend of mine, and Maggie was—I can't tell you how unpleasant her voice was."

I stood and smiled down at Cissy, a nice woman with a conscience. "Don't worry, Cissy. Angel's okay, but your telling me has been very helpful."

I went directly across the street to the president's office.

Tucker's secretary took in the note I'd quickly scrawled, and in a moment I stood in his office.

Tucker rose. He held my card between his fingers. "Yes, Mrs. Collins?"

I didn't sit down. "I'll be very brief, Dr. Tucker. What I need to know—and I am not carrying a recorder—is the tenor of your conversation with Maggie Winslow last Wednesday."

He didn't hesitate. I appreciated that.

"She was quite strident, Mrs. Collins."

"Did she threaten an exposé kind of story, with or without your cooperation?"

His glance locked with mine. Finally, his massive head nodded. "Yes. Yes, she did."

"Thank you, Dr. Tucker."

As I walked to my office, I had a clearer than ever picture of Maggie's last day, Maggie and her in-your-face journalism. Although editorial writers often bemoan what they see as an increasing lack of civility both in public discourse and its coverage, that phenomenon is nothing new. Joseph Pulitzer's *World* and William Randolph Hearst's *Journal* were simply the forerunners of today's checkout-stand cheap sheets. Jenny Jones titillates viewers just as Arthur Brisbane titillated readers. In the Sunday magazine section of the *World* under Brisbane's editorial direction, readers were invited to send letters discussing "Why I Failed in the Battle of Life." The willingness to bare all for fifteen seconds of fame is nothing new.

So I knew where Maggie was coming from. But she was too young, too brash, too confident to assess accurately the danger of directly challenging a man who'd successfully gotten away with murder.

I paused and looked across the lawn at Evans Hall. I knew something important now. No wonder Stuart Singletary had been unnerved by my visit. Had Maggie shouted at him, too, threatened to reveal what she'd discovered about Singletary and his roommate? That she'd discovered something I was absolutely certain.

I carried that thought upstairs to my office.

I closed my door, but I didn't settle with a file or at my computer. Instead, I looked out the stone-framed window at the parking lot and, past it, the back entrance to Evans Hall.

Singletary was nervous.

I needed to make him more nervous.
I could do that.

sixteen

I packed a small duffel bag with toiletries and clothes. I am, I hope, a good deal cannier than Maggie. The years have taught me that. I'm certain I'm more cautious. Back on campus, I used a pay phone in the Commons to call Margaret Frazier, who is on the general news faculty. Margaret is a good friend. She was quite willing to expect me as an overnight guest whose presence must be kept secret.

"Thanks, Margaret. I owe you."

Before I could hang up, however, she said sharply, "Henrie O, would it help if I came with you? Safety in numbers?"

Margaret had been a longtime correspondent in Paris for INS. She keeps on top of the news. She knew I was working on Maggie's series, and what that meant.

"It's okay. I'll be careful. But sometimes you have to get out in front."

Her warning was swift. "Not too far in front."

"I know. Thanks, Margaret."

I crossed the street to Evans Hall.

The light was on behind the pebbled glass of Dr. Abbott's door. So Tom Abbott had come in to his office today, even though he didn't keep daytime hours on Wednesdays. Was it because he needed to talk with his son-in-law—away from Cheryl?

When I stepped into the English department office, a spiky-haired coed immediately asked, "May I help you?" Her voice was firm. A corporate secretary in the making.

"I'm here to see Dr. Abbott."

"Do you have an appointment?" Her expression was pleasant but distant.

I didn't intend to be stymied. Once again I took a card and scrawled a brief note. "Please give this to Dr. Abbott," I told her. I, too, can be firm.

She returned in only a moment, looking faintly surprised. "Yes, ma'am, Dr. Abbott will see you."

Glass-fronted bookcases, seventeenth-century maps, a fine old walnut desk—and a distinctly icy reception.

Abbott stood by the corner of his desk, eyes dark with hostility, hands clasped behind his back, feet apart. "Mrs. Collins"—that dramatic, accomplished voice was dangerously low—"you have absolutely overstepped yourself." He crumpled my card in his hand.

I considered my note quite artful, certain to gain me entrée to a man who had no interest in talking to me. On the card, I'd written:

Dear Dr. Abbott,

There is a distinct possibility that the body of Maggie Winslow was hidden in Evans Hall

285

before it was abandoned in Lovers' Lane.
Let's discuss this. Before I go to the police.

Sincerely,
Henrietta Collins

"This is outrageous." His voice was taut with fury. "I intend to contact President Tucker if you do not cease these irrational accusations."

"Not irrational, Dr. Abbott. In fact, this is quite logically reasoned. Maggie was last seen walking toward Evans Hall." This was being a bit creative with the truth, but I thought it was fair enough. "The assumption is that she had an appointment in this building and that she died here." It sounded rather official. Of course, I didn't have to tell him it was my assumption, not that of the police.

"An appointment in this building?" He didn't like that suggestion, didn't like it at all. "With whom?" His blue eyes probed my face.

"Professor Singletary."

It took a moment too long for his response. His voice grated, "That's absurd. You have no right to say that." And then some of the tension seeped out of his shoulders. "Besides, Stuart had already spoken to her. That morning."

"So you and Stuart have talked about Maggie's murder?"

Once again his reply was slow in coming. Finally, he said cautiously, "In passing." He cleared his throat. "Mrs. Collins, I simply will not allow you to besmirch Stuart's reputation. Upon what basis are you suggesting this young woman came to talk to Stuart?"

"The timing is right, Dr. Abbott. Maggie was last seen walking toward Evans Hall about six o'clock. She was dead by six-thirty—"

His eyes widened at that.

"—but her body wasn't dropped in Lovers' Lane until later that night. Stuart Singletary had a seven-o'clock class. I'm certain that Maggie was strangled and her body hidden somewhere in this building until it could be disposed of. Stuart's class ends at nine."

"That is a dreadful accusation." Abbott's voice was husky with shock.

"I intend to prove every word of it."

They were brave words.

Words I expected Dr. Abbott would soon share with his son-in-law.

I climbed to the third floor. I'd timed it carefully. It was five minutes to four. Stuart Singletary's class was from three to four.

I stood outside his office, looking toward the adjacent closet.

Singletary hurried up the stairs. He was halfway up the hall before he saw me. He jerked to a stop.

I reached out for the knob of the closet door.

I rattled the knob, then dropped my hand and faced him.

His sharply angled face was absolutely without expression. I could see each feature as distinctly as the chisel marks in a sculpture: a bony forehead above deep-socketed eyes, a beaked nose, jutting cheekbones. His chocolate-brown eyes stared at me. Singletary's ears were small and laid tight against his skull. His mouth was small, too, the thin lips almost a straight gash in that still face. His chestnut hair was thick and shiny. Today his sweater was the color of a lion pelt. His slacks were stylishly pleated. His cordovan loafers glistened like polished glass.

We stood so close I could smell cinnamon aftershave and see the bristly texture of his neat black mustache.

He forced out the words, his reedy voice harsh. "What are you doing here?"

"Maggie came to see you before class Wednesday night, Dr. Singletary." I made it a definitive, declarative, accusatory statement.

"No. No, she didn't." His Adam's apple wobbled in his thin neck.

I looked from his office to the closet door.

His gaze followed mine. I saw a flare of panic.

"You have a key to that closet." Faculty are routinely issued keys for storage areas near their offices.

"What are you saying? What are you suggesting?" He took a step toward me.

I stood my ground.

A tiny tic flickered at the edge of his right eyelid.

I reached out, as if absentmindedly, and rattled the closet knob one more time.

That tiny telltale flutter continued. "I've got

288

papers to grade." He strode past me, unlocked his office door, slammed it behind him.

I started downstairs.

As I turned at the landing, I came face-to-face with Dr. Abbott.

"Give my regards to Dr. Singletary," I said as I passed him.

I walked swiftly down the stairs.

I felt I had made a good beginning.

I drove fast to the Singletary house.

The two-story Tudor brick house stood on a rise with a long sweep of lawn to the street. Oak trees and an occasional maple provided a parklike atmosphere. A white wooden fence marked the boundary on either side.

I parked at the front curb and walked up the flagstone path.

Midway to the house, I stepped around a doll buggy. On the porch, a Saint-Bernard-size stuffed lion with a red felt tongue was draped in a wooden swing.

I stopped at the door. I remembered so clearly the vivid portrait over Dr. Abbott's Adam mantel, the lively cheerful young woman brimming with vitality.

If I lifted my hand, if I rang that bell, I was taking one more step on the road to destroying her home, breaking her heart.

The wind ruffled the fluffy brown mane of the lion.

On the last morning of her life, Maggie Winslow had placed on her pillow a scruffy, limp teddy bear with a blue cravat.

Some years ago, Howard Rosen and Gail Voss lifted plastic champagne glasses in celebration.

I reached up and pressed the bell. I heard the cheerful ring of high chimes.

The door opened.

Masses of bright-red hair framed Cheryl Abbott Singletary's cheerful face. Her green eyes were lively and inquiring. Her pink lips curved in a welcoming smile. She had the lovely glow of good health and good humor. A bronze silk blouse was an excellent foil for alabaster-fair skin. The spatter of freckles across her cheeks added piquancy.

"Who is it, Mommy? Who is it?" The little girl galloped into the foyer, her wooden hobbyhorse clattering on the parquet.

"We'll see, Cindy. Take Mr. Ed down to the playroom, please. We don't want to scratch our lovely floor." The sweetness of her tone turned the command into a gentle suggestion laced with love.

"Hi-O, Silver," Cindy trumpeted in a high cheerful voice so like her mother's. She wheeled, stick held aloft, and galloped down the hallway to disappear through a doorway.

Cheryl laughed. "We have a Cheyenne outpost in the basement. I'm sorry. What can I do for you?"

I took a deep breath. I've found it hard many times over the years when I've asked questions and demanded answers that could transform or destroy lives.

None was more difficult than this moment,

with the sun spilling into the lovely foyer, capturing this young wife and mother in a pool of golden light. Happiness shimmered before me. I knew it was as insubstantial as a mirage, as easily destroyed as the wavering image reflected from baking sands.

"I'm Henrietta Collins, Mrs. Singletary. I teach—"

"Oh. Oh, yes, of course." Her recognition was immediate. "I saw the story in *The Clarion*. About the reporter, Maggie Winslow, and the series she was writing. You know, I told Stuart I thought she must have found out something! And you're trying to find out what it was, aren't you?"

"Yes. Yes, I am." I steeled myself to look pleasant, agreeable, non-threatening. "And I'd appreciate it so much if we could talk for a few minutes about the murders in Lovers' Lane when you were a student."

"Howard and Gail." Cheryl's voice quivered. "Oh, I still hate to think about it. They were so happy. They loved each other so much." Sorrow softened the brightness in her eyes, turned down the corners of her rosy lips. "I'd do anything to help catch the awful person who killed them. Come in, Mrs. Collins."

Cheryl led the way down the spacious hall to a library with crammed bookshelves and easy chairs and a fire flickering in the fireplace. We sat in matching Windsor chairs on opposite sides of the fire.

She held out her hands toward the heat, then

her head swung toward me, her green eyes intent. "I've always felt there was something behind Howard and Gail being killed. Lovers' Lane! That was silly. Nobody ever went to Lovers' Lane."

"You don't think they might have gone there—"

She interrupted impatiently. "To make love? Of course not." She put her elbow on the chair arm, propped her chin on her hand. "No, somebody made them go there. Or was going to meet them. Or something!"

"Do you have any idea what it could have been? Why they would meet someone there?"

Slowly, she shook her head and her shiny red hair glistened like Christmas tinsel.

"Did you ever hear either of them mention a Joe Smith?"

"No. Never. Stuart and I talked a lot about that. It didn't make any sense to us." Her diamond wedding band glistened in the firelight.

"Did Stuart mention that Maggie had asked him about Joe Smith?"

"No. He said she was curious about Howard, what he was really like."

"How did you meet Howard and Gail?"

"My dad—"

I nodded.

"He's chair of the department. So he invites the graduate students over, oh, once a month or so. And I helped him with those evenings after my mom...left. I met Howard at one of those parties. And I introduced Howard to Stuart."

Her tone was so casual, so relaxed. If there

was something odd about that meeting, she'd never known about it.

"Did you ever talk to Howard about his thesis?"

She shook her head firmly. And grinned. "Mrs. Collins, I never talked to anybody about their thesis! God forbid. If you let that get started, it's downhill from then on."

"Not even Stuart's thesis?" I made my tone light.

"Believe me, I didn't go out with Stuart to talk about his thesis."

I heard a creak from the hallway.

Cheryl was still smiling.

"I suppose Stuart was terribly upset about the murders?"

Her smile fled. "It was devastating. He was trying to get ready for his orals and the police were always underfoot, wanting to talk to him all the time. But there wasn't much he could tell them. He saw Howard about seven or so, and that was it."

"You were at their apartment that evening?"

"We had pizza. Stuart brought me home about eleven. We'd just started dating and I think he was scared to death of my dad. He always got me in so early."

An antique mirror on the wall behind Cheryl reflected a portion of the hall and a man's arm. In a tawny cashmere sweater. Abruptly the image disappeared.

Suddenly the front door slammed.

Cheryl looked around. "Stuart, we have company. Mrs. Collins is here."

"Yes. So I see." Her husband walked into the library, his angular face as rigid as a slab of concrete.

Cheryl's voice lifted in dismay. "Why, Stuart, what's wrong?"

He ignored her. "What are you doing here?"

I feigned surprise. "I thought you realized my next stop would be here. Of course I wanted to talk to Cheryl."

"I don't want you bothering my wife."

Cheryl looked from him to me, puzzled, her face suddenly wary.

I stood. "Is it a *bother* to try and discover what happened to Howard and Gail?"

Cheryl pressed a hand against her mouth.

"But I'm all through. I won't *bother* you any further. You see, Dr. Singletary, I've gotten what I came for." I met his gaze directly. "What I needed. Everything is much clearer to me now." I moved past him, stepped into the foyer.

I opened the front door and stepped onto the porch.

I was halfway down the walk when the front door slammed. Stuart Singletary caught up with me as I reached my car.

I unlocked the driver's door.

He stood on the other side of the MG. "What do you think you're doing, Mrs. Collins?"

"I think you know, don't you, Stuart? I'm hunting for a murderer, a man who's murdered three people."

"Damn you, you've got it all wrong. I—I didn't kill anybody."

For an instant, I was surprised. I didn't sense fear. Or even anger. This man was worried, nervous, uncomfortable. Not afraid. But, dammit, he should be. No one else had pursued him as I was doing.

I decided it was time to be absolutely clear. "I think you did," I said gravely.

"Listen." His voice rose. "There would have to be a reason. Wouldn't there?" Now he watched me closely, intently. "Why?" It was a demand, harsh, violent. "Why? I had no quarrel with Howard. I *liked* Howard." Singletary was gaining confidence with every word. "Why would I shoot Howard? And Gail, too?"

"I don't know, Stuart. Yet. But I will find out."

As I drove away, I saw him in the rearview mirror, standing on the curb, staring after me.

I wasn't quite sure how to score that encounter.

I hadn't won.

But if Stuart Singletary thought I'd lost, I'd teach him otherwise.

I drove slowly, my mind whirling with the central question, the important question, the question that seemed to have no answer.

Why? Why? Why?

There had to be a reason, a real, concrete, specific reason for Stuart to kill his friends.

Motives for murder cannot, perhaps, be reduced to a list, but any journalist knows only too well that anger, hatred, jealousy, greed, fear, revenge, and betrayal would head such a list.

Anger. Roommates often don't get along, but murder?

Hatred. If Stuart and Howard had quarreled, no one knew of it.

Jealousy. There was no hint that Stuart cared at all for Gail, Howard's girlfriend. And certainly no one had suggested that Howard was interested in Cheryl Abbott.

Greed. Certainly Howard's death didn't matter financially to Stuart. No one profited from Howard's death except his faraway brother.

Fear. What possible reason could Stuart have to be afraid of Howard?

Revenge. No, this was not Shakespeare with hidden identities and family passions to be played out.

Betrayal. That argues a close, intense relationship.

And how had Maggie known? What had tipped Maggie to Stuart Singletary's guilt? And not merely his guilt, but the *reason* for the murders. I could be certain that Stuart was a murderer, but if I never knew *why*, I couldn't prove it.

Somehow Maggie had discovered the reason why. And that knowledge was deadly.

I stopped at the library. But it only took minutes to satisfy myself that Stuart's thesis, as Dr. Abbott had indicated, was about the work and life of a minor American poet.

So that was a dead end.

I took the Rosen-Voss file with me to the Green Owl. Even this early it was crowded. I had to wait ten minutes for a small table. As I skimmed the file, I ate an old-fashioned hamburger and fries with ketchup.

But there was nothing in the file I had not already considered.

I walked back to my MG and sat for a moment before turning on the ignition. I had a definite feeling I could quite safely return home tonight.

Stuart Singletary had no fear of me.

I might be convinced of his guilt, but I had no proof.

Proof.

I turned on the motor.

Whatever Maggie had known, whatever she had surmised, it must have been linked to proof that would destroy Stuart Singletary's assured position.

When I'd rattled the knob to the third-floor closet in Evans Hall, I'd had Singletary worried. That's where he must have put Maggie's body until his class was done.

Could I persuade Lieutenant Urschel to get a search warrant and have the lab technicians scour that closet? Surely there was a trace of dust, some fiber that would link Maggie and the closet.

Urschel had to have more reason than I could provide.

No, that wasn't a possibility at this point.

But that didn't mean I was without recourse. I definitely would keep up the pressure on Singletary.

And maybe he would crack.

seventeen

I walked into Evans Hall slightly after seven. I passed Abbott's office. The light once again gleamed behind the glass. Wednesday-night office hours. I would have given a great deal to know whether he and his son-in-law had spoken together since I'd visited the Singletary house.

I hurried down the central stairs. Singletary's class was held in Lower Level 1. I stood behind the swinging door and looked through the small window. This was one of the large theater-style classrooms, with seats sloping down to a well and a stage. There were two entrances. About seventy-five students were scattered about the auditorium. But I'd known he was a popular teacher.

The young professor stood by the lectern, relaxed and confident. In fact, he had the air of a performer enjoying himself immensely.

I pushed through the door. I was halfway down the center aisle when Singletary saw me.

His reedy voice faltered for just an instant and then he continued. "...if we ever need reminding that the American humor of today has deep roots, we have only to go back to the works of authors such as Artemus Ward and Mark Twain to recognize that laughter is indeed a universal language and there is a particularly American..."

I slipped into a seat next to Sally Cummings, one of my editorial students this semester.

She gave me a sharp, quick look.

Sally is an excellent student. I saw the class syllabus neatly tucked in the front of her notebook.

I tapped it. "May I?" I asked softly.

She handed it to me.

"...let's think for a moment of Ward's wonderful *London Punch* letters. Here's an excerpt from number five, published in 1866. Ward wrote: 'The Puritans nobly fled from a land of despotism to a land of freedim, where they could not only enjoy their own religion, but could prevent everybody else from enjoyin *his*.'"

There was a burst of appreciative laughter.

"Class, let's think for a moment about the political expression of today and how talk-radio hosts..."

I glanced down the syllabus. I was impressed. Singletary covered the period in depth and the requested list of reading should keep any lazy students out of his class.

"...compare with Twain's comment in *Pudd'nhead Wilson's Calendar*: 'It could probably be shown by facts and figures that there is no distinctly native American criminal class except Congress.'"

He waited until the laughter subsided.

"It should be clear that..."

For Mark Twain alone, Singletary expected his students to read *The Adventures of Tom Sawyer*, *Adventures of Huckleberry Finn*, *Pudd'nhead Wilson's Calendar*, and Twain's autobiography.

I looked toward the stage. The faded blue curtains were closed. As Singletary gestured, his shadow moved against the curtain. Although his eyes occasionally jerked toward me, his voice didn't falter again. He had hit full stride now and was deep into the importance of *Huckleberry Finn* to American literature.

I glanced at the rest of the syllabus. It was a star-studded survey of great American writers. My lips quirked a little when I saw the title *Listen to Me*. Okay, so maybe, as some critics had said, it really was the defining novel of the last decade of the twentieth century. But it certainly didn't do any harm to family relations for Singletary to list his father-in-law's book as required reading in this survey of the greatest of American literature.

From that list, Singletary expected his students to read at least one book by each author. So many books, so many wonderful authors.

"...Mark Twain..."

I looked again at the syllabus.

Singletary had listed all of the books by each author.

I scanned Twain's titles; more than a dozen.

Many authors had from five to twenty books to their credit.

One book.

Mark Twain.

Artemus Ward.

Two of the most famous pen names in American literary history.

Pen names.

I handed the syllabus back to Sally.

Singletary moved away from the lectern, walking to the edge of the stage. "I want you to think about Huck and Jim," he told his students. "And then I want you to tell me why this passage is one of the great moments in American literature: 'I was a-trembling because I'd got to decide forever betwixt two things, and I knowed it. I studied it for a minute, sort of holding my breath, and then says to myself, "All right then, I'll *go* to hell."'"

The class got into it, with vigor. I had to admire Singletary's skill as a teacher, his love for his task.

One of my favorite passages from Twain is from *Life on the Mississippi*: "Your true pilot cares nothing about anything on earth but the river, and his pride in his occupation surpasses the pride of kings."

I had more than a little in common with Twain's riverboat pilot.

I care only for justice.

There is a danger in true passion, an inexorable progression. It will not rest with anything less than fulfillment.

Tonight I would see justice done, no matter the cost.

I didn't look toward Singletary when I rose and walked up the aisle.

For an instant, Singletary paused, then his voice picked up again.

I didn't have to look back to know he was watching me every step of the way.

I wondered if he realized that now I knew. I understood—and I would do what I had to do.

Maggie Winslow was a writer. That's how she had figured it out, the heart of one writer understanding the heart of another, the sensitivity, the passion, the reluctance to be hurt. And Maggie must have understood that yes, Gail Voss had loved Howard Rosen, and Gail had known Howard better than anyone, had known all about Howard and Joe Smith and the reason for a grand celebration.

All I had to do was prove it.

I pushed through the swinging door, hurried up the stairs, then out the main entrance into the cool darkness. But I wasn't worried. Stuart might guess the reason for my departure, but what could he do?

The newsroom was silent.

Eric March hunched over his computer keyboard. Dennis Duffy wasn't at his desk. Buddy Neville gave me a languid wave. Kitty Brewster slumped in her chair and stared dully toward the main doorway. Waiting for Dennis?

I unlocked my office, hurried to my desk, and picked up the phone. I glanced at my wall clock.

I called an old friend in New York who covers publishing for *Newsweek*. She gave me a list of a half dozen names and numbers.

I made call after call.

The minute hand continued its jerky sweep. Seven forty-five.

Seven-fifty. Time for Singletary's class to take a ten-minute break. I wanted to be outside Singletary's class when it ended at nine. With what I'd learned or surmised, I was certain I could make Singletary reveal what he knew.

Eight o'clock. Time for class to resume.

Eight-ten.

Eight-twenty.

I located Coleman Shelby at his home in suburban Connecticut at eight thirty-seven. I spoke fast and hard and waited tensely for his answer.

The editor's precise voice was matter-of-fact. "Mrs. Collins, I have every piece of correspondence since the initial submission."

I thanked him.

I slammed out of my office.

Eric lifted his head at the sound of my hurried steps. "Mrs. Collins—"

"Later." I was moving at a near run.

Once again I plunged out into the night. As soon as I reached Evans Hall—

But I never reached the building. I was still in the thick shadows of a line of cedars, their branches rustling in the north wind, when a fast-moving figure bolted out from the shadows.

I knew who it was, of course.

I'd made a grave miscalculation.

I'd been confident that Stuart Singletary was

powerless. Though I'd realized Stuart was worried about what he feared might happen, I didn't expect him to take action. But he'd had that ten-minute break at eight o'clock.

My mistake.

Perhaps my fatal mistake.

A creamy light sifted down from the golden-globed street lamp.

The figure was almost upon me now. His steps gritted on the sidewalk.

At almost the same instant, I heard faintly the asthmatic wheeze of the J-School main door.

I had to pray that this deadly attacker didn't know that sound, that his attention was focused utterly on me.

I said clearly, distinctly, and I hoped loudly enough, but not so loud as to provoke attack, "Is that the face you wore the night you killed Howard and Gail?"

The rubber mask, the head of a lion, glistened yellow and brown in the chalky glow. It looked almost charming atop the light tan of his trench coat. "Shut up, Mrs. Collins." It was a sibilant whisper.

"You saw them that night at the Green Owl. He'd told you earlier in the day, of course, about the wonderful news, that the publishing house was going to buy his book, the book he'd submitted over the transom using the pen name Joe Smith. A pseudonym, like Mark Twain or Artemus Ward. Howard used it because he was still hiding his true interests from his financier father. But Gail knew. Yes, Gail loved Joe Smith because she loved Howard

Rosen. So the double murders in Lovers' Lane came down to greed. *Listen to Me* received one of the highest advances ever paid for a first novel. The letter came that day, didn't it, Dr. Abbott? We can verify that, the date of the letter to Joe Smith, offering riches and success and fame far beyond anything you would ever have. When the letter arrived, Howard must have been so excited. He immediately called Gail, to go and celebrate. But he met with you that day and he told you his great news. After all, he'd written that novel as his graduate-school thesis. And you knew Howard, knew how secretive he was, so you could be confident that no one else in the world was aware of the offer from the publishing house—except you and Howard and Gail. And who knew that Joe Smith was Howard Rosen? Only you and Howard and Gail. Before the night of April 15 ended, no one would know but you. We can prove what happened. All we have to do is get the letter signed by Joe Smith in submitting the manuscript. That signature will prove to have been written by Howard Rosen. And Dr. Abbott, I just talked to your editor—that letter exists."

I wondered how Tom Abbott felt inside that hot, stuffy mask. Was sweat turning his red hair into tight ringlets? Or was his skin clammy and icy?

"What did you want most, Dr. Abbott—the money? Or the fame? Was it at the Green Owl that you made up your mind? Did you go home and get your gun? Were you waiting in the shadows by Howard's car when they came

305

out of the café? Did you make them drive to Lovers' Lane?" I shook my head in disdain. "Lovers' Lane. That was such a tip-off. Only someone as old as you would have hoped to make their murders look like kids caught in a romantic moment on a remote road."

"Nobody knows." It was a vicious whisper.

I almost challenged that statement.

Because Stuart Singletary knew. At the very least, Stuart had realized, when *Listen to Me* was published, that he'd seen scraps of that work before. On the desk of his roommate. But what could Stuart do about it?

What was he willing to do?

Stuart had looked the other way.

Tonight, he had not. He must have gone downstairs, warned his father-in-law, perhaps straight out, perhaps obliquely.

Perhaps he meant only to warn him to escape.

What would Stuart do when my body was found?

I didn't say anything about Stuart.

Was that rustle just the wind?

I lifted my voice. "Maggie Winslow figured it out, didn't she? You had an appointment with her at six, a time when no one was likely to see her in the building. And if they did, well, she had a seven-o'clock class at Evans Hall. Maggie was a writer. She talked to Howard's brother and she thought about the notebooks Howard always kept and she knew he was working on a master's in creative writing."

306

"She said she knew I hadn't written it—that no old man could have written *Listen to Me*. She laughed at me." The whisper was low and ugly, shaking with fury.

"You struck her down. You strangled her, shoved the body in your office closet. Then you kept your office hours. But later that night you took her body to Lovers' Lane. Did it amuse you to leave her body there?"

Abbott raised his hand. The gun gleamed dully in the milky light. "Nobody knows."

The sudden onset of brutally loud noise was bewildering, shocking, disorienting, a high piercing buzz alternating with a siren's wail.

The sound came from behind the cedars.

That huge rubbery head jerked toward the trees.

Eric March exploded from the other direction, slamming into Abbott's back.

Then the deep hoarse violent yell began, an ungodly, mournful howl.

I will never forget that sound.

Eric was astride Abbott, the scream coming from deep in Eric's throat as he pounded the lion head against the sidewalk.

Abbott's gun flung loose from his hand. I was on my hands and knees, scrabbling toward the weapon. I picked it up by the barrel. But I was prepared, fingerprints be damned, to grasp it properly if need be.

The shrill buzzing sound—I recognized it as the kind of small safety alarm often carried by female students at night—suddenly ceased its clamor.

Buddy Neville plunged toward Eric. Kitty Brewster panted up beside them.

It took Kitty and me and Buddy to grapple with Eric and pull him away from the motionless figure sprawled on the sidewalk.

I didn't have to worry about how I held the gun.

Tom Abbott didn't move. Blood oozed from beneath the lion mask.

From the unnatural angle of his neck, I knew he would never kill again.

eighteen

It was fairly late Thursday morning when I reached my office. I had *The Clarion* tucked under my arm. I'd scanned it at breakfast. I didn't need to read it. I'd lived it.

The lead story, of course, was Eric March's rescue of me from Dr. Thomas Abbott. Most of the story was Kitty Brewster's eyewitness account, then her subsequent interview with me at the Derry Hills police station. I made it clear that Abbott was guilty of three murders and that he was lifting the gun to shoot me and only Eric's intervention saved my life.

Additional stories focused on Maggie Winslow's murder, Rita Duffy's release, my efforts to clear Rita, and the expected revelations about the book that Howard Rosen had written and Tom Abbott had stolen from him.

But I was finished.

In, of course, more ways than one.

I unlocked my office door.

Two envelopes addressed to me had been slipped beneath the door.

The first bore the letterhead of the Office of the President of Thorndyke University.

I opened the thick envelope. The University's crest in gold and blue was emblazoned in the top center of a thick white notecard. There was a single line written in a heavy, looping script:

Dear Mrs. Collins,

You have served the University well.

Sincerely,
David Tucker

I crossed to my desk, dropped the note in the wastebasket. I sat in my chair and opened the second.

Henrietta O'Dwyer Collins
Assistant Professor of Journalism
School of Journalism and Mass Communications

Dear Henrie O:

The School wishes formally to recognize your extraordinary efforts on behalf of both students and faculty. We are delighted with your commitment to justice. You have demonstrated the highest levels of professional achievement.

Very truly yours,

Susan Dillon
Director
School of Journalism and
Mass Communications

Smooth words. But I knew I'd made an implacable enemy of Susan. I was sure there would be a budget difficulty in the spring which would, regrettably, of course, mean that my position could not be filled in the coming academic year. Her letter was simply a feline means of ensuring I could not complain that I was being dropped because of malice on her part.

No, my days at Thorndyke were over. But that was all right. I know that nothing—for good or ill—lasts forever. I'd had fun here, made good friends, fought a good fight. That was as much as I could ever ask of any job.

I've had many jobs. It might be tough to find a new one at my age. But I had enough savings to be independent and I could always freelance. I could go anywhere, write anything.

Or I could—my fingers closed around a carnation—I could try a new and different life, a life of leisure in a lovely land with a man I enjoyed.

But I had one more task to complete before I called Jimmy.

The greenhouse was moist, the air rich with the scent of growing things. The tabby lifted her head. Emerald eyes watched me benignly.

Kathryn Nugent sat behind a worn desk. A cracked leather ledger lay open before her. Slowly, she put down the ballpoint pen. Her oval face was haggard. She said brusquely, "I don't want to talk to you."

"Mrs. Nugent, I know what happened to your husband."

Those slender, dirt-grimed hands opened and shut spasmodically, but her face remained empty, walled against invasion.

I told her, as quickly, as kindly, as gently as I could.

And when I finished, I watched those hands open and shut, open and shut. Tears trickled down her pale cheeks. "If he'd only come home..."

I left then, understanding the depth and breadth of her love.

If he'd only come home...

At the door I paused. There was a vase filled with carnations.

I reached up and broke one off.

I didn't think she'd mind.

I stepped outside into a dull, raw, gun-metal-gray November day, the carnation nestling in my hand. In the car, I brought the carnation to my face, smelled its rich woody scent.

I thought of Jimmy and sunny days.

I thought of Richard and the incredible joy

it had given me to be near him.

I reached for my mobile phone.

"Hello." Even in that single word, Jimmy's voice was boyish, eager.

"Jimmy."

"Henrie O. I'm leaving in an hour. You'll—"

"Jimmy, you're a wonderful man. I wish you every kind of happiness."

"You're saying no, Henrie O?"

I liked Jimmy. I enjoyed him. I treasured him. I did not love him.

A man deserves a wife who can say, "I love you," and mean it with every fiber of her being.

"Jimmy, go to Mexico and be happy. I want you to be happy."

"I would be happier with you." But, as always, his voice was kind and reasonable.

We talked for a moment more, old friends and now former lovers, and then we said good-bye.

My hand rested on the telephone after I hung up. My eyes ached with tears.

But if I went to Mexico, it would be for all the wrong reasons.

So I wasn't going to Mexico.

I wondered where I would go.

Have laptop. Will travel.

CAROLYN HART is the author of two other best-selling Henrie O mysteries, including *Dead Man's Island*, which received the Agatha for Best Mystery of the Year and was made into a movie for television. She is also the author of nine Death on Demand mysteries featuring Annie Laurance and Max Darling, the third of which, *Something Wicked*, was an Agatha winner. Carolyn Hart lives in Oklahoma City with her husband, Phil, and is presently working on her next Henrie O mystery, which is set in Hawaii.

If you have enjoyed reading this large print book and you would like more information on how to order a Wheeler Large Print Book, please write to:

 Wheeler Publishing, Inc.
P.O. Box 531
Accord, MA 02018-0531